Praise for Jenifer LeC

Death in the Blood Moon

"Full of beautifully detailed descriptions of Lake [Superior] as well as interesting facts about the native Ojibwe . . . Wonderfully written characters throughout the book made me feel deeply connected to the story-line. . . Even though this is a work of fiction, LeClair's characters and their ability to put all differences aside for the greater good gave me a hopeful feeling in what sometimes feels like a time of such division in the real world today. . . Characters, locations, storyline—every aspect of this book was completely enjoyable. I look forward to reading the other books in this series, as well as future books by this very talented author."

—Reader Views

Dead Astern

"A great, bounding thrill ride . . . *Dead Astern* is the book Agatha Christie might have written if she'd loved the sea and had known how to trim a sail. Jenifer Le-Clair offers readers an engaging tale that is a strong, seagoing version of the locked-room mystery. With several well-plotted twists, lots of riveting scenes on the bounding main, and plenty of fascinating sailing information along the way, *Dead Astern* is an exciting excursion sure to please anyone willing to sign on for the voyage."

—William Kent Krueger
New York Times Bestselling Author

Apparition Island

"With a mastery of details and a sailor's sense of land and sea, LeClair has given us another memorable story on an eerie island off the coast of Maine . . . a real gift for those who like their mysteries straight from the sea."
—Steve Thayer
New York Times Bestselling Author

"LeClair handles the island's rugged terrain and its rugged inhabitants equally well."
—*Publishers Weekly*

"LeClair skillfully brings the setting into the mind's eye with wonderfully descriptive detail."
—*Foreword Magazine*

Cold Coast

"Brie is so likable and the plot so involving, it's not surprising this series has won several awards."
—Mary Ann Grossmann
St. Paul Pioneer Press

"This engaging police procedural vividly captures the Maine background. . . . The eccentric Mainers add depth to a fabulous step-by-step investigation."
—*Midwest Book Review*

"*Cold Coast* is superbly written. The characters are easy to follow and well developed. . . . Brie is a strong female protagonist but in an endearing way, not the stereotypical hard-nosed female law enforcement officer. The descriptions of the harbor and the coast are exceptionally vivid. . . . 5 Stars—excellent read!"
—*Reader Views*

"Tense . . . keeps the reader guessing until the final outcome . . . full of wonderful descriptions of life on a sailing vessel."

—*Armchair Reviews*

Danger Sector

"If you love sailing, grab this title and prepare to be immersed. . . . A strong sense of place and a fine little closed-room drama make this seafaring read a real pleasure."

—*Library Journal*

"Intelligent and well-written . . . The strong, smart protagonist is Minneapolis homicide detective Brie Beaumont."

—*St. Paul Pioneer Press*

"Recommend this agreeable mixture of adventure and crime."

—*Booklist*

"LeClair combines police procedure, finely-honed investigative skills, psychological insights, and suspense . . . in this haunting story of unrequited love, deceit, and murder [that] involves all five senses. A creative imagination, a love for sailing, and gifted communication skills combine to make Jenifer LeClair a top-notch storyteller."

—*Reader Views*

Rigged for Murder

"A winning combination of psychological thriller, police procedural, and action adventure. It's a five-star launch for [LeClair's] aptly named sea-going series. . . . Tightly written and intricately constructed, LeClair's

Rigged for Murder is first-class storytelling in a setting so authentic you can hear the ocean's roar and taste the salt from the sea."

—*Mysterious Reviews*

"An engaging New England whodunit."

—*Midwest Book Review*

"A strong plot, non-stop action, and first-class character development combine to make this an exciting, page-turning adventure novel."

—*Reader Views*

"A debut mystery that is so well written you will hunger for more . . . well-developed characters and superbly good writing."

—Once Upon a Crime Mystery Bookstore

"*Rigged for Murder* is an exciting mystery with a little romance thrown in. The setting for this novel is unique and gives the reader insight into life aboard a sailing ship."

—*Armchair Reviews*

"The characters have depth and movement . . . LeClair gets the sea and the sailing just right."

—*Books 'n' Bytes*

"*Rigged for Murder* is a fast-paced story which rings true both aboard and ashore on island communities. The characters are real, the situations are downright scary, tension is palpable."

—John Foss, Master/owner,
Schooner *American Eagle*, Rockland, Maine

DEATH IN THE WOLF MOON

ALSO BY JENIFER LECLAIR

DEATH IN THE WOLF MOON

A Claude Renard Mystery

JENIFER LECLAIR

FOG HARBOR PRESS
St. Paul, Minnesota

Sale of this book without a front cover may be unauthorized. If this book is coverless, it may have been reported to the publisher as "unsold and destroyed" and neither the author nor the publisher may have received payment.

This book is a work of fiction. Names, characters, places and incidents either are products of the author's imagination or are used fictitiously. Any resemblance to actual events, or to actual persons living or dead, is entirely coincidental.

Copyright © 2023 by Jenifer LeClair

All rights reserved. No part of this book may be reproduced in any form or by any electronic or mechanical means, including information storage and retrieval systems, without permission in writing from the publisher, except by a reviewer who may quote brief passages in a review.

Fog Harbor Press
4411 Wood Duck Drive
St. Paul, Minnesota 55127

Cover Design: Rebecca Treadway / ATRTINK

Library of Congress Control Number: 2023916739

LeClair, Jenifer.
   Death in the Wolf Moon: a novel / by Jenifer LeClair – 1st ed.

ISBN: 978-1-7336084-6-6

10 9 8 7 6 5 4 3 2 1

Printed in the United States of America

For my wonderful father, Fred Thibodeau, posthumously.
Archivist, historian, philosopher, WWII veteran, POW.
A brave, kind, and gentle man who loved the North.

"In the deep snow moons of winter, there are stories hovering around us. They are whispered by the voices of our ancestors, told in ancient tongues, told in the hope that we will hear them. Listen. In the drape of moon-beams across a canvas of snow . . . our ancestors speak to us, call to us, summon us to the great abiding truth of stories: that simple stories, well told, are the heartbeat of the people. Past. Present. Future."

Embers: One Ojibway's Meditations
by Richard Wagamese

Chapter 1

Claude Renard lay in that uncharted territory between wake and sleep. Outside, the wild elements both lulled and excited, drawing him toward the surface, then pulling him back to the restful depths. Lake Superior churned away, and a strong wind shook the frail glass panes in their worn sashes. His weathered frame house sat right on the stony beach of East Bay, where it took the brunt of the storms rolling in from the northeast. Claude wouldn't have had it any other way. He had grown up on Grand Portage Bay, on the tribal lands of the Anishinaabe, and the vast and ancient heart of Gichi-gami beat deep within him.

He was slipping once more beneath the surface of consciousness when the phone rang. He rolled to his right and fumbled for it on the nightstand. Caught it on the third ring. Deputy Gunderson's voice cut in and out until Claude sat up on the edge of the bed and leaned toward the window.

"Say again, Hank. You're cutting out."

He heard the words "You need to . . . folk school" and the final word that brought him fully awake—"murder."

1

Claude was already reaching for his prosthetic leg as he set the phone down. Bone-embedded metal snapped into the socket of his titanium appendage—a wonder of modern technology paid for by the U.S. military. He reached over to the chair where his uniform pants lay folded, slipped them on, and headed for the bathroom, where he brushed his teeth, ran an electric shaver over his face and a comb through his straight dark hair. He emerged fully dressed and headed down the stairs, where he slipped on his boots and uniform parka and was out the door.

A cold January sun barely struggled above the eastern horizon to shine its dim lamp over the frozen world. A fresh dusting of snow had fallen in the wee hours. Chief Deputy Renard climbed into his SUV squad and backed out onto Broadway Avenue. Behind him the road ran out to the Coast Guard station and Artist's Point—now a winter wasteland, save for the occasional aged gull, too old to migrate south. At the corner he turned left onto Wisconsin Street. To his way of thinking, neither of those names belonged on a street in Grand Marais, Minnesota, but there it was.

Since receiving the call, the single word "murder" had been flashing behind his forehead like an occulting red light. It was never a word expected in Grand Marais, even when you were the law.

The Northern Arts Folk School was just a few blocks away. No need to alarm the villagers with siren or lights. Claude turned left onto Highway 61, aka Voyageur Highway. Two blocks down he made a U-turn and parked in front of the school campus that consisted of a collection of frame buildings where the classes were offered. Except for the bookstore/gift shop that fronted on the highway, the rest of the buildings were tucked down the hill next to the harbor. The driveway that ran down there had been cordoned off with crime scene tape, and that was beginning to draw attention.

Renard climbed out of the squad and walked down the hill. There was a deputy stationed outside the door to the building where the woodworking classes were held. He headed in that direction.

Renard greeted the deputy with a nod as he approached. "Len." He noticed the young man's eyes danced with a kind of hyper vigilance.

The deputy nodded back. "Morning, Claude."

Renard stepped inside the building. There was a bootie box and gloves just inside the door. He removed a pair of shoe covers from the box and slipped them over his boots and pulled on a pair of latex gloves. He stood for a few moments, taking in the scene.

The long-running coffin-making class, annually billed as "Bury Yourself in Your Work," was underway inside the building. A collection of six- and eight-foot tables was scattered around the large shop, each one holding a wood coffin in progress. At the far end of the room, Deputy Hank Gunderson was talking to one of the wood-working teachers at the school—Howard Grainfeld. Howard was his given name, but pretty much everyone in town called him Sandy, because pretty much everyone in town—Claude included—had had him as a teacher in high school woodshop or here at the folk school for a woodworking class. Sandy was a bit of a taskmaster when it came to sanding the wood. Comments like, "That could use more sanding" or "Keep on sanding there, son" or "Don't stop now—that needs more sanding" had earned him his moniker.

Sandy was turned away from him, but Renard observed his body language. He rocked back and forth, intermittently crossing and uncrossing his arms. Movements that signaled anxiety. Sandy was in his mid-to-late 50s and of average height, but one glance told you he had muscles. His light brown hair was shot through with gray, and he had a Wilfred Brimley-like mustache that shouted "trim me."

After a few moments, Renard headed toward them.

Deputy Gunderson nodded to him as he approached, causing Sandy Grainfeld to turn.

"Claude, I'm glad you're here," Sandy said, as if Renard might be able to reverse time back to a set point where things made some kind of sense.

"What have we got here, Hank?"

"The victim is Grant Silverton. He's a resident of the town. He was one of Sandy's students in the class here. Sandy identified the murder weapon as one of Grant's wood chisels."

"The students provide their own tools for the class," Sandy offered.

Renard stepped over to the coffin-in-progress on the table next to them and looked in. Grant Silverton lay facedown in the coffin. He laid a gloved hand on the body. It was in advanced rigor mortis. A wood chisel protruded from his back. Blood had run down and pooled under his body and had soaked into the interior of the coffin, leaving a macabre stain on the wood.

"It's a shame about the wood," Sandy Grainfeld said from behind him.

Renard turned and studied him for a few moments, finding it odd that Grainfeld's first concern might be for the wood and not for Grant Silverton.

"It's a shame about Grant here, too," he said.

"Of course. I just meant . . . Never mind." Sandy's voice trailed off. But then he appeared to hit restart. "This is a shock and a tragedy, and . . ." He paused a moment and Renard waited. "And, well, I feel responsible."

"Why's that?" Renard asked, watching him carefully.

"Because I allowed him to stay here last night and work after I left. He'd fallen a bit behind the rest of the class and asked if he could keep working. He offered to lock up when he left and, well, I didn't see any harm in it, so I told him 'okay.'" Sandy studied the dusty floor beneath his feet, as if the weight of remorse made it hard for him to lift his head.

"Look, Sandy. This is not your fault," Deputy Gunderson said.

Claude Renard refrained from saying anything, wishing Hank had not made that statement. Why? Because, according to his narrative, Sandy Grainfeld was the last one to see Grant Silverton alive. That automatically made him a person of interest. Sandy also had known that Grant was here alone, and that gave him opportunity. Did he have any kind of a motive? That would have to be investigated.

"What time did you leave here last night?" Renard asked.

"Just after eight o'clock."

"Did you see anyone near the building or parked on the street when you left?"

Sandy shook his head. "Nobody."

Renard turned back to Deputy Gunderson. "Who found the body, Hank?"

"That would be Sandy here."

"Tell me about that, Sandy."

"Sure, Claude. I came down this morning to open up. Do some paperwork, you know. I've got a new class starting next week, so I wanted to prepare some handouts for that and inventory the tools—see if there was anything I needed to get." He paused and looked at the two deputies. "I found the door unlocked, and that made me a bit angry. After all, Grant had told me he'd lock up. So, I came in and walked over to his station to see how he was coming along, and that's when I saw . . ." Grainfeld's words trailed off again, and he gazed toward the window.

Finally, he turned back to Renard. "I've never seen anything like this. I don't think I'll ever get the image out of my mind."

Renard understood. Most people were never going to come across a dead body, especially one that had been a victim of murder.

"I understand how you feel," he said. "How well did you know Grant Silverton?"

"I knew him mainly as a student. He'd taken several classes from me here at the folk school. He moved to Grand Marais a couple of years ago."

"How do you know that?"

Sandy shrugged. "Don't know. Common knowledge, I guess."

"And did you have any dealings with him outside of the classes here?"

"Well, I helped him set up a woodworking shop at his house. He used to call me with questions sometimes. I wouldn't say we were friends, though. But he had a friend in the class," Sandy volunteered.

"Who would that be?" Renard asked.

"Name's Paul Strauss. I have his contact information if you'd like."

"Please," Renard said. "Also, an address for Grant Silverton if you have one."

"Sure thing." Grainfeld headed toward the opposite end of the room, where a desk sat in the corner.

Renard turned to Deputy Gunderson, who had been writing in his small notebook as the interview progressed. "Did you call the ME?"

"Right after I called you. He should be here any time now. I also notified the BCA. They're sending an evidence response team."

"That's good, Hank. It'll take them several hours to get here."

The county sheriff's office did not maintain a full forensic division, so in the case of a homicide, the BCA was called in to process the scene and collect forensic evidence. The regional office of the Bureau of Criminal Apprehension was in Bemidji, Minnesota—more than a four-hour drive away.

Sandy came back with a sheet that held addresses and phone numbers of those in the class and handed it to Renard.

"Can I keep this?"

"Yes, I have more copies."

Renard ran his eye down the list. Jules and El Pierre, Erin Flanagan, Paul Strauss, and Grant Silverton. It was a small group, but Renard was sure Sandy would have had his hands full what with five students each working on his or her own coffin.

He looked around the shop. "I notice this coffin and a couple of others are on lower tables," Renard said. "Any reason for that?"

"There is," Sandy said. "When a student is working on the inside of the coffin, we usually move it to a lower table. Makes it easier to work on the inside, especially if the student is shorter."

Claude gestured toward Grant Silverton in the coffin. "How tall would you say he was?"

"He was about my height—maybe a little taller," Sandy said. "I'm five-nine."

Deputy Gunderson made a note of that.

Renard was thinking about how Grant Silverton's body had gotten all the way into the coffin, but that was not a topic for discussion here.

Renard looked around the workshop. "This wood is different from the others. It's walnut, isn't it?"

He caught the shadow of a look that slid across Sandy Grainfeld's face and then was gone. Anger, irritation, disgust? He wasn't sure which.

"That's right," Sandy said. "The standard wood used in the class is cabinet-grade pine, but Grant here wanted something different. He was insistent, so I ordered it for him. Walnut is a hard wood, though, one of the reasons it was taking him longer on his coffin."

"Was that a problem?" Renard asked.

Sandy hesitated for a moment, trying to keep his expression neutral. Then he looked straight at Claude. "I guess ultimately it was," he said, gesturing toward the coffin. "If he hadn't been here working alone, well . . ." His voice trailed off.

"Who else in the class knew that Grant Silverton had stayed here last night?" Renard asked.

"There were a couple of students still hanging around after the class ended." Sandy thought for a moment. "Erin Flanagan, for sure. Oh, and the Pierres —Jules and El."

"And what time did they leave?"

"Right before I did. Like I told you, it was just after eight o'clock."

"And where were you between the time you left here last night and when you arrived this morning?" Renard asked.

Now the look on Sandy Grainfeld's face was easy to decipher. It was alarm.

"I was at home, of course. Went straight there after I left here." He eyed Renard. "Why would you ask that?"

"Because I have to. You were the last one to see Silverton alive."

"So, am I a suspect, then?" Grainfeld's voice registered the stress of the question. "You can ask my wife. She'll tell you I was home by 8:20."

Renard nodded. "I'll be checking in with her. And what time did you go to bed?"

Grainfeld shrugged. "Between ten and ten-thirty. That's my usual bedtime."

Renard made some notes in his small book and then turned to Deputy Gunderson.

"Do you have Mr. Grainfeld's address and phone number written down, Hank?"

Gunderson nodded.

"In that case, you're free to go, Howard." Renard opted for Sandy's formal name, since this was serious business.

Sandy nodded, looking a bit at loose ends, as if he wasn't sure whether to go or to stay.

Renard sensed his consternation. "It's okay, Howard. We'll call you if we need anything else from you."

Grainfeld met his eyes for a moment, then nodded and headed toward the door.

* * *

Erin Flanagan was out for her morning walk when she came upon the crowd outside the folk school. She stopped and looked around, and spotting Maurie Fontaine, edged up next to him.

"What's going on, Maurie?" she asked.

"Something's happening down at the folk school." He nodded his red plaid bomber hat—ear flaps down—toward the building at the base of the hill.

"I was headed downtown to the hardware store when I spotted the group beginning to gather, so I stopped to see what was up. The deputies are here, and Doc Mosley just arrived." He turned and pointed toward the doc, who had just pulled up in his car on the opposite side of the highway.

"Is someone hurt?"

"Don't know," Maurie said.

"The EMTs haven't arrived?"

"Nope, not so far."

Erin turned up the collar of her North Face jacket and snugged her headband down over her ears. "That's the woodworking building." She nodded toward it. "I'm taking the current coffin-making class. It just met last night. I wonder what could be going on?"

Erin wasn't one to stand on ceremony. Her whole life was on her phone, along with the numbers of most of the townsfolk. She was organized and ready at all times, in all situations. Or so she believed, anyway. She brought up the class list and started calling people. It wasn't really much of a job since there were only five students in the class, including herself, and the teacher, Sandy Grainfeld.

She noticed that Maurie had moved closer to her and was listening. She held up a finger as if to say, I'll give you the scoop in a minute. Out of the corner of her eye, she caught sight of Fred Tittlehouse, from the *Cook County News Herald*, hurrying across the highway, notepad in hand and camera slung over his shoulder.

The first call Erin Flanagan made was to the Grainfeld house. Since Sandy was the teacher for the coffin-making class, she thought he should know that something was up at the school.

Sandy's son Ethan answered the phone. Erin identified herself and asked if Sandy was there.

"He's not here. Can I take a message?"

"Is your mom there, Ethan?"

"Sure."

She heard him say, "It's Erin Flanagan, asking for Dad."

A moment later Becca Grainfeld came on the line.

"He's not here, Erin. He went down to the school about forty-five minutes ago."

"There's something going on down here, Becca. I was out for my walk and came past the school and something's going on at the woodworking building. The deputies are here. And Doc Mosley just arrived on the scene."

Erin heard an indrawn breath and then a moment of silence.

"I'm calling Sandy now. Then I'm heading down there. Oh God, I hope nothing's happened to him."

The line went dead.

"You're welcome," Erin said under her breath. She paused for a beat and then went on to her next call.

Within fifteen minutes she had made the calls and talked to all but one of the students in the coffin-making class. Grant Silverton's phone had gone directly to voice-mail, so she hadn't been able to reach him. She pocketed her phone and was about to fill Maurie Fontaine in when she saw Ethan Grainfeld pull to the curb across the street in Becca's tattered blue Jeep. Becca was in the passenger seat. Both of them jumped out and ran toward the crowd, coming to a stop next to Erin Flanagan. Ethan put an arm around his mom's shoulder, and she leaned into him for support.

"Did you reach him?" Erin asked. "Did you reach Sandy?"

Becca shook her head no.

Just then Erin saw Sandy Grainfeld come out the door of the woodworking building. He paused to talk with Deputy Len Blake, who was posted at the door.

"Look, Becca. He just came out of the building. He's okay."

Becca craned to see past those in front of her and caught sight of her husband.

"Oh, thank God he's all right."

She turned and Erin saw there were tears in her eyes.

"I'm sorry I hung up on you, Erin. I was just so worried."

"I get it, Becca. I'm glad Sandy's all right. Look, here he comes."

Becca turned and, catching Sandy's eye, waved at him. He made his way up the hill, and Becca threw her arms around him as he came around the police tape.

As the three of them walked away from the crowd, Erin heard her say, "For heaven's sake, what's going on, Sandy?"

Erin whipped off her headband just in time to hear Sandy respond in a low voice, "It's Grant Silverton. He's been murdered." She turned to share what she'd heard with Maurie Fontaine, but he had disappeared. She craned her neck in time to see him beating it toward his car down the street. "Huh, you're welcome," she said under her breath.

*　　*　　*

Just after Sandy Grainfeld exited the woodworking building, Renard saw Dr. Erbert Mosley, the medical examiner, step inside and pull on booties and gloves. Mosley was carrying a black medical bag and had a serious camera slung over his shoulder. The doctor was slight of build, and his large dark-framed glasses dwarfed a face with fine-boned features. He came across the room with an agile and determined stride that belied his sixty years.

"Hello, Claude. Hank. Came as soon as I could." His light blue eyes sparked with intelligence.

13

"Morning, Erb. Wish it were better circumstances."

Mosley nodded. "What have we got here?" he asked, even though he was already surveying the corpse.

"This is Grant Silverton," Renard said. "He was taking the coffin-making class here at the folk school."

"And just in time, I guess," Doc Mosley said, showing a bit of dark humor that MEs are wont to engage in.

Every ounce of Claude's upbringing kept him from smiling.

Hank Gunderson started to say something jocular in response, but one look from Renard silenced him.

"Mr. Silverton was last seen alive shortly after eight p.m. last night," Renard continued. "Sandy Grainfeld found him like this when he came in this morning, just before eight a.m."

Mosley stepped over and felt the body. "Rigor is complete," he said after a brief examination. "Death could have occurred any time from just after eight o'clock last night up until around midnight. Cause of death appears obvious. Sharp-force trauma." He turned to them as if translating. "Stabbing. There appear to be two wounds. He would have fallen forward, but someone would have to have lifted him the rest of the way into the coffin."

"That was my thought as well," Renard said.

"Makes a bit of a statement, wouldn't you say?" Deputy Gunderson commented.

"I agree," Mosley said. "The killer had to take time to lift the body into the coffin before fleeing."

"Stabbing is often an act of anger or fury," Renard said. "But the positioning of the body in the coffin goes a step beyond that. It feels like retribution maybe."

"What's the timeline on the BCA?" Doc Mosley asked.

"About three and a half hours," Hank said.

"I'll take some pictures," Mosley said. "And then I'll need a couple of deputies to help move the body and get it on the way to Anoka County."

Renard nodded. Homicide victims in Cook County were transported to the Anoka County Medical Examiner's Office for autopsy.

"I'll call in a couple of extra men." He turned to Hank. "Did you bring the camera from headquarters?"

Gunderson nodded.

"I'd like you to photograph the scene before they move the body and then get a warrant for the Silverton property."

"Sure, Boss."

Renard turned back to the victim and nodded toward his back pocket. "We need to take his cell phone into evidence. Will you start an evidence log, Hank."

Deputy Gunderson walked over to the table that held the gloves and booties and came back with a clipboard that held an evidence log form. He entered the item to be logged, the time and place they were collecting the cell phone, and wrote in his shield number. They retrieved the cell phone from Grant Silverton's pocket, placed it in an evidence bag, and labeled that with the same information. It would go back to the Law Enforcement Center to their digital forensics division.

Renard drew the deputy aside as Doc Mosley went ahead with his work.

"Were you acquainted with Grant Silverton at all?"

"I was not," Gunderson said.

"Nor was I, but we need to locate his next of kin. I'm going now and interview his friend, Paul Strauss. See what I can learn about that. Let me know as soon as you have the warrant in hand, and I will meet you at the Silverton property."

"Will do. I'll get started photographing the scene right now."

"Good. I'll leave Deputy Blake posted outside until the team arrives from the BCA."

Before he left, Renard removed a small evidence bag from his pocket. He walked back to where Doc Mosley was working, squatted down and, using his pocket knife, collected a sample of the sawdust from under the coffin Grant Silverton had been working on. He logged it into evidence and left it with Hank Gunderson. Then he headed outside to talk to Deputy Blake.

Len Blake was at his post outside the door. Renard told him to help the other deputies with removal of the body to the transport vehicle and then to stay at his post until the team arrived from the Bureau of Criminal Apprehension.

"It's cold today, so you can wait inside if need be."

"I'm fine for now," Deputy Blake replied.

Renard followed his eyes to the growing crowd that was gathering beyond the crime scene tape, up on the sidewalk, next to the highway. He nodded toward them. "You may want to help with crowd control up there when the transport vehicle arrives."

"Will do," Blake responded.

Renard turned and walked up the hill toward his squad that was parked along the highway above the school. The wind was picking up, and the newly fallen snow sifted down from the trees like powdered sugar under an ice blue sky. The beauty and purity of the winter world so contrasted with the scene inside the folk school that it put a momentary ache in Claude's heart.

As he approached the townspeople gathered behind the crime scene tape, one of them called out.

"Sheriff One Step, can you tell us what's happening at the folk school? Is someone hurt?"

The rest of the crowd leaned toward him, waiting.

"I can't say anything right now," Renard answered. "We will release information when we are able." He spotted Fred Tittlehouse from the *Cook County News Herald* moving on an intercepting trajectory, somewhere between where Claude stood now and his squad. He headed toward the inevitable intersection and, sure enough, Fred beat him to the spot.

"One Step, can you tell me what's happened? Can you tell me who's involved? I saw Sandy Grainfeld leaving the building down there. Is he involved? I saw Doc Mosley arrive. Is someone injured? There's been no ambulance. Has someone died? Mosley's also the ME. Has someone died? Is it one of the townspeople?"

The questions rained down like a November gale.

Renard came to a stop in front of Fred Tittlehouse. "You know I can't comment at this point, Fred. I can't comment at all." He modulated his voice, trying to remain understanding but firm nonetheless. Without saying any more, he turned toward his vehicle, but not before he heard Fred audibly sigh in frustration.

He climbed into the SUV and couldn't help smiling to himself at the town's desire to cling to the moniker he'd been given years ago—Sheriff One Step. Although he was the chief deputy now, he had been sheriff at one time, before his reserve unit had been sent to Afghanistan.

And his moniker—One Step—that was from before, too. Before he'd come back quite literally as one step. He'd had a saying, known throughout the sheriff's office in those years— "One step at a time." So, he'd come to be known as Sheriff One Step, both inside the department and around the town as well.

Of course, there was great consternation about the name when he'd come back from the war without his leg. Until he let it be known that he was fine with his former moniker. What was more, being Ojibwe, it had always had a certain resonance for him.

Renard looked in his rearview mirror. The towns-people had surrounded Fred Tittlehouse, hoping to get the scoop. He smiled as he reached for the mike on his radio to call two more deputies to the scene. Then he turned over the engine and pulled out onto the road.

Chapter 2

Paul Strauss lived in a modest frame house up the hill several blocks to the north. He was outside shoveling snow off his driveway when Renard pulled up in his squad. He stopped and leaned on his shovel as Renard climbed out of the vehicle. Strauss had his hat off and his coat open. He had a fringe of gray hair around his bald dome, and a slight paunch hung over his belt. But he moved the snow with ease.

Renard watched Strauss's face to see if he seemed surprised or not, but Strauss was unreadable. They regarded each other for a moment and then Renard started up the driveway.

"Deputy." Strauss nodded. "What can I do for you?"

"Could we talk inside?"

"Sure." The answer came immediately, but Renard sensed hesitance, possibly driven by anxiety. He knew the response well—the desire to know but also not to know.

Paul Strauss planted his shovel in the snowdrift and slogged toward the front door, with Renard trailing.

Renard was pretty sure Strauss was new to the community within the last few years. For one thing, he'd called him deputy. Not surprising that he and Grant Silverton had found each other if they were both relative newcomers to Grand Marais.

Outside the door, they did the Minnesota stomp and then stepped through the door directly into the living room of the house. There was a throw rug there, and they shed their boots and walked further into the room. Strauss was squarely built and a little shorter than he was. Renard put his age at somewhere north of sixty.

The walls of the living room were adorned with all manner of fishing paraphernalia. Nets, fly rods—some of which looked quite old—display cases with dozens of hand-tied flies mounted in each. There were bucolic scenes of men fishing in Scottish rivers, as well as some sizable trophy fish, mounted to look like they had just leapt from the water only to find themselves in a sadly altered and waterless reality.

In Claude's Anishinaabe heritage, one took a living creature for sustenance only. Never for show. Never for bragging rights. When all life is believed to be sacred, it must be sacrificed for only the best of reasons—to be used as food or to be harvested to support one's family. He understood that to many, including some of his fellow deputies at the sheriff's department, hunting was a sport. But it was also predation. One animal taking advantage of—making sport of its ability to kill another. For Claude it blurred a boundary.

"So, I guess you like to fish."

Strauss smiled. "You caught me."

Renard wondered if he'd intended that. He would go on wondering as the interview unfolded.

Paul Strauss shifted from one foot to the other as if to say, *why are you here?* His face showed a kind of guarded urgency.

"I've been told you are friends with Grant Silverton," Renard said.

The confusion on Strauss's face appeared to deepen. "That's right. Why do you ask? What's this about, Deputy?"

"I'm very sorry to have to tell you this, but Grant Silverton is dead." He watched Strauss's reaction carefully.

Strauss opened his mouth, but nothing came out.

"What do you mean, dead? I just saw him last night. We take a class together down at the folk school." He stopped and studied Renard. "Was it his heart? My God, he's only in his fifties. What happened?"

Strauss seemed genuinely confused, but Claude knew it was way too early to judge if his reaction was genuine or not. After all, Strauss may have been one of the few to know that Silverton had stayed at the folk school last night. That alone made him a person of interest.

"Again, I'm very sorry to have to tell you this, but it appears he was murdered."

Strauss backed toward a chair behind him and sat down. Some of the ruddiness from the cold outside had seeped from his face.

"Murdered? Here in Grand Marais? That's just not possible."

It seemed Strauss was already entrenching himself in the denial stage of grief.

"While unlikely in a community such as this, sadly, murder can occur anywhere," Renard said.

Strauss gave him a searching look. "Where did it happen? How did he die?"

"I can't share the specifics of the case, but it occurred sometime last night."

"But . . ."

Renard preempted his next question. "Do you know anything about Grant Silverton's next of kin? I've been told he moved here within the past few years and that you were his friend. Do you know where he might have family that we could notify?"

Strauss shook his head slowly. "I'm sorry but I don't. I know his parents have both passed away. He told me once that he was an only child who came along quite late and very unexpectedly. He said his mother was in her forties when she had him. His parents, were they alive now, would be in their nineties."

Renard nodded. "I see." He took his small notebook out of his pocket and wrote some notes. "Do you know if Mr. Silverton was ever married?"

"Well, he never mentioned a wife or being married or divorced, so I would say no."

Renard nodded. "Any girlfriend hereabouts?"

"I've never seen him with anyone."

"Would you say you were his closest friend here in Grand Marais?"

"I guess you might say that. We spent a fair amount of time together. It was my idea to take the coffin-making class. I guess we did it as a kind of a lark. More of a thumb your nose at the Grim Reaper." Strauss suddenly stopped, looking horrified. "Is that where it happened? Is that where he died?"

Renard knew this piece of information would not stay under wraps for long, so he conceded that, yes, the death had occurred at the folk school.

"I guess we never should have done it. Take that class, I mean. We were tempting fate, weren't we? If I'd never encouraged him to take the class, he might be alive now." And just like that, Strauss had moved on to another stage of grief. Bargaining.

"I don't think you should blame yourself," Renard said. "We don't know that the murder had anything to do with the class, except that it presented an opportunity for someone to find Grant Silverton alone and maybe, in that way, vulnerable."

"Did you know that he had stayed to keep working after the rest of the group left last night?"

Strauss studied him for a moment. Caution had crept onto his face. "No, I did not. He was still working on his coffin when I left. That's all I know. Several others left after me," he hurried to say.

Renard took the class list that Sandy Grainfeld had given him out of his pocket. "Could you indicate who was still there when you left."

Paul Strauss took the list and studied it for a moment.

"Jules Pierre and his wife, El. Sometimes husbands and wives take the class together," he said as an aside. "Each person is allowed to bring another person with them to work on their coffin, if they so wish." He looked back down at the list and pointed to another name. "Erin Flanagan was still there as well, and of course, Sandy Grainfeld, the teacher."

Renard nodded. Those were the same names Grainfeld had given him. "Anyone else?"

Strauss thought for a moment. "I don't think so."

"So, you didn't know he was there alone last night?"

"No, I already told you I didn't. But why would you even ask that?" The question trailed a shadow of antagonism.

"Because it's my job to ask that," Renard said in a level voice. "I'll be asking the others the same question."

Strauss looked a bit sheepish. "Sorry, Deputy. Of course, you're just doing your job."

"Might you have a picture of Grant Silverton?" Renard asked.

Because Silverton had been facedown in the coffin, Renard had not been able to see what he looked like. He wanted to put a face to the victim, if possible, to humanize him.

"I do," Strauss said. He stood and walked across the room and picked a framed photograph off the top of a table, where it sat with some others. He came back and handed it to Renard.

"That was taken at the first woodworking class we took together at the folk school."

Renard studied it. There was a distinguished handsomeness about Silverton that said, "I'm secure in life and I know it." *But was he secure? Was he happy?* Renard wondered.

Scratch beneath any human being's outward façade, and you will find the real story. One that might include regrets, or desires unfulfilled, or guilt, or a longing to turn back time. Of course, there is the rare character-disordered person who feels none of this, and Renard, in his work, had certainly encountered them. But largely those emotions are the bane of the human race.

Renard pulled out his phone and took a picture of the photograph and then handed it back to Paul Strauss, who returned it to the table. He motioned toward the fishing paraphernalia on the wall. "Did you and Grant go fishing together?"

"Nah. He never got into the swim of it. City boy, through and through—that was Grant. You know what they say, 'You can take the boy out of the city, but you can't take the city out of the boy.'"

Renard wasn't sure that's what *they* said at all, but it didn't matter.

"How about other outdoor activities?"

Strauss shook his head again. "He was like a fish out of water when it came to nature. Interesting guy, though. Hooked on history and reading. And smart. Crazy smart. And a whale of a good sense of humor."

Strauss was deep in fishing tropes now and sinking fast. Renard found it somewhat amusing despite the gravitas of the situation. He did wonder why a guy like Grant Silverton would move to a place like Grand Marais, Minnesota, if he wasn't a nature lover. After all, it was what drew people to this part of the state—the raw power and beauty of nature on display here year-round.

"How long have you lived here, Mr. Strauss?"

"Three and a half years, give or take."

Strauss shifted from one foot to the other, and Renard got the sense he was tiring of the questions. No matter. The interview would go on as long as was needed.

"Where did you live before moving here?"

"Minneapolis. Edina, actually, but I worked in Minneapolis."

"And who did you work for there?"

Strauss seemed to bristle a bit. "Why do you need to know that?"

"Just crossing the t's, Mr. Strauss."

"I worked for Hanson and Fredrickson, CPAs."

Renard wrote the name down. "And what brought you here?"

Strauss gestured toward the wall. "All this. It's the best fly fishing in the state. I used to spend weekends driving up here. Eight hours round trip from the cities. Now I have myriad rivers and creeks within a half hour's drive."

Renard nodded like that made sense. "So you were a CPA."

"It's a good career, you know," Strauss said. "Allowed me to retire early."

Claude needed no convincing. He knew accountants made good money.

Strauss gestured around the room. "This is just my winter roust. I've got a log home up on Gunflint Lake. Go there every summer. This time of year, I do taxes for a few of the local folks. Once they found out what I used to do, people started asking if I might do their taxes. I finally gave in and took on a few clients."

"Was Grant Silverton one of your clients?"

"As a matter of fact, he was."

"And what did he do before he moved here?"

"He worked in the investment banking industry—mergers and acquisitions, I think. Had a graduate degree in finance, I believe. Did his undergrad at Yale. Like I said, he was smart."

"Do you know where Grant Silverton lived before moving here?"

"Chicago. Like I said, city boy. That city had its hooks in him. Grew up there and moved back there after college."

"Odd that he'd end up here, don't you think?" Renard asked.

Strauss shrugged. "Maybe. He told me once that he got to a point in life where he just hated the pace there. I really think he was looking for something. Maybe he thought he'd find it here."

"What do you think he was looking for?" Renard asked.

"Couldn't say. It was just a feeling I got."

"And he never said what it was?"

"No. Not sure if he knew. There was a part of Grant he kept to himself. You never really missed that part, though, because he was so clever and witty and, well, just downright interesting." Strauss seemed to remember something then. "He did tell me he'd had a chance to live in Switzerland for a few years and teach some finance classes there. He said Chicago never felt the same after that."

"Huh, interesting," Renard said. "Wonder how he learned about Grand Marais?"

"You know, I'm remembering something now, after mentioning about his living in Switzerland. Grant was a skier. I know I said he wasn't much into nature, but he did like to ski. Definitely a rich person's sport, wouldn't you say? Nothing like ice fishing or portaging a canoe through the Boundary Waters. For me, it always conjures up pictures of fancy chalets and girls in fur boots."

Renard shrugged. "Couldn't say. Downhill skiing maybe. Cross-country skiing seems like a sport of the people, though. I've done that and snowshoeing all my life."

"I think Grant may have mentioned that he had skied up here when he was younger. Something about a high school ski trip, I think. Probably to Lutsen Mountains. Maybe that's how he knew about Grand Marais. Maybe this place made an impression on him when he was younger."

"Maybe," Renard said. "You've been helpful, Mr. Strauss. Given me a sense of who Grant Silverton was. I appreciate it."

"No problem, Deputy. I'm happy to help in any way. Grant was a bright light. He will be missed by those who knew him."

"Do you know if he was on the outs with anyone? Maybe bad blood over something or other?"

"Not that I know of. Can't really imagine it, either. Grant kept to himself a lot. He and I made a good connection, partly because we were both new to the community. But we'd been in similar lines of work, too."

"How did you two meet, anyway?" Renard asked.

"It was at the folk school. Grant was interested in woodworking. Took several of the woodworking classes there. Told me once he'd spent his whole life using his head and now it was time to use his hands. He liked Sandy, too. Thought he was a good teacher. I think they had a bit of a friendship going, maybe."

Renard wondered if that were the case. Sandy Grainfeld had seemed very unnerved by what he had stumbled into this morning at the folk school. But Claude had not gotten a sense of sadness or grief from him—the kind he would have expected would accompany the violent death of a friend. He remembered Sandy's apparent concern about the wood being ruined by the blood. That was something that was bound to stick in the mind of any investigator at a crime scene.

"Well, I think that's all for now." Renard closed his notebook and put it in his pocket. He handed Strauss one of his cards. "I'd ask you not to discuss any part of this interview with anyone." He knew pretty well that was like asking the snow not to fall in Grand Marais in the winter, but he said it anyway.

"Of course, Deputy. I understand. Please let me know if there's anything I can do."

Renard agreed to do that and then headed out the door. His next stop was Grant Silverton's house. He climbed into the squad and radioed Hank Gunderson to see if he'd gotten the warrant for Silverton's property.

Chapter 3

Hank radioed Renard back immediately.

"I'm at the sheriff's office. The warrant just came through. Over."

"Great. I'm heading to the Silverton property now. Meet me there. Over."

"On the way, Boss. Out."

Claude Renard pulled up in front of an impressive log home on the northwest end of Grand Marais. The place reminded him of a mountain lodge. The skier in Grant Silverton would have been happy here, he thought.

Deputy Gunderson arrived right after him, and they made their way up to the door together through the undisturbed snow that had fallen in the early morning hours. They tried the door and were surprised to find it open.

"You'd think, for a guy from Chicago, the habit of locking his door would be slow to die."

"So, he lived in Chicago before coming here?" Gunderson asked.

Renard nodded. "I just talked to Paul Strauss, and he told me Grant Silverton had lived his whole life there except for a couple of brief sojourns. One while away at college and one when he lived in Switzerland for a couple of years."

They stepped inside and surveyed the interior carefully before proceeding.

Soaring windows flooded daylight into the rooms, so that even now, in the depths of winter, the house was filled with light. Through those windows, at the back of the great room, vistas of Lake Superior ran to the horizon. It had been a deep winter, and the lake was white with ice and snow, but in the summer it would again turn to a field of sapphire. It made Renard sad to think of the life of striving that had made all this possible—a life too soon snuffed out.

Large leather sofas and chairs ranged around a fieldstone fireplace, and a heavy oak dining table completed the great room. A log stairway ran up to the second floor, and off to the left of that, behind a half wall, was a roomy kitchen.

One corner of the great room held tall bookshelves and a free-standing desk. Renard nodded in that direction. "Laptop."

They bootied and gloved up. Even though this was not a crime scene, the same protocols existed for searching victims' residences.

"Why don't you take the upstairs, and I'll cover the downstairs," Renard said.

"What are we looking for?" Gunderson asked.

"Records, legal documents. Things that can give us a picture of Silverton's life before he moved here. Where he worked. Where he lived. Who his friends were."

Deputy Gunderson nodded and headed for the stairs.

Renard walked into the great room. He stood silently in the middle of the room, taking the emotional temperature of the place. Listening. Trying to sense what had been the essence of Grant Silverton here in this space. Was he happy—at peace? Or did something weigh on his heart—his mind? Often, in the stillness of a place, Renard could sense the echoes of what had once been. In stillness, things are sometimes revealed.

After a time he walked further into the room. The house was very clean. No dust was suspended in the air where light streamed in the windows. Either Grant Silverton was a tidy guy or he had someone who came in and cleaned for him. Renard ran his finger over a couple of surfaces. Everything had been recently dusted. He walked over to the mantel above the fireplace. There were several photographs there. One was a shot of Silverton and his parents in Paris when Grant would have been in high school or college. Another was a picture of him standing in front of a lodge with his skis somewhere in the mountains. And there was a shot of him with Paul Strauss. Renard recognized the inside of the woodworking building down at the folk school. Grant was using a draw knife on a log, and Paul Strauss was looking on. He wondered if the teacher had taken the photo.

Renard walked over to where the laptop sat on the desk in the corner of the living room. He opened it, and it came to life. A password prompt appeared. He closed the computer, logged it into the evidence log that Hank had handed him when they'd entered the house, and placed it in an evidence bag. It would go back to digital forensics at the Law Enforcement Center to see what kind of magic their guy, Merlin Waters, could work on it.

Renard searched the desk but found no correspondence. There were no back bills or recent ones, which told him that Grant Silverton paid his bills online or had them set up as auto payments. He did find a sheet of paper with passwords. Some were labeled as to what they connected to in the digital world, but some were not. And some were crossed out. Who knew how recent any of them was? He logged the sheet and bagged it. The passwords would go to digital forensics along with the laptop. Merlin would have to take it from there.

He walked over to the bookcases and studied the spines. History and economics appeared to hold sway there. American history and the history and evolution of finance. Chinese history seemed to have been an interest as well. Science appeared to run a close second. The shelves were filled with books on physics and astronomy, but then Claude came to the geology section. There were several volumes on Minnesota's geology. What was more, it looked to Claude as if Grant Silverton might have owned every book ever written on agates and agate collecting. He looked around the room. One would have thought, with such an apparent passion for the topic, that there would have been agate specimens on display. But there were not.

He was headed for the kitchen when Hank came down the stairs carrying an archive box.

"This looks encouraging. What did you find?"

Hank walked into the kitchen and set the box on the breakfast table.

"Records." He flipped the top off the box. "I found Grant Silverton's birth certificate and passport in this file marked Important Legal Records. He was fifty-seven years old. I also found tax returns going back six years. They contain his previous address in Chicago and also 1099 information for his previous employer. He worked for Harold Wallace Investment Banking in Chicago."

"That's good work, Hank. This gives us some jumping off spots for the investigation. With these leads we should be able to learn more about Silverton's life before he moved here. Did you find anything else upstairs?"

"Not really. It's neat as a pin. Just like down here. I checked the closets in the three bedrooms and under the beds as well. This was the only box of records I found."

"Looks like he cleaned house before he left Chicago. But what's in here gives us a starting point. I've taken his laptop into evidence as well. It's password protected."

"Merlin will make short work of that," Hank said.

"I think I'll take a quick look upstairs just to get the lay of things up there. Make sure we haven't missed anything."

Hank nodded and Claude headed up the stairs to the second floor. He'd only been up there for a couple minutes when he heard Hank calling. He went back to the top of the stairs.

"What's up?"

"There's something you should see down here, Boss."

When Renard arrived in the kitchen, he found Hank kneeling next to the mat that sat just inside the back door.

"This is wet," he said. "Too wet to be from Grant Silverton, who wouldn't have been here since yesterday evening."

Renard knelt on his non-mechanical knee and felt the mat. He looked up at Hank. "Someone's been here."

He stood and looked out the back window. The snow leading away from the door was in disarray. He opened the door and studied the situation. He couldn't make out any footprints. It looked like whoever had been here had worked at obliterating the tracks in the snow, either by scuffing his or her feet or by brushing over them with something.

"These tracks are recent, or the snow would have covered them. Get some pictures of this, Hank. I'm going to walk around the outside of the house and check things out." He nodded toward the yard. "There's an outbuilding back there. I'd like to see what's inside it."

He walked back to the front door, stepped into his boots, and headed around the house. There was a path that ran around the kitchen side of the structure. It had been kept shoveled, except for the couple of inches of snow that had fallen in the early morning hours. There were no tracks in the pristine snow, so whoever had entered the house had come from the back of the property.

When he came around the corner at the back of the house, he studied the ground carefully before moving forward. The trail ran from the back door, across the yard, and down a small slope at the back of the lot. Whoever had been here had carefully eradicated any footprints. It looked to Claude as if the intruder had brushed something across the tracks as he or she exited the yard, so that any shoe or boot imprints would be obliterated.

He thought about who might have been here and why. First off, it had to be someone who knew that Grant Silverton would not be at home. It is a brazen act to walk into someone's house, so Renard suspected the intruder knew that Silverton would not be here—that he would not be surprised or interrupted. Which implied that whoever it was may have known Silverton was dead and may, in fact, have been the killer. But why wouldn't the killer have come here right away last night? Why wait until this morning?

It also seemed as if the intruder might have been looking for something specific that was in the house, since no path had been blazed to the garage or the small outbuilding. And again, since the electronics—laptop, TVs, etc.—had not been taken, it ruled out a random break-in or robbery or crime of opportunity. Renard guessed that whoever had been here was looking for something specific, possibly something incriminating, but there was no way to know if the intruder had found what he or she was looking for.

Hank Gunderson had opened the kitchen door and was photographing the trail of disturbance in the newly fallen snow. Renard headed toward the garage, which sat off to the left of the house, at the end of a driveway, and was surrounded by pine trees. It was sided with half logs, stained to match the color of the house. There was a door around the side which he assumed would be open, since the house had been. He turned the knob and stepped inside. It was a large double garage with a loft space overhead. There was room for his car at the far end, but the rest of the space was set up as a woodshop with various saws and tools—all expensive looking. There was a worktable and a lathe, with wood shavings beneath it, and a partially turned piece of wood, set to one side. It seemed what Paul Strauss had said was true. That Grant Silverton had developed a serious interest in woodworking. He thought about what Grant had told Strauss—*that he'd spent his whole life using his head and now it was time to use his hands.* It was sad that he hadn't had more time to explore this next chapter of his life.

Renard walked outside and closed the door. He headed for the small outbuilding beyond the garage. In dimension, it was like an oversized shed. Maybe twelve by eight feet, with cedar siding. Renard stepped inside. Windows on the front and back walls let in an abundance of light. The space was heated by a wall furnace, and the thermostat read sixty-eight degrees. When Claude had seen all the books on geology inside, he'd wondered where the rocks were. Now he had his answer. The shed was entirely set up for rock cutting and polishing, with two rock saws and several band polishers. Again, apparently money was no object for Grant Silverton when it came to outfitting his hobbies. Rustic shelves were filled with specimens in various stages of finish. Many looked like practice attempts. A few stunning agates had been face polished to look professional. Claude wondered if Silverton had purchased these or actually finished them himself. One thing was for certain. He'd become a true Minnesotan, bewitched, like so many, by a near mythic obsession with the Lake Superior agate.

Renard exited the shed and, paralleling the trail left by the intruder, trudged through the deep snow toward the back of the property. The land sloped down through a wooded area, skirted by a road running east and west toward the lake. Renard knew the road dead ended a few blocks down. Whoever had been there knew how to get to the back of this property via this dead-end road. Whether it was the killer or not, it was someone who knew the town and its back streets. Renard made his way down to the road. There were no tire tracks in the fresh snow, which told him the intruder had parked elsewhere and walked here or else had come by foot. He headed back up toward the house. He planned to ask the Evidence Response Team from the BCA to process Silverton's house as well as the crime scene. The hope was that the intruder had left some trace.

Renard made his way back to the house and entered again by the front door. Hank Gunderson was waiting for him. He had finished with the camera and had collected the logged evidence. Renard had seen a hook with keys inside the kitchen door. He went to get them. There were three keys on the chain. As it turned out, one of them locked both the front and back doors. He sent Hank to lock both the garage and the shed while he ran crime scene tape across the house doors. Then they headed for their squads.

"I need to eat something, Hank. I sprinted out this morning when you called, and it's leaning toward lunchtime already."

"You go ahead, Boss. I'll bring the evidence back to headquarters and log it in."

"I'll be down at the café. When you're done log-ging and securing the evidence, I'd like you to head back down to the folk school with a couple of deputies and canvass the neighborhood down there. See if any of the neighbors near the school saw anyone near the wood-working building between 8:15 and midnight. Also, if the BCA arrives, tell them I want them to process Silver-ton's house when they're done down at the school."

Hank nodded. "I'll let 'em know, Boss."

Renard climbed into his squad and headed down the hill toward the Harbor Café.

Chapter 4

Willow Tall Grass moved effortlessly across the café—part juggler, part dancer. As she balanced a full tray of heavy dinnerware, bound for the table near the front windows, she sidestepped a young girl headed for the bathroom. On the way, a woman with dark hair, seated in one of the booths by the wall, raised her hand to signal, and Willow gave her a nod.

Willow handed the plates around the table to the group of older men who met at the café once a week, year round. "Here you go, Harve, Bob, Larry, Dave." She knew them all by name and personalized each plate as she handed it out. "Enjoy, fellows."

Pulling her order pad from her pocket, she headed for the booth against the wall where the dark-haired woman was waiting. Willow had noticed her when she'd entered the café, as had a number of men seated thereabouts. Early to mid-forties, tall and lanky, she had a very pretty face, framed by straight, shoulder-length hair and punctuated by large dark eyes. Since she hadn't seen her before, the woman fell into Willow's category *Not from around here.*

"Good morning. What can I get for you?"

"I'll have a veggie omelet and black coffee."

Willow nodded. "Any toast with that?"

"No thanks. Just the omelet. Say, what's going on at the other end of town?"

Willow shrugged. "Don't know. I've been here since six thirty this morning. What *is* going on?"

"There were several police cars down there, and a crowd has gathered. I think the sign said something about a folk school."

"Northern Arts Folk School," Willow informed her. "I haven't heard anything, but I'll get your order in and bring coffee."

"Thanks."

Willow was back at the woman's table in moments with a carafe of coffee and a mug. She poured out the brew for her. "Your breakfast should be up shortly." Since it wasn't tourist season she asked, "Are you visiting someone in town?"

"I just moved to the area in mid-October. My name's Maggie Norlund. I've taken an administrative job down at Lutsen Mountains."

"Do you live here in town?"

"I do now. I just rented the first floor of a house."

Willow nodded. "Welcome to our community."

"Thank you," Maggie said. "Happy to be here." She ran a hand through her dark hair and glanced around the café as if to check who else might have noticed her.

"Bit of a drive down to Lutsen in the winter," Willow said.

Maggie waved that off. "It's only twenty-five miles, and I have a four-wheel drive. At first I was living at

Lutsen Village, but I found I'd rather be where there are a few things going on. You live here?"

She asked the question, but Willow noted that Maggie Norlund didn't seem all that interested in the answer.

"No. Up in Grand Portage."

"Ah," Maggie said, but there was no indication she knew anything about Grand Portage—the community at the heart of the tribal lands of the Grand Portage Anishinaabe.

"I'll just go check on your order."

As Willow headed toward the kitchen to check the orders, the front door opened. She looked over and saw Claude Renard enter the café. He was sturdy and broad-shouldered, with a steady gaze and deep blue eyes the color of Gichi-gami on a sun-charged day. She guessed Maggie Norlund would notice him. He moved toward the first booth next to the windows. Willow considered that Claude's booth since he ate so many meals here. She gave him a smile and a small wave as she ducked into the kitchen. She came out a few seconds later and dropped off Maggie Norlund's order.

*　　*　　*

Renard took a seat in his regular booth next to the windows. The Harbor Café sat on the corner of Wisconsin Street and 1st Avenue in downtown Grand Marais. It was the gathering spot for locals and had been for many decades. Service was fast and the food felt home-cooked. It was Claude's go-to spot for most of the meals he didn't have time to cook for himself.

A hurricane-style lantern hung over each table, and a wall of windows brought in the low, winter sunlight. The opposite wall of the café was painted with a giant map of Lake Superior, or Gichi-gami—the Great Sea, as it was known to Claude's people—and the arrowhead region of Minnesota.

He looked out the window. Across the street beyond the small waterfront park lay the harbor. It was covered with pack ice, which often lasted through March and sometimes part of April. This far north, winter did not easily release its icy grip on land or water.

Renard was thinking about a different kind of cold, though. He was thinking of the crime scene and the coldness of the act that had led to it. It was the kind of cold that cannot be buffered against, no matter how many layers are put on. The kind of cold that creeps into one's psyche, pushing out all thoughts of hearth and home, friendship and civility, and tracing out a territory governed by chaos, not order. An irrational, senseless kind of cold.

As he stared out the window, one of the waitresses stopped by with coffee and poured it out for him. He wrapped his hands around the mug, as if it might drive the bleakness from his thoughts, and glanced around the dining room. Boyle Bouchard sat in a booth with Father Jim George on the other side of the café. Boyle smiled at him, and Claude gave him a nod.

Father Jim George was the pastor for the local Catholic church. Boyle Bouchard was a former felon who had found Buddhism while in prison, with the help of the prison librarian, who, according to Boyle, had recognized that he was seeking for something and had guided him toward books about the great spiritual traditions. Boyle had embraced Buddhism, which, according to his understanding, required one to let go of the wrong kind of attachment to things and people. "Since I had nothing and no one," he had once told Claude, "I thought maybe this was for me."

Upon leaving prison, Boyle Bouchard had become a kind of self-styled Buddhist monk. He lived fifteen minutes north of Grand Marais in the village of Hovland, where he had grown up. Claude had met and interviewed him while working a case with Brie Beaumont, a detective from the Minneapolis Police Department. Boyle lived in a small log house in the woods, the living room of which he had converted to a Buddhist shrine. When at home, he wore the garb of a Buddhist monk. Claude had been pretty much gobsmacked by the whole scene when he and Detective Beaumont had gone to interview Bouchard. But it had quickly become apparent that this was no game for Boyle. He was all in.

Who would have guessed that inside the rough hull of this former felon there dwelt an intellectually curious and reverent man, who had found a meaningful spiritual path. So, in Claude's mind, Bouchard's evolving friendship with Father Jim George was not unexpected. Both he and Father Jim had devoted their lives to what Claude's people, the Anishinaabeg, refer to as the Great Mystery. It was not surprising they had found each other. What was more, Father Jim was a wonderfully open-minded man who would have been both interested in and supportive of Boyle Bouchard's spiritual journey.

Renard surveyed the dining room again. A dark-haired woman two booths down from Bouchard intercepted his gaze and held it for a moment. A slow, sensuous smile lit her eyes. Claude had never seen her before, so he didn't think she was from around here, and it seemed an odd time to just be traveling through.

Willow Tall Grass arrived at the table to take his order. She followed his gaze.

"That's Maggie Norlund. She just moved here. Took a job down at Lutsen Mountains."

"Ah," Claude said. "I was wondering what she might be doing here in the middle of January."

"Say, what's going on down the street at the folk school?"

"I can't say much about it, Willow, but there's been an incident down there."

"That's okay, Claude. Working here, I'm at the heart of the grapevine. I'm bound to know as soon as the rest of the town does. What would you like today?"

"How about the Country Benedict?" He posed it as a question, knowing that Willow was apt to weigh in on his choice. As expected, she hesitated with her hand over her pad and studied him in a concerned way. The Country Benedict was straight-up comfort food with its eggs, cheese, and sausage patties laid atop an English muffin, smothered in sausage gravy, and snuggled up to a crispy pile of hash browns. Right now, it felt like exactly what he needed.

"We have a wonderful turkey club on rye today," Willow offered. "Maybe with a bowl of tomato soup?"

Claude smiled. "Sure, Willow. Sounds great."

He watched her as she walked away. Her long black ponytail moved in rhythm with her steps. Willow Tall Grass was neither tall nor willowy, yet she was one of the most graceful people Claude had ever known. Not just how she moved, but how deeply she cared for others. Not just her two sons, but the elders on the rez and, yes, for him. She had always watched over him, which was ironic because he was the older one. It was he who had babysat for her when he was a teen. And yet in many ways she had become the older. Watched over him when he'd come back from war not completely himself. Brought meals. Sat with him during that first long winter. Telling the winter stories; drawing the ancestors close during those difficult months. Burning the sacred medicines. Bringing hope.

He had often wondered how he could ever repay her. But he knew what Willow would have said to that. In their heritage you pass that love and care on. You watch over others as you have been watched over. Every day he attempted to walk that path.

In a few minutes Willow brought his lunch to the table, refilled his coffee, and laid down his ticket. Then she made her way around the café, checking on the diners. Claude was halfway through his soup and sandwich when he saw Father Jim George put on his coat and leave the café. A minute later Boyle Bouchard headed across the dining room toward him. Boyle was a short but sturdy man whose balding head sat directly on his shoulders. Away from home he dressed like any other middle-of-winter northern Minnesotan. Heavy boots, jeans, parka, and a colorful flannel shirt.

He stopped expectantly at Claude's table.

"Hello, Boyle. Would you like to sit down?"

"I wouldn't want to disturb your meal, Deputy."

Boyle was always quite formal when he addressed him.

"It's quite all right, Boyle. What can I do for you?"

Boyle sat across from him. He placed his hands on the table so they touched, forming a triangle.

"Father Jim and I were supposed to have breakfast this morning. We had just met here when the call came in asking Father to come down to the Northern Arts Folk School. The deputy said there had been a death and could Father Jim come and say some prayers before the body was loaded for transport. We met them outside the woodworking building where the vehicle was waiting. But as we passed through the crowd gathered up the hill, we heard what had happened."

"So, word has already leaked out," Claude said, resignedly.

"I'm afraid so."

"Well, I knew it wouldn't take long."

"I was hoping I might be of some help, Deputy."

"It sounds like you already have been, Boyle. I mean, going with Father Jim and praying for Grant."

Boyle seemed flustered by this expression of gratitude.

"It was the least I could do," he said humbly. "But I was hoping there might be something more. Some way I could help."

"Boyle, I know you mean well, but you know you can't interfere with the investigation."

Bouchard lowered his head in a repentant way. "I understand, Deputy. I just thought . . ." He looked up.

"I just thought there might be some way I could be of assistance."

Claude was aware that Bouchard had thoroughly integrated himself into the community after moving here last year and taking over his deceased father's small house in Hovland. He worked for a local logging company. He belonged to the town book club. He helped out up at Father Jim's church. And Claude had seen him coming and going from the folk school, so he knew he had taken classes there. It was always possible he might have some insight into someone connected with the case. Claude was always open to such possibilities. He knew that leads in cases sometimes come in the strangest ways and from unexpected individuals.

He studied Bouchard for a moment. "I appreciate your offer, Boyle, and thank you. If I think of any way you can be of help, I will let you know."

Boyle nodded respectfully and rose from the booth. "I will leave you to your meal then, Deputy. I wish you peace."

"Thank you, Boyle."

As Bouchard headed for the door, Claude contemplated the probability that today was unlikely to be a peaceful one, but on a deeper level he knew there was always peace to be found, and Boyle's words were a reminder of that.

*   *   *

Willow Tall Grass stopped by Maggie Norlund's booth to see how she was doing and fill up her coffee cup.

"Can I get you anything else?"

"No, I'm good. So, who's the hunky deputy over there by the window?" She nodded toward Renard. "You seem to know him."

"Oh, that's Claude Renard. He's the chief deputy for the sheriff's department. We here in town sometimes call him One Step, or Sheriff One Step."

"I noticed his leg. That seems rather cruel."

Willow heard a gentleness in Maggie's voice she hadn't expected.

"No, it's not like that. He had the name before he went to war and lost his leg. The name comes from a saying he had when he was sheriff. 'One step at a time.' When he came back from Afghanistan, we all felt funny about his nickname. He was the one who told us not to worry, that he still liked the name."

Maggie nodded as if the explanation satisfied her. "Well, that's different then."

"I don't call him that, though," Willow said. "I've known him all my life. We both grew up on the rez. I just call him Claude. Or his Ojibwe name, Blue Fox— *Ozhaawashko Waagosh*."

"I like the sound of that—like water moving." She glanced toward him. "I'll say one thing, they got the fox part right. I wouldn't mind smoking his peace pipe."

And just like that, the other Maggie was back. Willow kept her face neutral, but she was troubled by the irreverence of the comment.

"Does he have a girl?" Maggie asked.

Willow shrugged. "Don't know." She said it even though she knew he didn't. "I saw him around town a while back with a long-haired blue-eyed blonde gal."

"Huh, maybe a long-distance romance?"

"Could be," Willow said, but she knew full well it wasn't. The blue-eyed blonde she'd referred to was a detective from Minneapolis who had become involved with a shooting down at Cedar Falls cabins, south of Grand Marais, and had worked on the case with Renard and the Cook County Sheriff's Office. The detective's name was Brie Beaumont, and since then, Willow had heard that she had moved to Maine. It wasn't a complete lie, though—the part about her being Claude's girlfriend. She had seen the way Claude had looked at her the one time they'd come into the café for coffee.

Willow laid Maggie's ticket on the table, wished her a good day and moved on to her other customers. She saw Claude put money down on the table, stand up, and head out of the door.

Chapter 5

Renard was headed for his squad up the block when he heard someone hailing him from behind. He turned and saw Dave Isaacs jogging toward him. Dave was an ER nurse at Cook County North Shore Hospital that sat up the hill on the northern edge of Grand Marais. Renard knew him well from his many visits to the emergency room that had resulted from 911 calls.

"Hello, Dave. What can I do for you?"

Isaacs came to a stop in front of him.

"I was just down at the folk school, and Deputy Gunderson said I could find you here."

Renard nodded. "Go ahead."

"I've heard about Grant Silverton and what happened at the folk school last night. People are saying his death was a murder."

"I'd rather not talk about the particulars of the case, Dave."

"I understand that, Claude. But I may have witnessed something last night."

"Go on," Renard said.

51

"Well, I was out for my nightly run before heading to work up at the hospital."

"What time was that?"

"Just before 10:30 p.m. I was coming up to the folk school and was about to cross the highway and head up the hill toward my house."

"And what did you see?" Renard asked.

"I saw the Dinkovich boys come barreling out of the woodworking building. They headed around the back of the building, and after that I lost sight of them."

"Did you go down to the building?"

"No, I had to get home and shower. My shift started at eleven. But the lights were on, so I figured someone was down there, and that's why the Dinkovich boys came running out so fast. You know those two. Always looking for some kind of trouble to get into."

Renard nodded. Yes, he was quite familiar with the Dinkovich brothers and their antics.

"I'm friends with Sandy Grainfeld, so I gave him a call, just to let him know what I'd seen."

"Did you reach him?" Renard asked.

"No, his phone went to voicemail, and I left him a message. I figured if he was down there working, he might not have heard the call. After that, I headed up the hill for home so I wouldn't be late for work. But when I heard about Grant Silverton this morning, I knew I had to get in touch with you. Let you know what I saw last night."

"I appreciate that, Dave." He'd been jotting notes as Isaacs talked, and now he put his notebook back in his pocket. "I'd like you to stop up at the sheriff's office and give a written statement."

"Of course. I'll head up there now."

"Thank you, Dave. I think I'll drive up and speak with the Dinkovich boys right now."

"You don't think they had anything to do with Grant's death, do you?"

Renard understood where the question came from, but decided not to comment. "It's always best not to speculate," he said. "We will follow the case and see where it leads."

Dave nodded. "You're right. I'll let you get on with it, then." He turned and headed back down the block where he'd come from.

Renard continued in the other direction and was almost to his squad when someone tapped him on the shoulder. He turned and was surprised to see Maggie Norlund standing in front of him. She wore an arctic white down jacket that set off her dark hair and eyes.

Before he could speak, she said, "I just wanted to introduce myself, Deputy. I'm Maggie Norlund."

"Pleased to meet you, Maggie. Willow told me you've just moved here. Welcome to Grand Marais."

She slipped something into his hand and as she withdrew her fingers, they trailed sensuously along the back of his hand.

"I hope you'll call me sometime. I'd love to know more about your town here."

Claude studied the piece of paper in his hand, deciding how to respond, and when he looked up, Maggie Norlund was already walking away. He opened his mouth to say something but then decided not to. He tucked the note into his pocket and watched Maggie proceed down the block and enter the Sivertson Art

Gallery. While he felt flattered by the encounter, he was hesitant to act on it. With the murder of Grant Silverton, now was not a good time to divide his focus. What was more, the timing of the encounter seemed curious to him. Unfortunately, suspicion of human nature went hand in glove with being in law enforcement. But he felt something else, too. A longing, born of loneliness. He realized he was staring at the door to the art gallery, as if expecting Maggie Norlund to reemerge.

He turned away, walked around to the driver's door of his squad, and climbed in. He drove back through town and headed north, up the hill toward the Dinkovich homestead. The brilliant blue sky had run its course, and a slate-colored cloudbank advanced across the lake, blanketing the sun.

Darrell and Duffy Dinkovich lived on the outskirts of the town in a house with their aging mother. The Dinkovich name went back generations in the town. Back to the time when Grand Marais was a thriving fishing village. The Dinko boys, as they were colloquially known about town, came from honest, hardworking stock, but it seemed that by the time Darrell and Duffy arrived on the scene there had been some serious thinning of the gene pool.

Renard doubted that either singly or collectively they were capable of murder. But if they had startled Grant Silverton or he had startled them, well, who knows? Grant was new to the community and may not have realized that Darrell and Duffy, while into petty larceny, were quite harmless in other ways.

The Dinkovich boys generally took a passive approach to their misdeeds. They were big on what Renard referred to as crimes of opportunity, so when one presented itself, usually they were in. Tools left lying about. An open car that might offer a small bounty of cash or change. A wallet or phone left on a restaurant table. Often, there was no proof to be found that they were responsible, but the Dinko boys were always the chief suspects in such incidents.

The current sheriff, when once asked by a tourist if there was any crime in Grand Marais, had quipped, "Oh, we have our criminal element here, and we know who both of them are." Truth be told, it was hard to say whether Darrell and Duffy actually harbored any criminal intent, or simply lacked a judgment center in their respective brains.

He thought about the footprints in the snow at Grant Silverton's house and the moisture on the mat inside. If the Dinkovich boys had been to the folk school and found the body, they might have gone there. But it was hard to imagine that even they would be so foolish.

As he neared the Dinkovich homestead, Renard saw Darrell and Duffy puttering around in the yard outside the house. On approach to the property, one might be unsure just what they were seeing—junkyard or artistic endeavor. Upon closer inspection, though, the place was revealed to be but a humble abode with everything—yes, everything, including the kitchen sink—on display. A three-ring circus of all the basics of life. Old cars and appliances; bicycles that would pedal no more; lawnmowers, identified only by their handles sticking out of the snow; all topped off with an unusual display of garden art, here and there protruding from the snow.

Possibly Mrs. Dinkovich's attempt to pretty the place up a bit.

Renard parked the cruiser down the block a ways and observed the two men. Duffy was of prodigious girth and wore an old leather jacket that Claude had seen him in before. The front of the jacket was coated with thick black grime, as if he might have spent long hours beneath a vehicle—possibly one in a similar state of disrepair as himself.

Darrell, on the other hand, had a wiry physique, and with one missing eyetooth appeared equal parts pirate-rakish and backwoods hillbilly. He had long, stringy shoulder-length black hair that looked like it had been caught in an oil spill. Despite all that, the raw materials for handsome were there, but Darrell apparently had no idea how to marshal them into a cohesive whole, or maybe lacked the discipline to do so.

Renard got out of the cruiser and walked toward the property. When the Dinkovich boys saw him, they looked like they wanted to flee. Darrell even turned, as if to make his escape, but a washing machine blocked his route. Something had spooked them, and Renard guessed it was more than his presence.

He held up his hands to steady them. "I just want to ask you boys a few questions."

That seemed to settle them a bit.

Of course, they weren't boys. They were both men and well into their forties, at that. But considering their antics, it was often hard for Renard to think of them as anything *but* boys.

He walked up the driveway that led to a single-car garage and stopped about ten feet from Darrell and

Duffy. The two made no attempt to move closer, so Claude walked a bit further into the yard along a narrow shoveled path.

"How are you two doing?" he asked, deciding to start off in neutral territory.

"Yup. Fine. Weez fine," Duffy said.

"And your mom?" Renard asked.

"Yup. She fine too," Duffy pronounced.

Renard studied Darrell, who still looked like he wanted to bolt.

"I'm here because I had a talk with Dave Isaacs a little while ago." He looked from one to the other of them to see if anything registered. It didn't seem to.

"Dave told me he was out for his run last night, before heading up to his job at the hospital. Says as he came up to the folk school, he saw you two come barreling out of the woodworking building down there."

He paused to watch their reaction. Darrell and Duffy looked everywhere but at him.

"Is that true, boys? Were you two down at the folk school last night? Did you go into the woodworking building?"

"Weez looked through the windows and didn't see nobody, so weez thought weez'd take a look around," Darrell said in an offhand way, as if it was the most innocent thing in the world.

"The door warn't locked or anythin'," Duffy added with some urgency.

"So, what exactly were you boys looking for?" Renard asked.

They squirmed a bit and then Darrell said, "Weez just wanted to take a look around. See what was in there."

"I see. And what did you find?"

"There was a body in one of the coffins," Duffy blurted out. "A dead body. Looked like he'd been stabbed."

"Scared the begezzus out of us." Darrell stuck his hands under his armpits. "Weez hightailed it outta there."

"And you didn't think to call 911?"

"Huh? No," Duffy stammered. "I mean, they mightta thought we done it. Weez just hightailed it."

"And what time did all this happen?" Renard asked.

They both shrugged. "Dunno," Darrell said.

"You didn't check your watch or the car clock?"

"Don't gotta watch, and the car clock's broke," Duffy reported.

"Well, take a guess, boys. What time do you think it was?"

Duffy shrugged again. "Maybe around ten-thirty. Quarter to eleven."

Renard nodded. "Here's the thing, boys. There's another scenario I'd like to run by you. See what you think." He looked from one to the other and leveled his best cop stare on them. "I think maybe you looked into the woodworking building and didn't see anyone in there, so you figured, why not? Let's see what we might find. But Grant Silverton was there and you surprised him. He threatened to call the police. Maybe he got in a scuffle with one of you. The other one of you got scared and grabbed a wood chisel and stabbed him."

"No. No, Sheriff." Darrell waved his arms back and forth like he was trying to avert a disaster. "That ain't it. That ain't what happened. He were dead when weez got there. Like I said, scared us half to death."

"Weez'd never do such a thing as that, Sheriff One Step," Duffy pleaded. "You know weez wouldn't."

Renard had to smile inwardly at Duffy pleading their case based on their fine past record. But, even if he was inclined to believe them, by bumbling into a crime scene, at the very least, they could have compromised the scene. Out of the corner of his eye, he saw elderly Mrs. Dinkovich at the window, and his heart went out to her.

"Let me ask you this, boys. Did you see anyone else around the building when you first got there? Anyone who looked like they could have been inside?"

Darrell and Duffy looked at each other for a moment.

"Unh-uh." Darrell shook his head. "Weez didn't see nobody."

"How about you, Duffy? You see anyone?"

"No, sir. Not a soul." Duffy hung his head repentantly, like he wished he could report something. Anything.

"And when you saw that Grant Silverton was dead, did you take the opportunity to head on up to his house? See if a door might be open? See what you could lay your hands on?"

Darrell was waving his arms again frantically. Like he might be waving down a semi.

"No, One Step. We was freaked. Weez hotfooted it outta there. Never looked back. Drove home as fast as we could."

"Weez didn't go nowhere near Mr. Silverton's house," Duffy added. "We ain't ghouls. I know weez done some bad, but weez wouldn't prey on the dead like that. You know we wouldn't, Sheriff One Step."

Renard studied them for a long moment. "I'll tell you what, boys. I want you to stop in at the sheriff's office this afternoon and give your statements. And we'll go from there."

The Dinkovich boys looked sheepishly at one another, and Renard guessed that the thought of appearing at the sheriff's office was less than appealing. But they agreed to come. He put away his notebook and fixed them with a serious look.

"You boys really need to clean up your act. For your mom's sake. She's not getting any younger, you know, and she shouldn't have to be worried about you two all the time."

They hung their heads in apparent shame. Who knew if his words would have any effect. Maybe this was the close call they needed to shock them out of their larcenous ways. He turned and headed for his squad.

"Don't forget," he called. "This afternoon. Sheriff's office."

Back in his squad, he radioed headquarters to let them know that Darrell and Duffy Dinkovich would be coming in to give statements. Then he radioed Hank Gunderson to check on the progress of things at the crime scene. Grant Silverton's body had been removed and was on the way to the medical examiner's office in Anoka County. They were still waiting for the BCA to arrive. Renard told Gunderson that he was going to interview the students from the coffin-making class who were the last to leave the previous night.

Hank came back with, "I'll radio you when the forensic team arrives. Over."

"Copy. Out."

Renard took out the list of students and addresses that Sandy Grainfeld had given him and found the address for Jules Pierre and his wife, El. They, along with Erin Flanagan, were the students who were still there after class when Grant Silverton asked to stay and work on his coffin. That knowledge, of course, made them persons of interest. He decided to start with the married couple. Jules and Ellen Pierre. He tucked the list back in his pocket and drove toward their address on W. 2nd Street.

He was busy thinking about the Dinkovich boys, but also about what Dave Isaacs had said. Dave had told him that he had called Sandy Grainfeld to tell him he'd seen the Dinkovich boys hotfooting it out of the woodworking building, but the call had gone to voicemail. Unlike Dave, Renard knew that Grainfeld was not there at the folk school. He had said he'd gone home immediately after leaving the school and had been up until 10 or 10:30. But, if he was at home and still awake, why hadn't he answered his phone? There was probably a simple explanation, but it was the first incongruity to appear in the investigation. Renard knew it would not be the last.

Chapter 6

Jules Pierre worked as a ranger for the Gunflint Ranger District of the Superior National Forest. Claude Renard had known him for years, since the Forestry Service is one of several branches of law enforcement in the North Country, and success in criminal cases often depends on cooperation among these various agencies.

Jules and Ellen Pierre lived on the west side of Grand Marais in a simple two-story house with a porch on the side. The house was painted cobalt blue and sat comfortably in a landscape of deep snow and tall pines.

Jules Pierre was outside shoveling his walk when Renard drove up. Pierre looked like he might just have stepped out of a Montreal canoe and into the future. He was a short man with broad shoulders and thick, curly black hair streaked with gray. Renard placed him in his mid-fifties. The red stocking cap perched on the back of his head did little to keep him warm but certainly added to the jaunty French-Canadian air he seemed to personify. And, fact was, Pierre's forbears had been voyageurs back in the seventeen and eighteen hundreds.

The townsfolk were split fifty-fifty when it came to his name, with half of them calling him Jules and the other half Pierre. Renard always used his given name, despite the fact that, well, he looked like he should be called Pierre.

Renard climbed out of the squad and started up the driveway.

Jules greeted him in Ojibwe.

"*Boozhoo*, One Step. What brings you my way today?"

Jules seemed surprised to see him, which indicated to Renard that he'd yet to hear about Grant Silverton's death. The other possibility—he already knew about it but had decided to play ignorant. During any investigation, Renard constantly reminded himself that things were not always as they seemed.

"Good to see you, Jules. I just need to talk to you and Ellen. Is she home?"

"She is." He looked like he wanted to say something but decided against it. "Let's go into the house. El's baking."

Renard followed him up onto the porch, where they stomped off their boots and stepped inside. They removed their boots inside the door and walked into the living room. There was a fire blazing in the woodstove, and Renard could smell something wonderful baking. Something that featured cinnamon.

They walked through to the dining room, and Jules stuck his head into the kitchen. "Claude Renard is here, El. Can you come talk to him for a minute?"

Ellen appeared in the living room a few seconds later. She was a dark-haired beauty of French lineage, like Jules. Her hair was pulled up in a ponytail that made her look quite girlish, and her cheeks, rosy from the heat of the kitchen, matched her pink flowered apron.

"Welcome, Claude. What brings you by?"

"Good to see you, El. I guess I'll get right to it. I'm sorry to say that there's been a death down at the folk school—at the woodworking building. Grant Silverton has died."

"Oh, how terrible." El's hand came up to cover her mouth.

Pierre put an arm around her shoulder to steady her, but his expression was unreadable.

"I thought you might already have heard about it," Renard said. "Word gets around town pretty fast."

"There *was* a call this morning," El said. "It was Erin Flanagan. She's in Sandy Grainfeld's class with Jules and me. We're taking the coffin-making class. But you must already know that. That must be why you're here. Grant Silverton was in the class."

"I didn't know anyone called," Jules said.

"You were outside splitting wood. I guess I forgot to tell you when you came in."

"What did Erin say when she called this morning?" Renard asked.

"Just that something was going on down at the woodworking building. That the sheriff's deputies were there. And Doc Mosley. She was calling the rest of us in the class. I'm not sure why. Something about wanting to see if we answered. Maybe see if we were all okay, I guess."

"Did you go down to the folk school?" Renard asked.

"No, I was already into my baking. I couldn't leave."

"Look, Claude. What's going on?" Jules asked. "What happened to Grant Silverton? Is there something you're not telling us?"

"Normally I wouldn't be disclosing anything about a case at this point, but somehow the facts have already leaked out." He paused and studied them for a moment. "The truth is, Grant Silverton was murdered."

El's legs went out from under her. Fortunately Jules was hanging onto her, and he steered her toward a chair.

Unfortunately, the drama of the moment prevented Renard from reading Jules' reaction to the news. But he did find it odd, as the seconds ticked by, that neither Jules nor Ellen Pierre expressed any regrets over the situation or any sympathy for Grant Silverton's demise. It was also not uncommon, in the case of a murder, for people to ask how the victim died. But Jules and El did not ask. Renard would not have divulged this information, of course, but he found the fact of their disinterest curious.

"Does Sandy Grainfeld know about this?" Jules asked.

"It was Sandy who found Grant Silverton this morning."

Jules nodded solemnly.

El seemed to have recovered from the initial shock. She stood up and smoothed her apron. "What can we do to help, Claude?"

"I'd like to go over what happened at the class last night." He looked from one of them to the other. "Were there any problems? Did anything out of the ordinary happen?"

Jules and El looked at each other blankly.

"There was nothing different," El said. "We all went right to work on our coffins. Sandy moved about the room answering questions, solving any problems that would arise. It was just like any other class."

"And did anything happen after class?"

"Not really," El said. "Grant was still working on his coffin when we left."

"Did you know Grant was going to stay and keep working?"

There was a moment of silence and then El said, "I heard him talking to Sandy after class. Something about his project."

"How about you, Jules? Did you know Grant Silverton was planning to stay after class and keep working?"

"I think I heard him ask Sandy if he could stay."

"And was Sandy okay with that?"

Jules shrugged. "He seemed a bit irritated with Grant. I guess I could see why. He probably wanted to get home."

"Did you know that Grant stayed there alone to keep working? That Sandy Grainfeld left and told Grant to lock up when he left the building?"

Jules studied the floor between his feet. "I did not know that."

For whatever reason Renard wasn't convinced by his denial.

"And approximately what time did you two leave the folk school?"

"Must have been just after eight o'clock," El said. "We were the last ones out, along with Erin. Not including Sandy and Grant, of course."

"So, you didn't actually see Sandy leave the building?"

"No," Jules replied.

"Did you two come straight home?"

"We did," El said.

"And how late were you up?"

"I went to bed at nine. I like to turn in early, especially in the winter. I'm an early riser, you see. That's when I get my baking done."

"And what time did you go to bed, Jules?"

"About ten thirty, I guess."

"No, it was eleven," El said. "Remember, I woke up and looked at the clock and asked why you were still up."

"Oh, yeah. That's right. I'm usually in the sack by ten thirty."

"So, what was different last night?" Renard asked.

"He likes to stay up and read," El interjected. "Must have gotten caught up in his book."

"Must have," Jules said.

Renard waited for him to elaborate, but Jules said no more.

"Do you know of anyone in town who might have had issues with Grant Silverton? Anyone who didn't get along with him, for whatever reason?"

"Well, it's no secret. . . " El started to say. Then she seemed to read something in Jules' eyes and stopped abruptly.

"No secret that what?" Renard asked.

"Nothing. It's not my place to say."

"El, there's been a murder. If you know something that might be of help . . ."

El shook her head. "It's best not to engage in hearsay."

Jules Pierre checked his watch. A sign that he wanted the interview to end.

"Got somewhere you have to be?" Renard asked.

"Nope. Just checking."

"Did Grant Silverton get along with everyone in the class?"

"Seemed to," Jules said. "He had a friend in the class. Paul Strauss. So they mostly hung together."

Renard nodded. "I've already talked to Paul Strauss." He put his small notebook in his pocket, took out a card and laid it on the dining room table. "If either of you thinks of anything else that might pertain to the case, please call me."

"We will," El said definitively.

Renard headed back out to his SUV. A cold wind drove in off Superior. The sun, no more than a diffuse glow behind the cloud deck, held little sway over January in the Arrowhead.

He turned over the engine, cranked up the heat, and sat thinking about the interview with the Pierres. Something seemed off about their demeanor. But then he'd almost never seen a person of interest in an investigation act completely normal. They all knew they were being questioned because they had some connection to the victim, and that had a way of making people act squirrelly.

Add to that the fact of Claude's native heritage. Hardwired into present-day native peoples is a tendency to be suspicious of what is said or presented by those outside their heritage—the end result of being taken advantage of over 400-some years. Renard had worked on this distrustful part of himself his whole adult life, and the work continued. But beyond all of that, his law enforcement training had taught him to beware of the surface—the façade. Taught him to question first, even second, impressions of people. Were they actually who they made themselves out to be? He had learned that sometimes they were not.

But always there to save the day were those folks who practically crackled with goodness and authenticity —the kind that went bone deep. Renard tried to bring their faces to mind whenever he felt ready to give up on the human race.

The wind buffeted the squad, shaking him from his thoughts. He checked the next address on his list, put the car in gear and drove toward Erin Flanagan's residence.

Chapter 7

Erin Flanagan ran a bed and breakfast out of her home that sat up on the hill in the heart of Grand Marais. The address was just a few blocks from the Pierres' residence. Of course, everything in Grand Marais was just a few blocks from everything else.

Renard knew about Erin and the B & B because she was always a vocal presence at town hall meetings. His impression of her was that she knew a lot about everyone in the community, whether they liked it or not. So the fact of her being in the coffin-making class with Grant Silverton might prove useful. On the other hand, since she was one of the last to leave the woodworking building the night before, she may have known that Grant Silverton would be there alone. If so, that made her a person of interest and also gave her opportunity. Whether there was a motive remained to be seen, as it did with all of them. That was the job—his job. Get to the root of things. Find out who had a reason to want Grant Silverton dead.

He parked along the curb in front of the B & B. It looked a bit like a Swiss chalet with a small balcony that jutted out above the front door. It was a cedar structure, stained brown, and reminded Claude of a gingerbread house with its sloping snow-covered roof and cranberry-red shutters and front door. As he climbed out of the cruiser and started up the front steps, the door opened, and Erin stood there as if she'd been waiting for him.

"Sheriff One Step. I've been expecting you."

Erin Flanagan was a tall woman—five nine or ten—with thick brown hair that seemed to stick out in all directions. A headband swept severely back from her forehead appeared to establish some kind of order over the situation.

"Hello, Ms. Flanagan." But before he could say more, Erin preempted the next bit.

"I'm sure you must have questions for me."

"Yes, well, as a matter of fact, I do. Could I come in for a few minutes?"

"Of course. Please." She gestured with her arm, and Renard stepped inside.

Something was baking, so that now it also smelled like a gingerbread house. Erin Flanagan wore a red apron and under it a red checked shirt. He decided she had a penchant for red.

"Could we talk in the kitchen? I have some cookies in the oven."

"Sure. I can smell them. Do you have guests staying?"

"No, but things pick up in February and March, what with skiers coming up on the weekends."

Renard followed her to the left through the dining room and into a very large kitchen that looked like it had been bumped out the back of the house. Being a bed and breakfast, this kitchen would have been the heart of her operation.

"I know why you're here, Deputy. I know about Grant Silverton's death. Actually, it was murder, wasn't it."

She delivered the last statement rhetorically.

"How would you know that, Ms. Flanagan?" Renard watched her.

Erin Flanagan suddenly realized the implications of her statement. "I was there," she said hurriedly. "I mean, this morning. Outside the folk school, with the rest of the crowd. When Sandy Grainfeld came up the hill, I heard him tell his wife that Grant had been murdered."

Renard didn't respond. Erin Flanagan had a reputation for knowing what was going on. Which was a nice way of saying she minded other people's business. He went on to his next question.

"I've been told that you were one of the last students to leave Sandy Grainfeld's class last night."

"Told by whom?" Erin crossed her arms.

"Well, by Sandy himself. But also by Paul Strauss, who left before you, and by Jules and El Pierre, who were among the last to leave the woodworking building."

"Huh. Well, yes. I guess they would have known that," she said a bit grudgingly.

"And where did you go after leaving the folk school?"

"Why, home, of course."

"And what time was that?"

"I was home by 8:15. I know because I looked at the clock when I came in the door."

Renard recalled seeing the grandfather clock in the hallway when he'd come in.

"And did you go out after that, at all?"

Erin propped her fisted hands on her hips. "And just where would I be going on a Wednesday night in the dead of winter? Back down to the folk school, I suppose, to kill Grant Silverton." She gave him an icy stare.

Renard looked up from his notebook and held her gaze for a moment.

"Is that what happened?"

"How dare you ask me such a thing." Her face suddenly matched her apron.

"How I dare is that it's my job, Ms. Flanagan. Only a handful of people knew that Grant Silverton was alone down there last night. You are one of them. So, I am well within my rights asking you the question."

She let out an exasperated huff of air. "You should be looking for someone who actually had a motive to kill Grant."

"And who might that be, Ms. Flanagan?"

"Well, Maurie Fontaine, for one. I happen to know he had quite a bone to pick with Grant Silverton. And by the way, anyone driving by the folk school last night could have seen Grant's car down there. Could have easily found out he was there alone. Everybody knows he drives that fancy Mercedes SUV."

If everyone knew that, then Renard was farther out of the loop than he would have guessed, since it was only this morning at the crime scene that he had become aware of what kind of car Silverton drove.

"You mention Maurie Fontaine. What do you mean, he had a bone to pick with Grant Silverton?"

"I heard him going on about it one night, up at the Harbor Light."

The Harbor Light Bar and Grill was a hangout for the locals. They had a variety of beers on tap and affordable food.

"Go on. Tell me what you heard."

"Well, Maurie was there with a couple of his buddies. They were sitting at the bar, kitty-corner from where I was seated."

"So you were seated at the bar as well?"

"That's what I just said, isn't it?"

Actually it wasn't, but Renard let it go.

"So, anyway, there I was, well within earshot, and Maurie is going on about how Grant Silverton finagled him out of his prize agate."

She paused for effect. To build drama, Renard suspected.

"Well, the whole town knows what a rock hound Maurie is. So apparently he had this large agate that he'd found. That's what he said at the Harbor Light that night, anyway. I haven't seen it, but apparently it was a beauty. Eight inches in diameter, or that's what he said."

"And when did you overhear this?"

"A couple of months ago. It was in November, I think."

"Did Fontaine say anything else?"

"Yeah. He said, 'I'm going to get it back from Silverton, no matter what I have to do.'"

Renard felt his eyebrows go up. "You heard him say that?"

"Didn't I just say so?" Erin looked at him like he might be deaf.

Claude knew that Maurie Fontaine was an avid rock hunter and collector. He was a bit of a fixture in the town. He taught earth science at the middle school, where he ran a geology club for the kids, taking them on field trips to show them the geologic wonders along the North Shore. Claude and his friend Martin Running Wolf had accompanied him as chaperones on one of these outings recently, since Martin's son was in the club. Renard also knew that Maurie Fontaine had a couple kids in college — not an easy go on a teacher's salary. Maybe that had factored into the equation.

"What exactly do you mean by finagled him out of his prize agate?" Renard asked.

Erin looked at him like he was a few balls short of a full rack.

"Maurie obviously needed the money. Grant must have used that as leverage. He probably didn't see it that way. He probably thought he was making Maurie an extremely generous offer. But maybe it felt like leveraging to Maurie. Maybe he felt exploited. And even if he didn't feel that way initially, maybe it ate away at him over time."

Renard nodded. That was a lot of maybes, but he didn't discount any of it. He was thinking about the outbuilding behind Grant Silverton's house—the one with all the fancy rock cutting and polishing equipment. The scene framing up in his mind went something like this. Rich guy from Chicago moves to the North Shore of Minnesota. Land of the legendary Lake Superior agate. Rich guy hasn't developed the agate hunter's eye over decades of combing the beaches from childhood on. But rich guy wants in on the action, and can buy his way in, whatever the asking price.

But where was this prize-winning agate, he wondered? Wouldn't Grant have displayed it proudly and prominently? Why hadn't he seen it when he and Hank had searched Silverton's property? He was also thinking about the footprints in the snow and the moisture on the mat inside the kitchen door. Had Maurie Fontaine seen Silverton's car at the folk school last night? Had he decided to confront Grant about the agate? Had things gotten heated between them? Had Maurie Fontaine grabbed a wood chisel and stabbed Grant Silverton?

Renard had seen people kill over less, and he had the sensibility of one who had been to war. He knew how quickly things can escalate. How suddenly a scene can turn deadly. But if Maurie Fontaine *had* killed Silverton last night, why would he wait until this morning to go to the house and retrieve his agate?

He studied Erin. "Ms. Flanagan, did you happen to see Maurie Fontaine in the crowd outside the folk school this morning?"

"Sure. He was right next to me until he disappeared."

"Disappeared?"

"Yeah. He was there one minute and gone the next. I'd turned to say something to him, but he'd disappeared."

"Could he have known who the victim was down at the woodworking building?"

"Maybe. Just before he disappeared, Sandy Grainfeld came up the hill and met his wife. I heard him say that Grant was dead. Maurie was next to me. He might have heard it, I guess. Why does it matter?"

"Just trying to get a picture of what unfolded," Renard said. "Can you think of anyone else who might have

76

had a grudge against Grant Silverton? Possibly someone in the coffin making class?"

Just then, Erin was distracted by the timer going off. She went over and pulled the cookie sheets out of the oven and set them on the counter to cool.

"I can't think of anyone offhand, but if I do, I'll give you a call."

"Very well." Claude put away his notebook and handed Erin one of his cards. "Please feel free to call if anything comes to mind."

"I will. Let me give you some cookies, Deputy."

"Oh, no. That's quite all right. Really." But he could see he wasn't going to prevail. Erin Flanagan was already bagging up some of her cooled cookies.

"You have some hard days ahead with this case. It's the least I can do."

"Thank you, Ms. Flanagan. That's very kind."

"I know this is a formal inquiry, but you can call me Erin."

Renard nodded. "I'll do that, Ms. Flanagan."

He headed for the door and stepped into his boots, but Erin was right behind him.

"I think we're about the same age, you know."

Renard turned and nodded. "Important information, Ms. Flanagan." And then he was down the steps. He thought he heard her say something. It sounded like, "Huh, well, you're welcome."

Renard sat in his cruiser, thinking. Wondering whether the tracks in the snow around Silverton's house had been made by Maurie Fontaine. Whoever had been there had visited the house this morning, after it had snowed. Add to that the fact that the prize agate Erin had mentioned was nowhere to be seen in Silverton's house. Claude shook his head. He couldn't believe that Maurie Fontaine would be so foolish as to enter a murder victim's house and take something from the scene. Didn't he realize he'd be incriminating himself?

What was more, if he'd killed Grant Silverton over the agate, why hadn't he gone to Silverton's house last night to retrieve it? But then Claude thought about the Dinkovich boys, and that changed the complexion of things.

Assume for a moment that Maurie Fontaine killed Silverton. Maybe he saw his car there and decided to go talk to him. Maybe things escalated and one thing led to another. Enter the Dinkovich boys. Was it possible that Fontaine was still in the building—that he had just killed Silverton? And here come the Dinko boys bumbling into the scene of the crime. If Maurie knew the Dinkovich boys had found the body, he might have assumed the same thing Claude had. Namely that they would go up to Silverton's house to see what they could lay hands on. Maurie had lived here forever, so he would certainly know about the Dinkovich boys' predilection for opportunistic behavior. Maybe he thought it was safer to wait till morning to go after his agate. And, fact was, until someone proclaimed Silverton dead this morning, maybe Maurie Fontaine was uncertain whether he'd actually killed him.

The stream of possibilities flowed on with Renard along for the ride. He knew something else, too—that killers sometimes visit the scene of the crime after the fact. It gives them a chance to be seen acting surprised at what's unfolding. Fontaine could have simply been putting on an act by being part of the crowd this morning.

The radio squawked, shaking Renard from his thoughts. He keyed his mike. "Go ahead, Hank. Over."

"The team from the BCA has arrived. Thought you'd want to know. Over."

"I'll head down there right now. Who's the team lead? Over."

Hank came back. "Adrianna Tomebay."

Renard smiled. "Thanks Hank. On the way. Out."

He needed to get over to Maurie Fontaine's place ASAP. But as lead investigator, he also needed to make an appearance down at the crime scene now that the Evidence Response Team had arrived. And he hadn't seen Adrianna Tomebay for quite a while, which was reason enough to go there first.

Chapter 8

Renard pulled up along the curb, across from the folk school, and turned off the engine. He could see the van from the BCA down below, next to the woodworking building. He sat for a moment picturing Adrianna Tomebay in his mind's eye. They'd known each other since middle school and had become an item in high school.

Nowadays, she had straight, shoulder-length blond hair with neon blue streaks in it. They put him in mind of the fact that Adrianna'd had a wild side. But she'd also had a big brain, and that, not her looks, had been her ticket out of obscurity. A whiz at math and science, she'd landed a scholarship to Penn State and gone on to get her undergrad degree in biochemistry and a master's in forensic science.

Claude had always known why she'd gone that route. Or was pretty sure, anyway. It was because of her older sister. Alicia had disappeared when Adrianna was twelve and had never been found. Ria had never stopped trying to make up for that. Claude guessed she hadn't stopped yet. There was a part of her that broke that day—the day Alicia never came home. A part of her that Renard had always wished he could fix. But of course, he couldn't, and that had made him feel helpless.

She had drifted away. No, that was wrong. He had let her drift away. She'd written to him religiously from college, but he hadn't kept up the correspondence. And by Christmas break, when she came home, she had a new boyfriend. A guy with an Italian name and the looks to go with it.

She was forty-five now just as he was, but to him she would always look eighteen. The way she had looked that last summer when they'd been together. Back when everything still seemed possible.

He sometimes wondered now, how much the tragedy surrounding Adrianna's family had factored into his going into law enforcement. He had been sitting with the heat off, remembering. He climbed out of the cruiser and crossed the highway. The cold had penetrated the junction between his real and artificial leg. That sharp feeling always reminded him of the junction between his two lives—the one before and the one after losing his leg.

He had long ago made peace with the loss of his leg. He'd had to. His work was taking care of others—watching over the town. How could he do that if he invested his time in feeling sorry for himself? Accepting what is, even if you don't understand it, is the only way forward. And patience with oneself and others. His Anishinaabe heritage had given him that. His people had learned patience over many generations. And acceptance? That came easier to him than it might have to those from ancestry less oppressed.

At the bottom of the hill, Deputy Len Blake was still on duty outside the woodworking building. He didn't seem to be feeling the cold, but then there were twenty-three years that separated them.

Renard stepped inside the building and bootied up. The Evidence Response Team moved about the scene, looking like characters in a sci-fi film in their white hooded crime scene suits and blue booties. It took him a moment to locate Adrianna Tomebay among the amorphous figures. He caught her eye when she turned his way. She set her clipboard down and headed over to him.

"Hello, Blue Fox."

She had always used his Ojibwe name. But back when they'd been together, she had shortened it to Fox.

"Adrianna. It's good to see you."

"Same, Fox."

There they were, face to face, and for just a moment, it felt as if time had spun backwards. As if all things might still be possible. But then the spell broke. Claude noticed that while Ria's clear blue eyes still danced with intelligence, there were dark shadows beneath them and stress lines in her brow.

"We're just getting into it here," she said. "It could be a few hours. But given the nature of the scene—a class setting—and the number of people who were here last night, before the crime occurred, well. . ."

She didn't need to finish. Renard already knew what the likelihood was of finding meaningful evidence. And then there were the Dinkovich boys, who, even if not responsible, would have polluted the crime scene.

"I understand," Renard said. "I also need to ask you and the team to process the victim's house when you're done here."

"Okay. . ."

"Someone entered the victim's house this morning. There were fresh tracks in the snow around the house and moisture on the mat inside the kitchen door."

"Any sign of a break-in?"

"No. The doors had been left unlocked."

"All right, Claude. We'll get on it after we're done here."

She turned and headed back across the room, but called over her shoulder, "Good seeing you."

"You too, Ria."

She turned back, and they looked at each other for just a moment. A moment that somehow spanned the wide river of time. A moment filled with questions.

He removed his booties, placed them in the bag that would later hold the paper jumpsuits and booties from the team, and headed out the door.

She had used his first name. He tried to remember the last time that had happened. He couldn't. It had always been Blue Fox or just Fox. It signaled some kind of shift in her, he thought.

She seemed tired and stressed. Not hard to understand in her line of work, which served up new horrors daily that needed to be processed—studied and pored over. What toll did that take over time? he wondered. It was far different from his job as chief deputy with the county sheriff's office. There were other aspects to his work. Positive aspects like community interface and interaction. But for Adrianna Tomebay, it was always grim.

Always the remnants of a crime scene. Her branch of the BCA covered a large area of northern Minnesota. That meant exposure to bad things, almost daily.

He hadn't been able to see her blue-streaked hair under her crime scene hood, and that had brought into sharp focus the signs of stress on her face. He wondered now if the blue hair was maybe a way to divert the focus of those around her from a more stark reality. Away from what the inner Ria was coping with.

He had learned through the law enforcement grapevine that there were cracks in her marriage. The union had produced two children, so the thought of it going awry was painful to think about. But he knew one thing; because of those children, Adrianna would have hung in there with the tenacity of a pit bull, whether she should have or not.

He turned over the ignition, as much to restart his thoughts as to pump some warmth into the car. He needed to keep a singular focus on the investigation until they had their killer. The first forty-eight hours were critical. He pulled away from the curb and drove up the hill toward the western end of Grand Marais, where Maurice Fontaine lived.

Chapter 9

Maurie Fontaine lived on the outskirts of Grand Marais. In fact, technically his house lay beyond the town line, up on the bluffs across from Lake Superior. His property fronted on Highway 61, but the house was set back from the road up a long driveway. The house was kind of a split-level affair that Renard guessed had been built in the 1970s.

He saw the driveway coming up and turned right. He drove up toward the house and parked in front of the attached garage. The garage door was up, and Kristin's white van was parked in there. Maurie's Ford pickup was in the driveway, so Renard knew he was home from his teaching job for the day. He noted the time on the dashboard clock was 3:55. He climbed out and headed along the shoveled path to the front door.

Renard was thinking about the story Erin Flanagan had told him—about Maurie selling his prize agate to Grant Silverton—when Fontaine's wife Kristin opened the door.

"Why, Claude. This is a surprise. How nice to see you."

"Good afternoon, Kristin. I wonder if I could speak to Maurie?"

"Of course. Come in."

Kristin was in her late forties. She was tall and had a kind of no-frills Scandinavian beauty about her. One might have thought her shy, since her blue eyes seldom looked directly at you. But Renard knew better—had seen her outspoken side.

Renard stepped into what was the lower level of their house. Off the family room, where he stood, he could see a bedroom and a bathroom down on this level.

"I'll go get Maurie," Kristin said. "Would you like to come upstairs and have some coffee?"

"No, I'll just wait here, if that's all right."

"Of course."

She seemed a bit bemused by his visit, and Renard wondered if she knew about Grant Silverton's death. If not, he had to wonder why Maurie had not mentioned it to her. At any rate, he had decided that questioning Maurie down here might offer a bit more privacy.

"Claude, this is a surprise," Fontaine said on his way down the stairs.

He was far enough away that Renard could not read his expression. *Was* it a surprise? he wondered. He thought not. He decided to play it like he didn't know anything about Maurie being in the crowd that morning.

Fontaine came across the room and held out his hand. He was a burly guy, around six feet tall, with a neatly-trimmed beard and hair that shagged over his ears a bit. Renard decided he had the physical where-withal to have killed Silverton and hoisted him into the coffin.

"What can I do for you, Claude? Nothing has happened at the school, has it?"

Renard recognized it as an honest concern. One that constantly plagued parents and teachers in these times when children were senselessly gunned down in what should be the sanctity of school settings.

"No, Maurie. This is about something else entirely." Renard waited a beat for a response, but none was offered.

"Are you aware that Grant Silverton was found dead this morning?"

"Dead? What happened? That . . . That's terrible."

"He was found this morning, down at the folk school in the woodworking building." Renard studied him carefully. "You haven't heard about it?"

"No, sorry, I haven't. What happened?" he asked again.

"I'm not at liberty to talk about the case." Renard paused, surprised at Fontaine's denial. He knew this man, or he thought he did, anyway.

"Did you know Grant Silverton?"

Fontaine glanced to the side like he wanted to escape. But then he looked Renard in the eye. "I did know him."

"Tell me about your connection with him."

"Well, he was interested in rock hunting. Agates specifically. No surprise there, I guess. He'd moved here from somewhere else a few years ago. Chicago, I think. Someone in town directed him to me. He stopped up at the middle school one day, and that's how we met."

Renard wrote notes as Fontaine talked.

"So you became friends?"

"I wouldn't say friends, exactly. I helped him set up a space for working on rock cutting and polishing."

"Where was that?"

"He had a small outbuilding behind his house. That's where he set up his workshop. He got most of his specimens at rock shows. Moose Lake has a big one every summer. I think he went to that."

"And did you sell him any specimens of yours?"

"Me? No."

Fontaine crossed his arms and turned his gaze out the window. Renard was sure he was lying. He waited, hoping Maurie Fontaine would have a sudden attack of remembering. But it wasn't going to happen.

"I have a witness who places you in the crowd this morning, outside the folk school."

"So? What does that have to do with anything?" Fontaine said defensively. "I was driving into town to pick up some supplies. I didn't have any classes today until afternoon. I saw the crowd gathered up the hill from the folk school and stopped to see what was going on. That's all. No crime in that."

"No one has mentioned anything about a crime." Renard looked up from his notebook and held Fontaine's gaze for a moment.

Fontaine looked sheepish. "Like I said, I was there. But I never found out what was going on. I had to get on into town, so I left."

Renard recalled that Erin Flanagan had said that she'd turned to say something to Maurie, but he had disappeared. That was right around the time Sandy Grainfeld had come up the hill, met his wife, and whispered loud enough for others to hear that Grant Silverton had been murdered. He guessed Erin was not the only one to have heard that, because word had spread around town like wildfire. So, he was having a hard time believing that

Maurie Fontaine had not heard about it. But whether he had or not, it was apparent that he was trying to distance himself from any connection with Grant Silverton.

"I'm going to ask you again, Maurie, did you sell any of your agates to Grant Silverton?"

"I told you I didn't." The denial came out loud enough that Fontaine glanced toward the stairs, maybe hoping his wife hadn't heard.

"Look, Maurie, I have a witness who heard you up at the Harbor Light a while back going on about how Grant Silverton had bought one of your prize agates. Are you telling me that's false?"

Maurie let out a sigh. "No, it's the truth," he finally said. "But I didn't kill Grant Silverton," he blurted out.

"I didn't tell you he had been murdered. So how would you know that?"

"I overheard it this morning down at the folk school."

"So, why did you lie to me?"

Fontaine fell silent. Renard waited, matching his silence, but Fontaine did not answer the question.

"The witness up at the Harbor Light also overheard you say that you were going to get your agate back, no matter what you had to do."

"I was just blowing off steam. I'd had one too many that night. I don't remember what I said." He looked pleadingly at Renard. "Claude, you know me. Do you really think I'm capable of murder?"

"Maybe not premeditated murder, Maurie. But things happen in the heat of the moment. Did you know that Grant Silverton was taking the coffin-making class at the folk school?"

"Of course not. Why would I know that?"

"Where were you last night between eight and ten thirty p.m.?"

"Right here, of course. You can ask Kristin."

"I plan to, Maurie. So, you admit to being in the crowd this morning, near the folk school."

"Yes. I told you that."

"And that's where you overheard that Grant Silverton had been murdered?"

"I told you that, too."

"Well, not initially."

"Okay, okay. But I fessed up."

"Did you already know he was dead when you got there this morning?"

"Of course not. Why are you asking that? How could I already know he was dead?"

Then the light bulb went on. Fontaine's face went bright red.

"I have nothing more to say, Deputy. I've told you the truth. I certainly did not kill Grant Silverton, no matter what I said at the Harbor Light that night."

"Do you know where Mr. Silverton kept this prize agate after he bought it from you?"

"Somewhere in his house, I suppose. How would I know?"

"Here's the thing, Maurie. We did a search of Grant Silverton's house this morning. There was no evidence of a large agate. I saw some smaller specimens in his outbuilding—the one you mentioned helping set up— but nothing like the prize agate I've heard described."

"Well, who knows? Maybe he rented a safety deposit box for it."

"Here's the other thing, Maurie. Someone had been at Silverton's house this morning. There were fresh tracks in the newly fallen snow. And whoever it was had gone inside the house. There was moisture on the kitchen mat."

"What does any of this have to do with me?" Fontaine asked. He had crossed his arms on his chest and taken a step back from Renard, like he might be getting ready to bolt.

"Do you really think I'd go to Silverton's house, knowing he'd been murdered, and take that rock? I'm not out of my mind, you know."

Whether Fontaine was in or out of his mind was not readily apparent, but he did have motive, and Renard found it quite plausible that he would have gone to retrieve his agate. The big question was, had he killed Silverton first? Fontaine had lied to him twice in this interview. Why do that if you're not hiding something? It was possible he could obtain a warrant to search Fontaine's premises. But would it reveal anything? If Fontaine had retrieved the agate from the victim's house, Renard was pretty sure he wouldn't have it sitting around in plain sight.

"Look, I'm not the only one in this community that Silverton rubbed the wrong way."

"What are you saying?"

"Just that other folks took issue with the way he did stuff. Talk to the Pierres—Jules and El. There was no love lost there."

"Can you tell me about it?" Renard asked.

"Not my place to do that. All I'm saying is there are others here in the community who might have acted out of anger. I'm not the only one. And as to who ratted on me this morning—I'd guess that was Erin Flanagan. She was standing right next to me. That woman minds everyone's business, but she's not lily white either."

Renard listened from a place of neutrality. He was after facts, not hearsay.

"Look, Claude. I know you're just doing your job, and I don't envy you. It can't be easy to run an investigation in a town where you know most everyone. So, I have no hard feelings about this. I know you have to go where the evidence leads and ask the questions you have to ask."

"I appreciate that, Maurie. But I don't intend to let those relationships stand in the way of finding a killer." He waited a beat, holding Maurie's gaze. "Would you call Kristin down here, please?"

Maurie complied. He stepped over to the stairs and called his wife's name. Asked her to come downstairs. When she got to the bottom of the stairs, he nodded for her to go over and speak to Renard. He stayed at the foot of the stairs.

Renard gave Kristin the news of Grant Silverton's death, watching for any sign that she already knew about it. The look of absolute alarm in her eyes told him that she did not and, again, he had to wonder why Maurie had not shared what he knew with her. Renard did not mention that Silverton had been murdered. When he asked her where Maurie had been the night before, between eight and eleven, she looked purely confused.

"Why, he was here, Claude. At home. Why would you ask?"

"Just dotting all the i's, Kristin. Nothing to worry yourself about."

She nodded, but the look of confusion deepened. "Is there something you're not telling me?"

"So, he didn't go out at all during that time?" Renard said, ignoring her.

"Not that I know of. I was in here, sewing, and Maurie was out in his workshop for a couple of hours. He came in, and we went to bed around ten thirty."

Not an airtight alibi, Renard thought. Maurie could conceivably have left, and Kristin might not have known. To drive into town from where they lived, kill Silverton, and get back home could have been accomplished in fifteen minutes. Add in a few more minutes for the two of them to get into a heated argument and a half hour would be plenty of time for the whole thing to unfold.

Maurie Fontaine's responses had been, at best, a patchwork of half truths. Renard was not at all convinced that he'd had nothing to do with the crime. He closed his small notebook and thanked Kristin for her time. She went back upstairs, and Maurie walked over to where he stood.

"I hope you're being truthful, Maurie."

"About what?" Fontaine asked defensively.

"About not having that agate in your possession, for one thing. I'd hate to have to come back here with a search warrant."

Fontaine gave him the stink eye.

"Think carefully about it, Maurie. You can save yourself and Kristin a lot of embarrassment by being truthful here."

Maurie looked him straight in the eye. "I don't have that rock. I regret selling it to Silverton, but everything you're suggesting is insane."

Renard pocketed his notebook. "I'll be in touch, Maurie."

Fontaine wasted no time opening the door and, with an extended hand, ushering Renard out.

Claude sat in his car, thinking about the interview. Were Maurie's initial lies just designed to distance himself from the fact that he had a connection to Grant Silverton—one that had led to bitterness between them? Or had they been an attempt to mask something much darker?

He took out his notebook and looked at the notes he'd written. Maurie Fontaine had made reference to the Pierres having some kind of grudge against Grant Silverton. Sometimes he was amazed at what he didn't know about the inner workings of the town—the secrets that seemed to be common knowledge. But, truthfully, it was territory he tried to stay far away from—gossip and hearsay. Too much of that can cloud one's impressions of those around him. Whatever was happening in Grand Marais, he preferred to find out about it firsthand. Because he wore a badge, anything else felt like dangerously shaky ground.

The big question was, how would Maurie Fontaine have known Silverton was there at the woodworking building last night? He claimed not to have known that Silverton was taking the class. But then again, having had dealings with Silverton, Fontaine would recognize his car. And since the folk school sat right off the main highway through town and, coincidentally, on the route to and from Fontaine's house, he could easily have been aware that Silverton was taking a class down at the school, as well as knowing what nights he was there.

Renard checked his watch. He needed to get back to the sheriff's office and write his reports, but Maurie Fontaine's insinuation about Jules and El Pierre felt like a hanging thread. One that needed to be addressed. If they'd in fact had a grievance against Grant Silverton, Renard needed to know about it. Until any concrete information came back from either the autopsy or the BCA, his job was one of discovery. Find out who had a grievance against Silverton, ergo, a motive to do him harm. He started the engine and headed back into town to revisit the Pierres.

In the west, the sun generated little more than a faint glow behind the thick cloud deck. These days, in the deep of winter, it set just after 4:30. In his rearview mirror, Claude watched that ghost of a sun slip below the horizon.

Chapter 10

As he drove toward the Pierres' house, Renard was thinking about his interview with them earlier in the afternoon. He had asked them if they knew of anyone in town who had an issue with Grant Silverton. He remembered that El had started to say something and suddenly stopped, as if Jules had sent her a silent signal not to speak. He remembered her words, "Well, it's no secret . . ." and then nothing. He had prodded her to continue but gotten the line, "It's not my place to say." Almost, if not the identical line he had gotten from Maurie Fontaine.

Seemed folks were reluctant to cast aspersions, at least when he was present. They all seemed to know things about others in the town but were reluctant to speak about those things. Was it because he was the law? He had to believe that, as in all small communities, the townsfolk gossiped about each other. So, why the self-righteous act with him? He was sure the answer had a lot to do with the badge he wore.

As he pulled up in front of the Pierres' house, he noticed their pickup truck was gone. It had been in the driveway earlier. He got out and went up to the door.

After ringing the bell twice and waiting, he headed back to his squad. He would have to catch them later — if not today, then first thing tomorrow.

What if they denied that there was an issue between them and Grant Silverton? What then? *One step at a time,* he told himself. *No point in getting ahead of yourself.* He turned over the engine and drove through town toward the sheriff's office. On the way, he radioed Deputy Hank Gunderson to check on the BCA's progress at the crime scene. He was told that Adrianna Tomebay had sent a few members of the team, with one of the extra deputies, up to Grant Silverton's house to get started there.

The Cook County Sheriff's Office sat on the eastern edge of town on a hill, where the Gunflint Trail began its steep climb north from Lake Superior toward the Boundary Waters. It was a fairly large facility, housing offices, the evidence collection and storage area, the county jail, and 911 communications, as well as outbuildings and a fueling facility for their small fleet of SUV squads.

Renard let himself in the front door with his pass code, and used it again to pass from the lobby into the secure area of the facility. His office was in the middle of the long corridor. His desk was stacked with work that would have to wait. This investigation would now take precedence over all else.

He signed into the system, took out his notebook, and started writing reports on the interviews he'd held. First, with Sandy Grainfeld at the crime scene. Then, proceeding chronologically, through his interviews with Paul Strauss, Darrell and Duffy Dinkovich, the Pierres,

Erin Flanagan, and finally, Maurie Fontaine. He also entered into his reports what they had found at Grant Silverton's house, as well as the information Dave Isaacs had given him about seeing the Dinkovich boys running from the woodworking building last night, around the time Silverton would have been murdered.

It was approaching six o'clock when he got up from his desk and went to see if Merlin Waters, their digital forensic tech, was in the facility. Merlin had been out with Covid and was expected back today or tomorrow. Katie Hill, one of the administrative assistants, was just packing up to leave and informed him that Merlin had tested negative for the second time and would be returning to work tomorrow.

Renard walked back to the evidence lockers and looked at the log. As instructed, Deputy Gunderson had brought Silverton's cell phone, collected at the crime scene, and laptop, taken into evidence when they had searched Silverton's house, back to the sheriff's office. He had logged them in and placed them in an evidence locker, along with the sawdust sample Renard had collected at the crime scene.

Renard checked his watch. He needed to head home and change. There was a special gathering tonight up at Grand Portage. It was one of the winter storytelling evenings on the rez, and his father, Joseph Renard, one of the tribal elders, was the storyteller for tonight. There would be a drum circle, which he was scheduled to take part in, and tribal dancers. He walked back to his office, logged out of the system, and shut off the light as he left.

His house was just minutes away. He turned right onto Highway 61 and at the traffic light—there was only one in town—made a left and drove down the long stretch of Broadway Street to where it fronted on East Bay. At this end of town, storms regularly crashed in from the northeast to flow up onto the streets of Grand Marais, occasionally closing businesses in their line of fire. Claude parked the SUV in front of his house and headed inside.

There wasn't time to make dinner, so he grabbed a protein bar from the kitchen and headed upstairs to change out of his uniform. He pulled on a pair of jeans and a clean tee shirt, brushed his teeth, and ran a comb through his dark hair. He put on a heavy red flannel shirt with the emblem of his band. Gitchi Onigaming. The Grand Portage Band of Anishinaabe. Willow Tall Grass had embroidered the emblem onto the shirt with her beautiful handwork and given it to him the winter he had come home from war. He always wore it to gatherings at the Grand Portage community, especially if he thought Willow would be present. It was a small way to show his continuing gratitude for all she had done for him.

He headed downstairs. There were a few minutes left before he had to leave, and he used them to prepare a spirit bowl for the ancestors. He took out the small wood bowl he had turned from a piece of maple many years ago in his high school woodworking class. He always used it for his spirit bowl offerings. He poured in a handful of *manoomin*, or wild rice, a few nuts, and some dried cranberries. The spirit bowls varied depending on what he had on hand, but he always incorporated *manoomin*—the food that grows on water— which was a sacred food to his people.

He slipped on his coat and went out the back door and down toward the lake. He set the spirit bowl at the edge of the trees that bordered his property and whispered a short prayer in Ojibwe. Darkness and cold pressed in on him, but he walked down to the edge of the water and squatted there. While Grand Marais harbor, a stone's throw west of him, was solid pack ice, here, the bay was open. He could hear the movement of water, the murmurings of Gichi-gami, as it washed over the stone beach, drawing back with a thousand whispers.

His mind was preoccupied with the case, and he offered a silent prayer to the Great Spirit for wisdom and that he would find a way to the truth. As he listened to the murmurings of the dark water, he felt the hairs rise on the back of his neck. He was not alone. He could sense someone nearby. He slowly stood and turned toward the trees, but the darkness there was complete. He stood for a long minute, staring into the woods, hoping to detect movement, but there was nothing.

He turned away, walked to the back door of his house, and slipped inside. He turned off the lights and waited by the window, but no one appeared. Claude was not easily spooked. He wanted to tell himself it was nothing, but his life had served up plenty of dangerous situations. Ones that had taught him to trust his instincts.

He walked to the front of the house, grabbed his keys from the small table, and headed out the door, locking it behind him. His pickup truck sat in the driveway. He climbed in, and within minutes he was heading out of town for the forty-minute drive northeast to Grand Portage.

Chapter 11

As he drove northeast toward Grand Portage, Renard was thinking about the case, while a subliminal part of him kept constant watch for deer that might dart out onto the highway.

Bits of the interviews rolled through his mind as he considered who qualified as a suspect in the murder of Grant Silverton. Maurie Fontaine topped the list with his grudge against Silverton for leveraging him out of a prized agate specimen. But the Dinkovich boys, innocent as they pretended to be, could have scared Silverton. After all, he may not have lived here long enough to develop a tolerance for them, the way the rest of the community had. One thing could have led to another.

But what about the unknowns? And there were always unknowns in any case. Things that came to light that never would have been suspected. What about those? That was territory yet to be explored. Four people knew Grant Silverton had been at the folk school last night. Sandy Grainfeld, the woodworking teacher, Erin Flanagan, and the Pierres—Jules and El. And though he claimed otherwise, Renard had not ruled out the possibility that Paul Strauss, Silverton's friend, also knew he had been there. Of course, there would have to be a motive, which seemed unlikely if they were as close as Strauss had said.

Twenty minutes along, just beyond the Reservation River near Hovland, Renard passed the sign identifying these as the tribal lands of the Grand Portage Anishinaabe Nation. He looked at the car clock. It would be close, but he'd make it on time. His mind returned to the case.

There was the possibility of someone passing by the folk school and seeing Silverton's car there. Again, making it a crime of opportunity. Maurie Fontaine fell into this category, but so could virtually anyone else. It boiled down to motive, and that would keep Renard awake at night until the murder was solved. Could he find the motive and evidence to prove culpability? Or would the case go cold and a killer slip away, figuratively speaking?

The principle of truth was the last of the Seven Sacred Laws, also known as the Seven Grandfathers Teachings —principals foundational to the Anish-inaabeg through untold generations. The search for and the upholding of truth had been Claude's guiding light all of his adult life. Along with the other Grandfather principles— wisdom, respect, love, honesty, humility, and bravery —it sat at the heart of what had saved him in the really dark times.

He had been driving for over a half hour when the lights from the Grand Portage Trading Post came into view in the distance. A few minutes further on, he turned right into the community, drove past the trading post, where a semi was fueling up, and followed Mile Creek Road around the bay for about a mile. He turned left and made his way up to the elementary school, Oshiki Ogimaag Charter School, where the evening's gathering was being held.

Claude headed into the school. Just inside the doors to the gym, he stopped and looked around. Some of the band were in their ceremonial dress for dancing. He saw his friend Martin Running Wolf across the gym. Martin waved and headed toward him. When he got closer, Claude could read his T-shirt. It said, *Don't wait too long.* Claude wanted to ask, "Wait for what?" or "How long is too long?" But he didn't. Running Wolf liked wearing shirts with cryptic sayings, and if you asked him to explain, the answer was often even more enigmatic.

"*Anin,* Claude. Thought maybe you weren't going to make it."

"*Boozhoo,* Martin. I wasn't sure I would. Long day."

"I heard about what happened down at the folk school." He shook his head slowly. "Unbelievable. I'm surprised you're here."

"We're in a bit of a holding pattern until the BCA finishes their work."

Martin nodded. "It's good you came."

Claude took a deeper meaning from those words. He knew Martin Running Wolf to be wise. Not one for casual comments.

Martin was a teacher here at the elementary school. He also occasionally taught at the folk school in Grand Marais. Native drum making and traditional weaving techniques. Claude hoped Running Wolf might have some insight to contribute, since he knew the staff at the folk school.

"We should take our places, Claude."

Martin gestured toward the drum circle, where one of the elders was sprinkling the traditional tobacco around the drum, and the men were taking their places around it. Claude followed him, and they took their seats. Across the gym he saw his father, Joseph Renard, and Edna Beaumont talking to one of the dancers. The children and teens sat in a semi-circle on the floor near where the storyteller would stand. Adults behind them were seated in chairs.

The lights went down, and torches, secured in buckets of sand, were lit. The mood was set, and the drum circle commenced with a slow drumbeat and low rhythmic chant. The drumbeat represented the heartbeat of Mother Earth—the heartbeat of his people. Claude let the vibrations travel through him, become one with him, and the stresses of the day—of the case—grew fainter and fainter until, finally, there was only the drumbeat and the chanting as he felt a weight lift from him. What replaced it was breath and sound and the deep vibration of the drum. It was like a cleansing, every time he joined the drum circle.

After about five minutes the chant ended and the drum quieted. Joseph Renard took his place in front of the band members gathered there and began the story. Storytelling is a winter occurrence for native peoples. It is often said that stories are only told in the winter months, but in earlier times they were told throughout the year, as the seasons turned. But, for Claude, winter had always seemed the appropriate time for the telling of stories. A time of year when the frenetic pace slows and focus on inner things is somehow easier. That is the time for stories and reflection on the morals and messages they carried.

Tonight Joseph Renard was telling the story of Pukawiss, one of the *manitous*. The *manitous*, or *manidoos*, are spirits who often have both godlike and human qualities. The legend tells how Pukawiss, the third son of Winona, daughter of Nokomis, was the inventor of dance, as well as the regalia worn in the performance of the dances. Joseph told how Pukawiss, as a child, was interested in the movements and habits of all the animals. He would watch them and mimic their movements and learned to bend and shape his body into many forms in his attempts to imitate the animals. As he grew, his love of dramatizing the natural world in movement grew as well, and he traveled far and wide, teaching his dances to the many tribes.

Pukawiss also observed human behavior, and as the dances evolved, they were used to demonstrate human dilemmas and problems and sometimes their solutions. Joseph told the audience that the hoop dance was one such dance. It demonstrates how humans become entangled in difficult situations both physically and psychologically and how they must learn to cope with and free themselves from these situations.

As the storytelling drew to an end, the drum circle commenced, and the dancers, in their regalia, gave their performances, with Joseph introducing each group or individual. Many of the children got up and danced on the sidelines, imitating and emulating the experienced dancers.

When the drumming concluded, Claude went to find his father and Edna.

Edna spotted him first and hugged him.

"That was wonderful, Dad. It's been many years since I've heard the story of Pukawiss and the invention of dance."

"It was good to coordinate with the dancers and give the children a treat. January is a month that needs some color and movement."

Joseph studied his son for a moment. "We've heard about what happened at the folk school. I'm very sorry."

Claude nodded but refrained from saying anything.

Edna must have sensed his discomfort because she took him by the arm. "I baked blueberry pies today, Claude. Would you like to stop by the house for pie and coffee?"

"That would be fine, Edna. I'm actually famished."

"Good. We're leaving soon," Joseph said. "So, we'll see you up at the house."

Claude went to locate Martin Running Wolf and say goodbye. He had a question he wanted to ask him. He found Martin surrounded by a group of students from the school and waited off to the side until he was free.

Martin walked out of the school with him, which gave Claude a chance to talk to him privately.

Outside they paused next to Running Wolf's pickup truck. He must have sensed that Claude was seeking something, because he asked, "Is there anything I can offer that might help with the case?"

"I can't talk about the case, but I'm wondering if you've had any dealings with Sandy Grainfeld?"

"Well, I don't have anything to do with the woodworking classes, but I've been around the folk school long enough to have a sense of the man."

"And what is your sense of him?"

"He has certainly played an important role in fostering the development of the school over the years. So, he's very loyal to the mission of the school. Maybe too loyal, if that's possible."

"Why do you say that?"

"It's just that between his running the woodworking program at the high school and his commitment to the folk school, well . . ."

Running Wolf didn't finish the statement, but he didn't have to. Claude caught the drift of what he was saying. Running Wolf was a family man, devoted to his two sons who lived with him here in Grand Portage.

"You think his family may be getting the short end of the stick?"

Martin shrugged. "Not my place to judge that. His son Ethan is grown, and as far as he and Becca go, well, they work it out, I suppose."

"Anything else?" Clausd asked.

Martin shifted from one foot to the other as if making a decision.

"He's quick to anger," he finally said.

Claude nodded slowly. "Can you say any more about that?"

"Not much to say, really. I've just witnessed it a number of times over the years when something rubs him the wrong way."

"Or someone?" Clause asked.

"That too."

Before he could say more, a group of boys burst forth from the school, laughing and jostling each other. Two of them split off and headed toward the pickup— Martin's sons. Claude knew they were ten and twelve years old. The older son, Simon, had been part of the drum circle tonight.

"I'll let you go, Martin. Thanks for the input."

"It's not much, but I hope it helps."

"All information is valuable in an investigation."

Martin nodded, and Claude watched as he climbed into the truck with the boys. He gave his friend a wave and then headed across the parking lot and climbed into his own truck. He drove down the hill, turned left, and followed the road that arced around Grand Portage Bay out toward his father's house on Hat Point, where Joseph and Edna lived.

Edna Beaumont was the mother of Detective Brie Beaumont, with whom he had worked a case in October of last year. Edna had been the target of a killer, and Claude had suggested placing her with his father in Grand Portage, thinking the tribal lands would offer a safe refuge. To date the killer was still at large, and they had all decided that Edna was safest where she was with Joseph Renard, for the time being.

Claude's mother had died ten years ago, and Joseph Renard had been on his own since then. Edna had lost two husbands. Her first husband, Brie's father, had died when Brie was twenty, and Edna's second husband had passed just last year. Suffice it to say that both Edna Beaumont and Joseph Renard were feeling their way in this new and unusual situation. But one thing had become clear to Claude in the past three months. The two of them enjoyed each other's company.

Claude pulled up the driveway and climbed out. The tang of wood smoke met him. The wind chime on the porch beckoned in the frigid January air. The log house sat high on the point, and the northwest wind sliced at his face as he headed for the porch. He took the steps two at a time, paused at the door to knock and stepped inside.

Joseph already had a fire blazing in the stone fireplace, and the flames cast shadows across the walls and high ceiling. The air smelled of coffee and fresh-baked pies.

Joseph turned at the sound of the door. *"Anin, ningozis."*

It was the Ojibwe greeting for *Welcome, my son.*

"Come sit by the fire. Edna will be down in a minute."

Claude slipped his boots off and headed into the living room. All the warmth of home and family engulfed him as he sank onto the soft leather sofa in front of the fire. Up on the chimneybreast, light and shadow played over his mother's painting of the mystical golden eagle, soaring over Grand Portage Bay. Claude still missed his mother dearly, but he'd noted that a new spark flickered in his father since the arrival of Edna. Claude was glad of this. Ten years was a long time to be alone. Joseph and Edna had both been teachers, so they shared a built-in love of books. And Edna, having been a history teacher, had a deep respect for and interest in Joseph and Claude Renard's Anishinaabe heritage.

"I talked to Martin Running Wolf at the school this evening." Joseph studied his son for a moment. "He told me what has occurred in Grand Marais. Did you know the man who died, Claude?"

"I've seen him around town, but I did not know him personally. He's new to the community. Moved to Grand Marais a couple of years ago." He couldn't talk about the investigation and was glad when Edna came down the stairs and joined them. Her long hair was gray, not blonde, but she had the same fiery blue eyes and fine bones as her daughter Brie. She sat in a chair by the fire, opposite Claude.

"Have you learned anything about who might be responsible?" Joseph asked. "Will the BCA be involved in the case?"

Edna came to the rescue. "Joe, you know Claude can't talk about an active investigation."

She would know this, being the mother of a homicide detective, Claude thought. "You're right, Edna. I know you both understand that I can't talk about the case. But to answer your other question, Father. Yes, the BCA is processing the crime scene. In fact, I met with Adrianna Tomebay earlier. She's in charge of the Evidence Response Team for this case."

"How is Adrianna?" Joseph asked. There was warmth in his voice at the mention of her name.

"She seems well," Claude said. "Dedicated to her work, as always."

"I would expect that." He turned to Edna. "Claude and Adrianna went to school together."

Edna nodded, but Claude sensed she was reading between the lines.

"What do you hear from Brie?" he asked, going for a redirect.

"Well, she continues to work with the Maine State Police on special assignments. Even more so at this time of year, since *Maine Wind* is berthed for the winter. And of course, she calls more often during these months, when she's not at sea."

Claude nodded. "Tell her I said 'hello' and tell her to remain watchful."

"I'll do that, Claude."

They all knew what was being referenced. They all knew a killer remained in the wind. One who was obsessed with Edna's daughter.

"So, how about that pie and coffee?" Edna asked, trying to lighten things up.

Claude smiled. "I'm hungry enough to eat a whole pie by myself."

"Good. I'll serve it up."

The three of them went to the kitchen, and Edna plated up blueberry pie. Claude poured out coffee, and they headed back in to sit by the fire. Edna had started to volunteer at the tribal charter school and lit up when Claude asked her about it. She had been a high school history teacher in her career, and as she talked, her connection to the children was evident.

It was ten o'clock when Claude said goodnight and headed out the door. Edna had boxed up the second blueberry pie and sent it with him. Everything about the night had been therapeutic, from the drum circle and the storytelling to his time with Joseph and Edna. All of it had helped to temper the feeling of tragedy surrounding Grant Silverton's murder and the gravitas of the unfolding investigation.

Anxiety is an ever-present emotion during such cases. Investigators must battle the thought that they will fail at the task and a killer will slip away. Renard's headlights caught a deer on the side of the highway. It stayed fixed in place as he passed, but its presence seemed to say, sideline those thoughts and move forward. He drew in a breath and let it out, the memory of the drum circle still a vibration in his heart. He would work the case. It was all he could do. He hoped it would be enough.

Forty minutes after leaving Grand Portage, he pulled into the driveway next to his house and got out of the truck. He headed for the front door but then remembered the pie. He had just turned to go back to the truck when Adrianna Tomebay stepped out of the shadows. She startled him, and his mind flashed back to the spirit bowl he had placed outside earlier and the sense he'd had of someone watching him. He dismissed the thought. If someone had been there, it wasn't her. She had been with her team at the crime scene.

"Ria. What's up? Did you and the team find something? Did you try to call? I was up at Grand Portage, and I had my phone turned off for a short time."

She stepped closer to him. "It's not that, Fox. Everything's fine."

She laid a hand against his face and now he saw—understood. He knew the hand was cold, yet it felt like a fiery brand on his face. Desire, loneliness, wonder, the sense of time spun backwards—far back. He read it all in her eyes and knew she read it in his too. And then she was in his arms and they were kissing and, for just a moment, he actually smelled dry leaves and the early nip of fall that had been in the air the day she'd left for college. And then she was pulling him toward the door and he was trying to think straight enough to stop her. She took the key from his hand and put it into the lock.

"Ria, wait. You're married. We can't . . ."

"We're separated, Fox. It was over long ago."

He started to say something else, but she laid her finger on his lips.

"We're good together, Fox."

"That was a long time ago, Ria."

She stopped at the foot of the stairs and looked at him. "Was it, Fox? That's not what your kiss said just now."

Those were the last words they spoke as she drew him up the stairs and into the bedroom. The rest of the night was spent in blissful surrender to each other, as the wind whispered around the eaves and sent ice crystals tapping a wintery Morse code against the window panes.

Chapter 12

Renard woke in the still chill of predawn darkness. The north wind howled along the eaves at the back of the house. He reached for Adrianna, already knowing she would be gone. He sighed, sat up on the edge of the bed, and snapped on his prosthetic leg. He headed for the bathroom. A shower would be his only warmth this morning.

By 6:45 he was out the door, headed for the law enforcement center. The polar express was steaming in, straight down off the North Pole. He'd felt it muscling up last night, outside his father's house on Hat Point. They would be in for multiple rounds of sub-zero January air. Maybe the bone-chilling cold would keep the snow at bay. Living in the frozen North, one looks for any small ray of hope.

He was the first one in, except for the personnel back in the detention center and the 911 operator, who'd been on duty overnight.

Renard settled in at his desk in his office and brought up the Grant Silverton case file. He opened the file and reread the reports that he and Hank Gunderson had written yesterday. Howard (Sandy) Grainfeld had stopped in to give a statement. Renard read it carefully, looking for any discrepancies between it and the information he'd collected in the interview with Grainfeld at the crime scene. He didn't find any.

As instructed, the Dinkovich boys—Darrell and Duffy—had also stopped in to give their statements. Renard couldn't help but smile at their creative use of grammar. And then there were Darrell and Duffy's justifications for, if not breaking—the door had been unlocked—then at least entering the woodworking building at the folk school the night before last. When it came to the Dinkovich boys, Renard truly believed there was no such thing as malicious intent. When opportunity knocked, they simply bumbled in. What was more, there was a kind of naïve sincerity to their denials and justifications. If they said it happened or didn't happen, Renard was inclined to believe them, ironic as that seemed.

Dave Isaacs, who worked up at the hospital and had been out for a run before going to work the night of the murder, had also stopped in to give a statement. Renard reread it carefully, looking for any tidbits of information he might have missed. The only point of interest there was that Dave Isaacs had tried to call Sandy Grainfeld to tell him he'd seen the Dinkovich boys running out of the woodworking building at 10:30 p.m. But Sandy's phone had gone to voicemail.

Now, cell reception was pretty much nonexistent up on Devil Track Lake, where Sandy and his family lived. So, if Isaacs had called his cell phone, it might have gone to voicemail due to lack of reception. It was a detail he would have to check on. Most everyone up that way, and for that matter here in Grand Marais, had a land-line, so he'd have to see if Dave Isaacs could remember which number he had called. Hopefully, he had only one number for Sandy Grainfeld in his contact list, so that would answer the question.

Renard sat back in his chair and ran through the possible suspects he'd identified as well as potential motives they might have—at least the ones he knew something about. It was the tip of the iceberg, but at least it gave him a sense of having some kind of foot-hold in the case.

Sandy Grainfeld had been irritated by Grant Silver-ton's demands in the coffin-making class at the folk school. He'd also learned from Martin Running Wolf that Grainfeld had a quick temper. And then there was Maurie Fontaine and his prize agate that Silverton had managed to leverage him out of. Whether there was any leveraging or not was yet to be seen, but that was Maurie Fontaine's take on it.

Apparently, according to Fontaine there had also been some bad blood between Silverton and the Pierres—Jules and El. Coincidentally, Jules and El were in the coffin-making class and knew that Silverton had stayed late to work on his coffin the night of the mur-der. What was more, in his interview with them, El had started to say something and then stopped—changed her mind. He'd have to circle back around to them today and try to get to the bottom of it. But anyone who was there after class at the folk school Tuesday night was a person of interest. That included Sandy Grainfeld, the Pierres, and Erin Flanagan. Any one of them would have had opportunity, knowing Silverton was there alone.

At 7:30 Deputy Hank Gunderson stuck his head in the door.

"Come in, Hank. Sit."

"So, where are we at?" Hank asked.

"Well, the BCA will be finishing up this morning at Grant Silverton's house."

Gunderson nodded. "They were at it till almost ten o'clock last night. Finally, Adrianna Tomebay called it and told the ERTs they'd finish in the morning."

Renard was aware of this, of course, but said nothing.

"As soon as Merlin Waters gets in, I'll have him start working on Grant Silverton's laptop and cell phone."

"Do you want me back at Silverton's house while the BCA is finishing processing it?" Gunderson asked.

"Yes, I'd like you there in case they need anything from us. Also, Grant Silverton had a landline. I'd like you to find out what company supports that line and obtain a call log from them. The warrant covers acquisition of those records."

Hank nodded. "I'm on it."

"Before you leave, could you head back to the evidence room and bring me the employment records we found at Silverton's house from the time he lived and worked in Chicago? I'm going to contact the company he worked for—see what I can learn about his time there. See if I can track down anyone he was close to at the company. Learn more about his personal life during that time, and also about his moving to Switzerland."

Gunderson nodded again and swung his lanky frame out of the chair. "Be back in a few minutes."

Renard reached for a pad of paper on the side of his desk and jotted a list of what he needed to accomplish in the next few hours. Besides filling in background on Grant Silverton's life before he had moved to Grand Marais, he needed to revisit Jules and El Pierre. If they'd had a grievance with Grant Silverton, he wondered if they would admit to it. And if not, he wondered who else might know about it. Maurie Fontaine knew something, but he wasn't talking.

He also needed to visit the Grainfelds. Talk to Sandy and his wife Becca. Find out why Sandy had not answered his phone the night of the murder, when Dave Isaacs had called him. Isaacs' statement was still in front of him, and Renard sent a text, asking Isaacs to call him so he could clarify something.

Dave Isaacs worked the night shift at the hospital, so Renard figured he might be getting off about now. Sure enough, within a couple of minutes his phone rang.

"Chief Deputy Renard."

"Hi, Claude. I just got your message. How can I help?"

"I was just reading your statement, Dave. I'm wondering if you can tell me what number you tried to call Sandy Grainfeld on the night of the murder, when you saw the Dinkovich boys running from the woodworking building at the folk school?"

"Hang on. I'll check. I think I only have one number for him."

There was a moment or two of silence and then Dave was back.

"I only have his cell number in my phone. So that's what I called."

"Good. Thanks for that info, Dave."

"Did you learn anything about whether the Dinkovich boys were involved?"

"I can't talk about any of the particulars of the case, Dave."

"Sorry. Of course not."

"I appreciate your coming forward with that information, though. Every bit of information is crucial in a case like this."

"Glad I could help, Claude. If there's anything else I can do, let me know."

"Thanks, Dave."

They ended the call. Renard checked his watch and got up to go see if Merlin Waters was in his lair. The Digital Forensics Division consisted of a small office with a work room attached. Waters had been out with Covid for the past five days and was busy settling back in.

Renard knocked on the open door, and Merlin looked up. His face was even more gaunt than usual—probably a result of his bout with Covid. His super curly hair lent a tennis ball look to his head. His glasses sat slightly askew on his face and, behind them, he had a perpetually panicked look in his eyes, as if there was way too much to do and not enough time to do it. He always kept a jar full of gummy bears on his desk and a case of Mountain Dew on the floor at the ready. Renard wondered how much all that sugar contributed to his high-strung manner.

Renard filled him in on the Grant Silverton murder case, asking him to read the reports on the case. Then they went to the evidence room to sign out Silverton's cell phone and laptop. Renard left Merlin to his work, noting that he'd already shifted into gear. There were pass codes to crack; data to be mined. Merlin Waters was in his element.

Renard headed back to his office to place the call to Silverton's former employer in Chicago. His thoughts were on Ria—the magic of last night was juxtaposed with a feeling of guilt that he might be leading her in the wrong direction. But then he realized—no, remembered—that no one had ever led Adrianna. She knew her mind. Always had. More than anyone else he had ever known. She was like a comet, blazing through life. If you joined her—caught the tail of that comet—you had to know that she would be doing the driving. He had known that when they were young and together. Was that why he had gone in a different direction? He couldn't say. Was it different now? Maybe. At this point in life, he didn't feel he had anything to prove. He knew who he was. Maybe now he was secure enough to let her do the driving.

At this point in time, though, there was nothing for it. Ria's work was based in Bemidji. His was here. They would remain two ships that had passed in the night. He did want to see her before she left, but right now, he needed to follow up on Grant Silverton's former employer in Chicago. He would try to catch her later. Maybe they could share a meal before she left.

Hank Gunderson had left a manila folder with records from Grant Silverton's former employer in Chicago on Renard's desk. He sat down and flipped it open. Harold Wallace Investment Banking was the name of the company Silverton had worked for in Chicago. Renard found a phone number for the company on one of the documents. He reached for paper to take notes on and dialed the number.

A voice at the other end answered. "Harold Wallace Investment Banking. How may I direct your call?"

Renard asked for the Human Resources department. Within moments, a woman came on the line.

"Human Resources, Stephanie Weber speaking. How may I help you?"

"This is Chief Deputy Claude Renard with the Cook County Sheriff's Office in Grand Marais, Minnesota." He gave her his shield number and then continued. "I'm trying to obtain information on a former employee of yours as part of an ongoing investigation. His name is Grant Silverton."

"Let me see if I can access his employment records. I recognize the name, so he has worked here during the time I've been employed," Ms. Weber offered.

Renard heard her clicking away on her keyboard and within a few moments she said, "I have his record up here now."

"Can you tell me how long he worked for your company?"

"It looks like he was here for twelve years. He was employed by the firm from 2006 to 2018."

"Do you know who his boss was during that time?"

"Let's see what I can find. He worked in our Mergers and Acquisitions division. Looks like that would be Anthony Martin."

"Does Mr. Martin still work there?"

"I believe he does." Her keyboard clicked again. "Yes. He's still working here."

"Do you have his email, Ms. Weber?"

"I do. It's a.martin@haroldwallace.net. Would you like me to transfer your call?"

"Please," Renard said. "Thank you for your help, Ms. Weber."

"Of course."

Renard heard ringing on the line. Anthony Martin answered on the third ring. Renard introduced himself and gave his shield number.

"What can I do for you, Deputy?"

"We are involved in an investigation relating to Grant Silverton. I've spoken to Ms. Weber in Human Resources. She gave me some background information on Mr. Silverton's employment at the Harold Wallace Firm and told me you were his boss at the time he left there."

"I remember him well, Deputy Renard. How can I help? I hope Grant is well."

"I'm very sorry to tell you that Mr. Silverton was murdered the night before last, here in Grand Marais."

"Murdered! My God. How awful. Where did you say this happened?"

"In Grand Marais, Minnesota. It's a small town here on the north shore of Lake Superior. He moved here two years ago after he retired."

"I can't believe this. It's something you might expect to happen here in Chicago, but not in a small town in the middle of nowhere."

Renard restrained himself from saying what he really wanted to and instead replied, "Murders can happen anywhere, Mr. Martin."

"Well, yes. I suppose they can. The whole country's like the Wild West. Shootings everywhere, every day. Terribly disheartening."

Renard realized that Anthony Martin was making an assumption. Grant Silverton had not been the victim of gun violence, but he was not about to share any particulars of the case.

"We're trying to fill in background on Mr. Silverton, since he has only lived in this community for about two and a half years."

"How can I be of help?"

"I know it was a while ago, but were you aware of any problems in Grant Silverton's life? Or for that matter, any problems on the job? Any relationships gone bad, or employees he didn't get along with?"

"I'm looking at his employee assessments right now. To my recollection he was a model employee—a team player. He wasn't married, at least during the time he worked here. His employee reviews all mention that he was an arch-professional. And that's how I remember him. We weren't friends outside of work, so I can't comment on his personal life.

"It looks like he left here to take a teaching position in Switzerland. I do remember that it was the talk of our division at the time. Pretty sweet opportunity. I don't recall if he had sought out the position or if they came looking for him. Grant was super smart, though. I see here he graduated from Yale and had a master's degree in finance from Northwestern University."

"I've been told by someone he knew here that he moved back to Chicago for a short time after Switzerland. Did he come back to work at Harold Wallace?"

"Not to my knowledge," Martin said. "There is no employment record for him here after he moved to Switzerland."

Renard jotted a note and then continued. "Do you recall anyone he was friends with at the company there? Someone who might have spent time with him outside of work?"

"As I recall, there was someone he was friends with here. Let me do a little digging, ask around the division. See if anyone knows more about that. I'll call you back."

"I appreciate your help, Mr. Martin."

They ended the call.

Renard had been writing notes as Anthony Martin was talking, and he read back through them now. He checked his watch. It was 8:20. He had several interviews to get to but decided he would wait a bit to see if Mr. Martin got back to him with a name. He started a new report on Grant Silverton's former employment at the Harold Wallace Investment Banking Firm in Chicago and began typing up his notes.

Twenty minutes later his phone rang.

"Mr. Martin. Thank you for getting back to me."

"I've got a name for you, Chief Deputy. It's Owen McGraw."

Renard jotted the name on his notes.

"He doesn't work here anymore, but one of the guys in our division is still buddies with him. Said McGraw was pretty tight with Grant Silverton when he worked here. I've got a number for you, as well."

"Go ahead," Renard said.

Martin gave him Owen McGraw's cell number. "If I can be of further assistance, please let me know, Chief Deputy."

"I will. Thank you for your help, Mr. Martin."

Renard set his notes from the Anthony Martin interview to one side and reached for some more blank paper. He dialed the number for Owen McGraw, thinking that if he kept banker's hours, he might still catch him before his work day began.

He answered on the fourth ring.

"McGraw."

"Owen McGraw?" Renard asked.

"That's right. Who is this?"

Renard identified himself and gave his shield number. It sounded like McGraw was on a train. Renard guessed he was riding the "L"—a commuter train that would take him into downtown Chicago.

"I'm calling to make inquiries about Grant Silverton. I got your name and number from someone you worked with at the Harold Wallace Firm."

"That must be Ted Trumbell. But as to Grant Silverton, we fell out of touch several years ago."

"But I've been told you were friends with him during his time at Harold Wallace."

"That's correct. What's this about, Chief Deputy?"

Clearly, McGraw was not one to mince words, so Renard didn't either.

"Grant Silverton was murdered the night before last, here in Grand Marais, Minnesota."

"Murdered!" There was a moment of silence. "Look, I'm sorry I was brusque with you, Deputy Renard. Grant *was* a friend. This is terrible news. Just terrible. How can I help?"

"We're just trying to assemble the pieces of his life, Mr. McGraw. Grant Silverton had only lived here in Grand Marais for a couple of years. As the investigator,

I need to understand his life and background as much as possible. Through employment records discovered at his home, we were able to trace him back to Chicago, and to the Harold Wallace Firm specifically. I've interviewed Anthony Martin there, but he only had a work relationship with Mr. Silverton. Whereas I've been told you knew him on a personal level."

"That's correct. We were friends outside of work as well."

"How long did you work with him at Harold Wallace?"

"For about five or six years. He was well established at the company when I came in. I was assigned to his team in Mergers and Acquisitions, and he made me feel welcome. I'd say, more than anyone else there, it was Grant who helped me get in sync with the work and the team. That was the beginning of our friendship."

"Were you two about the same age?" Renard asked.

"Grant was a little older, I think. I couldn't tell you how much, but I'm fifty-three now."

Renard knew from Silverton's driver's license that he was fifty-seven.

"Did you ever get the sense that Grant Silverton had issues with anyone at Harold Wallace? That he rubbed anyone the wrong way—metaphorically speaking, of course."

McGraw actually laughed at that. "In corporate America, work is just the time between sexual harassment seminars. Not like the old days, that's for sure. But to answer your question, no. Grant was an arch professional—a team player if ever there was one. Most likely, he would have been the one to mediate issues between others. And if Grant did rub someone the wrong way, as you say, it was probably because he expected people to measure up to his standards. And I would say he set the bar pretty high for himself."

"And what about outside of work? What was he like?"

"Definitely not a party animal like a lot of guys that work in our business. Grant was a private guy. Liked his space. Kept to himself. But we did go sailing together. And out there, well, he was like a different person."

"Tell me about that." Renard heard the train come to a stop and doors open and close. Then McGraw was talking again.

"I'm a sailor, Deputy Renard. Grew up sailing. I work in downtown Chicago, and here, you're five minutes from Lake Michigan and some of the best sailing in the Midwest. I keep my boat in a marina right near the south loop. If the wind's good, I can be out on the lake and under sail in less than an hour. I used to invite Grant to come along with me and help crew. I was teaching him the ropes."

"You said he was like a different person out there. Can you tell me more about that?"

"Well, like I said, Grant was a private guy. I always felt like there was a part of him he kept locked away. But out on the water, sailing, it was like his guard came down. He was funny, and he would talk about his time growing up. If you're not a sailor, Deputy, you may not know this, but sailing is freedom. You get out there, and it's just you and the wind and the water and your boat, and everything else falls away. It's always felt the same to me, even when I was a boy and especially as a teenager. Those years are filled with such angst, but when I was out sailing, all that would just magically melt away. I think that's what happened to Grant as well.

"He used to tell me about his skiing—going out west to the mountains. I always thought he'd retire out there. But he admitted it was different from sailing. He seemed to like that you could physically separate yourself from humanity out on the water."

Renard tapped his pen. "It seems like he was well-regarded at Harold Wallace. Do you know why he decided to move to Switzerland or how all of that came about?"

"As I recall, he got wind that one of the universities there was looking for someone with a background in finance to join the faculty. I can't remember if it was a guest teaching position, which would have been for a limited amount of time, or whether they were looking to fill a permanent faculty position. At any rate, Grant got wind of it, and it intrigued him. I remember him telling me about it. I always thought that maybe the allure of skiing in Switzerland was too much to resist. Grant wasn't married. Had no kids. So it would have been relatively easy for him to up stakes and move. Maybe he just needed an adventure. That certainly would have been one."

"What did you hear from him after he moved there?" Renard asked.

"That's just it, Deputy. I heard nothing. He said he'd send me his address once he got settled, but he never did. I have to admit I was a little hurt by it. He changed his phone number too, so there was no way to contact him. I guess I could have tracked him down by calling universities, but I figured he wanted to be left alone. Why else would he have done what he did?"

"I'm sorry to hear that, Mr. McGraw. To me, as a cop, it almost sounds like he was running from something and didn't want to leave a trail."

"I guess I never thought of it that way," McGraw said. "Maybe I took it too personally."

"Was there anything you can recall that troubled Grant Silverton? Anything he might have wanted to get away from? Anything he ever talked to you about? You mentioned that it was like his guard came down when you were out sailing. Do you know what that might have been about? Did he ever talk about his past, or anything that might have haunted him?"

There was silence at the other end of the line. "There was something, now that I think about it. My stop is coming up, Deputy Renard. Could I get back to you in a few minutes? The wind is fierce today, and once I step off the train, I'd like to make a dash for my building."

"I would appreciate that, Mr. McGraw." Renard gave him his cell phone number and his number at the sheriff's office, and they ended the call.

Chapter 13

Renard needed to get on to his interviews. Jules and El Pierre were first on his docket, since they lived right here in town. After that, he planned to head up to the Grainfelds' place on Devil Track Lake. But he decided to remain in his office for a little while, hoping that Owen McGraw would call him back from Chicago.

Fifteen minutes passed, and he had just stood up to put on his coat when the phone rang.

"Chief Deputy Renard."

"Owen McGraw here, Deputy. Sorry about the wait. I ran into a colleague in the lobby of my building and got caught up with him for a few minutes."

"Quite all right, Mr. McGraw. I appreciate you calling back."

"So getting back to your question about whether Grant Silverton might have been haunted by something from his past. There was something. Or, more specifically, someone."

"Go on," Renard said.

"There was a woman that Grant had had some issues with."

"What kind of issues?"

"It may sound overdramatic, Deputy, but it sounded like she was stalking him."

"Being a law enforcement officer, I would never consider that overdramatic, Mr. McGraw. It happens more than one would think, and we take it seriously. What can you tell me about this woman?"

"Not a lot. Grant only spoke about it once, while we were out sailing. Remember I said he seemed to let his guard down out on the water."

"I do. Go on."

"He told me he had met this woman on one of his skiing vacations to Colorado. They had a fling. One of those things that happens on vacation. I don't think Grant ever meant it to be any more than that. They had each other's contact info, and he told me they stayed in touch. And then, lo and behold, she moved to Chicago. Didn't tell him she was moving. Just showed up at his door one day."

"That's pretty startling," Renard said.

"Grant found it really unsettling and said he immediately started to distance himself from her. But Grant was courteous and, well, apparently this woman was quite a looker, which made it hard for him to reject her advances. My read—he was equal parts flattered and alarmed by it."

There was a moment of silence at the other end and then Owen McGraw continued. "I've actually known someone like this in my past, Deputy. I don't know what it is that attracts us men to someone like that. Maybe an element of danger."

Although it was different because Renard had known Adrianna Tomebay most of his life, still, he couldn't help thinking of her and the night of passion they'd just spent together.

McGraw was talking again. "Anyway, when this woman started showing up at the brokerage firm, that was it for Grant. He changed his phone number. But he owned a home north of the city, so he couldn't easily move."

"Do you recall what suburb or town he lived in?"

"Sure. It was Winnetka. He had grown up there. It's the wealthiest suburb in Chicago."

Renard made a note of that. "Do you know if he ever took out a restraining order against this woman?"

"I told him to, the day he shared all this with me. But I don't know if he ever did. But I could tell that just sharing the situation with me helped Grant to decompress a bit. So, when he landed the job in Switzerland, I guess I wasn't that surprised. And looking back, maybe that's why he broke all ties with me and everyone else at Harold Wallace. Maybe he was afraid Crazy Pants would somehow track him down."

"What was this woman's name?" Renard asked.

"That's just it, Deputy. I've been wracking my brain, trying to remember, and I can't. I'm sure I'll remember it, though, and when I do, I will let you know."

"Do you know where in Colorado they met? Which ski resort?"

"I don't know. Vale, maybe?"

"Was she vacationing there, or did she work there?"

"Vacationing, I think, but I really don't know."

"You've been very helpful, Mr. McGraw. Please let me know if you happen to remember that name."

"I'll text it to you if I do. You don't think that woman could be responsible for his death, do you? I honestly can't think of anything scarier than that."

"There's no indication of that, Mr. McGraw. But this is valuable information nonetheless."

Renard thanked him again and they ended the call. As soon as he hung up, he looked up the number for the police department in Winnetka, Illinois, and put through a call. He was hoping that Grant Silverton had taken out a restraining order on this woman, but there was no record of it at the Winnetka PD. The officer on duty did a thorough search going back ten years, but found nothing on record.

Renard started typing in a report on the information he had gathered in his interviews with Ms. Weber and Anthony Martin at the Harold Wallace Firm, and with Owen McGraw, former work colleague and friend of Grant Silverton. It was 10:20 when he finished the last report. Three and a half hours had flown by since he'd stepped through the door of the law enforcement center this morning. He stood up, grabbed his coat and headed for the door.

He was eager to get on to the interviews with the Pierres and the Grainfelds. Once the frame of the puzzle was in place, he and the rest of the team could work their way toward the center, toward the heart of the case where, hopefully, the truth awaited.

There were any number of people who'd had opportunity, since the victim had been all by himself in a public building with the door unlocked. And the means, the weapon, was right there at hand. One of the wood chisels Silverton had been using. The fact that the killer had not brought a weapon suggested that the murder was not premeditated, but had possibly escalated from an argument to a sudden act of violence. And maybe Silverton had made the mistake of turning his back on the perpetrator. In the final analysis, though, it all boiled down to the "why." What grievance had motivated the killer to go to the folk school the night before last? What had motivated him or her to confront Grant Silverton?

Renard climbed into his squad and headed west on 5th Street, back into town to the Pierres' residence. Five minutes later he pulled to a stop in front of their house. The house, with its striking blue color, came to life against the arctic white background.

Renard took out his notebook and glanced through his notes from the interview with Jules and El yesterday. He remembered that while they'd been shocked at the news of the murder, neither one of them had expressed any regrets about Silverton's death. That had struck him as odd. It had also emerged in the interview that Jules had come to bed a half hour later than normal.

El had said she was always in bed by nine, but Jules had not come to bed until 11:00 that night. When asked about it, El had volunteered an answer—said Jules was into a book he was reading and had stayed up later than usual. But it left two hours of unaccounted time on the night of the murder, after El went to bed. Jules could easily have slipped out of the house, gone down to the folk school, and killed Silverton during that time.

But what had brought Renard back here today was El's reaction when he'd asked them if they knew of anyone in town who had issues with Grant Silverton. El had said, "Well, it's no secret . . ." and had suddenly stopped. That's why he was here. He needed to know what had been left unsaid.

Renard stowed his notebook and got out of the squad. He walked up the driveway, climbed the steps to the porch, and rang the bell. A few moments later Jules Pierre opened the door. Though a short man, Jules was built four-square.

"*Boozhoo*, One Step." Jules always greeted him in Ojibwe.

"*Boozhoo*, Jules."

Pierre opened the door. "Come on in. Too cold to stand on ceremony."

Renard stepped inside. He smelled something wonderful. El had been baking.

"How's the case progressing?"

"It's early days, as you might suspect," Renard said.

The question was not unexpected. As a ranger with the Forestry Service, Jules Pierre was part of law enforcement here in the North.

"I wanted to stop back and talk to you and El some more."

Jules nodded. "I suppose everyone in the coffin-making class is a person of interest, since we knew the whereabouts of Grant Silverton that night. El isn't here right now. She went down to the market to do the shopping."

"Well, why don't I talk to you then, Jules. I can always circle back here if I need to see El."

Jules nodded. "Come on out to the kitchen. There's warm coffee cake that El just baked."

Renard hesitated for a beat and then said, "Sure." Maybe El's coffee cake would be just the icebreaker he needed.

Jules Pierre poured out coffee and plated up coffee cake.

"El won't mind if we dig into this, will she?"

Jules shook his head. "Nah. She always says it's here to be eaten."

Renard had left the house without breakfast that morning, so the coffee cake was welcome. Jules must have seen he was hungry and offered him a second piece, but Renard restrained himself from saying yes.

"So you must have more questions for us, Claude. I know you're not here just for El's baking."

Renard smiled. "No, but it would be a good enough reason."

He set his plate aside and took out his small notebook. "I just need to clarify something from our interview yesterday."

"Sure," Jules said. "Shoot."

"During the interview I asked if you or El knew of anyone in the community who had issues with Grant Silverton. Anyone who didn't get along with him." Renard referred to his notebook. "El started to say, 'Well, it's no secret. . .' and then stopped abruptly. I got the feeling you had sent her a signal to stop talking, Jules. If that's the case, I need to know what she was about to say."

Jules shifted uncomfortably in his chair. "You really should ask her," he said.

"I'm asking you, Jules. I think you know the answer. And before you say anything aye or nay, I need to remind you that keeping back information that may aid in an investigation is obstruction of justice."

Jules let out a sigh and ran a hand through his dark curly hair.

"I may as well tell you. Otherwise someone else in town probably will, and that would be bad."

Renard didn't say that someone—Maurie Fontaine —had already intimated as much.

"There *was* bad blood between Grant Silverton and us. It had to do with the house he lives in, or I guess I should say, lived in."

"Go on."

"Well, that fact is, El loves that house. Always has. For years she's said if she could live anywhere in town, it would be there."

"It's a pretty expensive property, I would think. Could you and El have afforded it?" Renard refrained from saying, "on your salary."

"No. It was a pipe dream. But then two and a half years ago, El's father died. She received a very nice inheritance. It was enough that, coupled with the sale of this house, we could have afforded the place.

"A few months after that, El had gotten wind through the grapevine that the owner was thinking of selling. The day the house went up for sale, we called the agent."

"Let me guess," Renard said. "It had already sold."

"Yeah. For cash, what's more. We begged the agent to ask the owner to reconsider and sell the place to us, but apparently Silverton had already signed the contract.

"El was furious. Demanded to know who the buyer was, but the agent would only say it was someone from out of town."

"Did you ever confront Silverton about buying the property?" Renard asked.

Jenifer LeClair

"No. But he somehow found out, which wouldn't have been hard to do. Our anger about it had become common knowledge here in town. Part and parcel of living in a small community, I guess."

"Did Silverton ever talk to you or El about it, express regret about how things had worked out?"

"Never. It was always the elephant in the room whenever we'd pass him in town. So, when we signed up for the coffin-making class and then found out he was in it, I actually wanted to quit. Avoid any uncomfortable feelings. But El said, no—that we weren't going to let his presence drive us out of a class in our own town."

Renard sat back in his chair and looked Jules straight in the eye. "Did you go down to the folk school the night before last, Jules? Maybe to confront Grant Silverton? And maybe things got out of hand and an argument ensued?"

"I swear to you, I did not. Nothing would have made me do that. Truth is—and I'd never want El to know this—but I was relieved we lost out on that house. Even with the money El inherited, it still would have strained our budget. Taxes, upkeep. You know."

Just then they heard the front door open and the rustle of bags as El came in. Jules gave Renard a pleading look that said, *I'm telling the truth, so please don't question El about this.*

Renard put his notebook away, deciding he was done for now. If he needed to, there were plenty of ways he could check out the truth of Jules' story, starting with the agent who had sold the property.

Within moments El came into the kitchen.

"Well, Claude. This is a surprise."

"Just a couple of t's to cross from our interview yesterday, El."

She gave Jules a quizzical look.

"We just finished," Jules said. "I think Claude has everything he needs. Right?"

"That's right." Renard stood. "Jules gave me some of your coffee cake. It's delicious."

El nodded. "You're welcome any time, Claude."

He pulled on his coat, thanked her, and headed out the front door. But he had caught the look of concern in her eyes. She was wondering what had just passed between him and Jules. He wished he could hear what they were saying right now.

He headed for his squad, climbed in, and pulled away. Grant Silverton had had one good friend here in town. It was time to double back and talk to Paul Strauss—see what he knew about the Pierres. And also if he knew anything about this unnamed woman Silverton had dealt with in Chicago.

Chapter 14

Renard was fairly close to Grant Silverton's house and decided to swing by to see if the BCA had finished processing the premises. As he turned the corner and approached the house, he saw the ERT loading up their equipment. He pulled to a stop across from the house just as Adrianna Tomebay walked out the door carrying a large black bag. She stowed it in the BCA van and crossed the street toward him. She was smiling, and there seemed to be a spring in her step, despite what he knew was a significant lack of sleep. He hoped he was the reason.

He rolled down the window and she leaned on it.

"Ria. You okay this morning?"

A mischievous twinkle ignited in her eyes. "I'm fine, Fox. You?"

Her voice set up a vibration in his heart like a ceremonial drum. "There's no way I could not be fine. Do you have time to talk?"

"It's a long drive back to Bemidji, Fox. The team and I need to get on the road. The case has to take precedence."

"You're right. It does. That's why I didn't come by earlier."

"As you know, even under a rush order for homicides, DNA evidence can take two to four weeks to process. But we *will* talk."

She glanced behind her. Some of the ERT members stood by the van waiting for her orders. They both knew a kiss was out of the question, but the look that passed between them more than made up for it.

Adrianna turned and crossed the street toward the BCA van. Renard watched her for a moment, then put the squad in gear and pulled away. He made a U-turn at the end of the block and headed back toward the center of town, where Paul Strauss lived.

Renard pulled up in front of the small wood-sided house—certainly a modest abode for a former CPA, but Strauss had said yesterday that this was merely his winter residence and that he owned a log home up on Gunflint Lake. Renard had gotten the impression that the lake home was a more lavish place. He climbed out, headed up the walk, and rang the front doorbell.

He stood there for a good minute before ringing once more. He was about to leave when Strauss opened the door. He held a small needle-nose pliers in one hand.

"Deputy Renard. This is a surprise. Please, come in."

He opened the door and Renard stepped inside.

"Looks like I caught you in the middle of a something."

Strauss motioned toward the kitchen with the pliers. "I was in the middle of tying a fly. Sorry it took me a minute to answer the door."

"No problem." Renard had learned from his visit yesterday that Paul Strauss lived to fish. His small house was pretty much a shrine to the sport.

"I suppose you're here about Grant. I still can't believe he's gone."

"I understand," Renard said. "It's a shock, and you were close to Mr. Silverton. I'd like to ask you a few more questions, if you have time. You were his closest friend here in town and so, might be in a position to help confirm a couple of things for me."

"Of course. Let's sit down in the kitchen. Would you like some coffee?"

"No, I'm fine." Renard slipped off his boots and followed Paul Strauss.

There was a small dine-in kitchen beyond the living room. Renard took off his coat, and they sat down across from one another at the wood table where Strauss had been tying his flies. There was a large magnifying glass on a gooseneck clamped to the edge of the table that he looked through when working.

Renard nodded toward it. "It's exacting work."

"Yes, but I enjoy it," Strauss said. "And I get to make use of the fruits of my labor."

"A good winter hobby," Renard said.

Now that the ice was broken, he took out his notebook and turned to the notes from yesterday.

"You told me yesterday that you didn't think Grant Silverton had ever been married. Nor did you think he had a girlfriend here in town."

"I did say that, but you know, I remembered something last night. Something very minor, but . . ."

"In a murder investigation nothing can be considered minor, Mr. Strauss."

"Well, it was a few months ago. I called Grant on a whim one night to see if he wanted to go out and grab some food. While we were talking, I thought I heard a cell phone ring in the background and woman's voice say hello. That was all I heard, but I know I wasn't mistaken. I even asked Grant a few days after that if he was seeing someone, and he said no, and why would I think that? I figured, if he *was* seeing someone, he wanted to keep it a secret, at least for the time being."

"So he turned you down—about going out for food that night you called?"

"Yeah. He said he'd already eaten but suggested we go out another night. He ended the call pretty quick. Said he was in the middle of something."

"Interesting." Renard finished writing.

"Over the time you knew him, did Grant Silverton ever mention any problems from his past? Specifically, anything that might pertain to problems with a woman in his past?"

Paul Strauss reached for his mug of coffee and took a swallow. Renard could see him turning something over in his mind.

"You know, there was something. It stands out in retrospect, because even after knowing Grant for over two years, I feel like I knew very little about his past."

"Tell me about it," Renard said.

"Well, Grant and I met in a class at the folk school. That was shortly after he moved here. We hit it off right away. Just one of those things that sometimes happens. Anyway, we started spending time together. He was setting up a woodworking shop in his garage, and I'd go over and we'd work on that together. We were both new to woodworking, and I didn't have room here to set anything up. There were a lot of laughs about how much we didn't know, and some dark humor about who might cut off a finger first.

"Anyway, one night after being out there with the tools, we went back into his house and had a few beers, and out of the blue he started talking about this woman from his past. I could tell right off the bat that it was something troubling, because the laughs we'd been sharing just evaporated and he became deadly serious."

Renard listened as Strauss told him a very similar story to the one he'd heard from Owen McGraw—Silverton's friend from Chicago. Strauss recounted how Silverton had met this woman on vacation, where they'd had a fling, as Silverton had described it. How they'd kept in touch and then one day she showed up at his door in Chicago and told him she'd moved there.

"I could see that even years later, it freaked him out."

"So, did he feel like she was stalking him?" Renard asked.

"That's how he made it sound, but. . ."

"But what?"

"I don't know, maybe she was just that in love with the guy that she was willing to give up her life somewhere else."

"Interesting," Renard said. "What would make you think that?"

"Well, here's the thing, Deputy. I lost my wife to cancer the year before I moved here. Our big house had become so lonely and empty, I decided to sell it and move up to this part of the country I'd always loved. But Celia—that was my wife's name—she loved it here too. She would often travel up here with me and, though she didn't fish, she'd come down to the river with me sometimes. Bring a picnic, sit and read. Other times she'd go shopping in town. We always stayed at a motel here in Grand Marais. Anyway, when I would tell Grant about all of it, it always felt like I was speaking a foreign language. I could tell that the idea of marriage freaked him out a little."

"So, he had commitment issues," Renard said.

"I don't know. Maybe."

"So, you think maybe the problem might have been him, not the woman? That maybe he was running from commitment?"

"I think it's possible. I'll tell you one thing, though. As he talked about this woman from his past, it was clear he was attracted to her. You could practically see his heart rate go up. So, why would he have pushed her away?"

"Do you know what her name was?"

"I asked him. He wouldn't say."

"Did you get the impression he moved to Switzerland to get away from her?"

"I have no idea. I just know he left Chicago to take a teaching position in Switzerland. At the University of Geneva."

"This has been helpful, Mr. Strauss. Just one more thing. Was there any bad blood between Grant Silverton and Jules and El Pierre?"

"You mean over the house? Yes, I guess you could say that. They thought he'd somehow cheated them out of an opportunity to buy the house he owned. It was crazy, really. All the guy did was buy a house, sight unseen."

"Tell me what you know about it."

"When he left Switzerland, he moved back to Chicago for a short time. He connected with a real estate agent up here and told him he was looking for a house. When that house came on the market, the agent contacted him. He liked what he saw and bought it. That's all there was to it. The Pierres made a big stink about it, but fact is, Grant hadn't done anything wrong."

Strauss sat back and sipped his coffee. "It's funny, though. A few weeks ago, Grant said something really odd. Said he was thinking about selling out, moving elsewhere. Letting the Pierres have his house for a good price, since they felt he'd somehow robbed them of it originally. I said, 'You're joking, right?'"

"And he said?"

"He said, 'Yeah, just joking.' But you know, after what has happened, I wonder if maybe he wasn't joking.

"I'll tell you one thing. I'm sure he didn't want to leave. He once told me that, until he came here, he'd never lived in a place where the people around him felt like family. So, what would drive him to think of leaving? Had to be something bad enough."

"This is all very helpful information, Mr. Strauss."

"I'm glad. If I can help in any way . . . well, it makes me feel less helpless, frankly."

"I understand those feelings, Mr. Strauss. You've lost a friend."

Renard flipped back to his interview with Sandy Grainfeld at the crime scene. "Just a couple more questions about the coffin-making class. In interviewing Sandy Grainfeld yesterday at the folk school, I picked up a bit of irritation that Grant Silverton had wanted to use different wood from the rest of the class on his project."

"I guess that might have been the case," Strauss said.

"What can you tell me about that?"

Strauss sat for a moment, thinking. "It just seemed like he was impatient with Grant sometimes. Short with him in how he'd answer questions. Not all the time, but I did notice it on several occasions. It was such a change from his demeanor in other classes that Grant and I had taken from him."

"Any idea why?" Renard asked.

"None, really. Unless Sandy thought Grant wanted some kind of special privileges in the class. You know, what with wanting the different wood for his coffin. Maybe Sandy felt it was setting some kind of precedent, and now other students would want to change things up too. I can see how that would be irritating for the teacher."

Renard flipped back in his notebook. "You said in our interview yesterday that Grant had a bit of a friendship going with Sandy Grainfeld."

"That's how it seemed. I know Grant would call him with questions when he was setting up his woodworking shop in his garage."

"How long ago was that?"

"A year—year and a half ago. He always said how helpful Sandy was. I know he liked him. They seemed to hit it off. But just lately, in the class, it seemed a bit strained between them."

Renard made a couple more notes. "I think that's all. I'll let you get back to your flies." Renard pocketed his notebook and stood up. He took out one of his cards and handed it to Strauss.

"I'm here if you need anything else, Deputy."

"I appreciate that."

Strauss walked to the door with him. Renard stepped into his boots, headed outside and down the steps.

He turned on the engine, cranked up the heat, and sat thinking about the interview. The gravity of the situation had set in for Paul Strauss. There'd been no more fishing idioms. Just the soberness of one who'd lost a close friend.

Renard had confirmed some things. Sandy Grainfeld *had* been irritated with Silverton. Renard had seen that irritation in his interview with Grainfeld at the scene of the crime, and Paul Strauss had confirmed that something between them had changed. Was it just Silverton's requesting different materials in the class? Silverton appeared to have been a man who got what he wanted. Had that started to rub Sandy Grainfeld the wrong way, to the point that it had soured their friendship?

Then there were the Pierres and the tension over the house Silverton had bought, sight unseen, out from under Jules and El. Another case of Silverton getting what he wanted. But in all fairness, when he bought the property, he would have had no idea they wanted it. And once the contract had been signed, well, Silverton was a corporate guy from Chicago. He'd have a very different mentality from the people native to a place like Grand Marais. He wouldn't have been likely to relinquish the property.

Renard took out his notebook and flipped to his notes about the mystery woman from Grant Silverton's past. Silverton *had* talked to Paul Strauss about her, but it was curious the take Strauss had on the topic of this woman. That maybe she was just so in love with Silverton that she had decided to move to where he was. That wasn't the sense he'd gotten from Owen McGraw, Silverton's friend in Chicago, but then again, his view of this woman, whoever she was, would have been seen through Silverton's eyes.

Human nature is an interesting thing, Renard thought. How the same situation can be interpreted quite differently by two people, depending on each person's point of view. Did the mystery woman's behavior actually pose a threat to Grant Silverton? Or were his fears motivated by some form of commitment phobia? Was she the problem or was he?

"So many questions," Renard said to himself. Peel back the surface of any person or situation and you will find surprising and unexpected layers. He knew that any one of those layers can become the catalyst—the motive for a crime.

Yet another curious question had been raised by something Paul Strauss had remembered. A memory that had been triggered by the first interview Renard had had with him yesterday. It had been the question about whether Silverton had a girlfriend here in town that had triggered Strauss to remember hearing a woman in the background one night when he had called Silverton to suggest dinner out.

So who could *that* have been? Renard made a mental note that he and Hank would interview the neighbors near Silverton's house to see if anyone had seen a woman coming or going from his place.

Renard closed his eyes for a moment, listening to the thrum of the engine. The weight of the investigation sat heavily on his shoulders. Fear always crept in for the investigators of a violent crime. Fear that they would miss something, or accidentally overlook some piece of evidence, some nuance in the case that could lead to the truth.

He reflected on the Seven Grandfathers Teachings of his Anishinaabe heritage. Teachings or principles that can be applied to any situation in life to help one stay on his path. Bravery is the principal juxtaposed with fear. The word for bravery, *zoongide'e*, means to have a strong heart, to be courageous. It is the state of having a fearless heart. Renard repeated the word in his mind. When he opened his eyes, a weight seemed to have lifted, and he felt a kind of clarity.

"One step at a time," he said to himself.

As he started to put the car in gear, he realized he had forgotten to ask Paul Strauss what he knew about Grant Silverton buying the prize agate from Maurie Fontaine. He turned off the engine, climbed out of the car, and went back up to the door.

Strauss looked surprised when he opened the door.

"Did you forget something, Deputy?"

"I did. If I could have a few more minutes of your time. . ."

"Of course, no problem. Come in." He held the door open, and Renard stepped in and stood on the rug in front of the door.

He pulled his notebook out—a signal that they could wrap things up right here by the door.

"In my interviews yesterday, I learned that Mr. Silverton had purchased a large agate from Maurie Fontaine. Not sure whether you know him, but he teaches earth science up at the middle school. Runs a geology club for the kids at the school."

"I know of him," Strauss said.

"Among other things, he's a keen rock collector. He sold one of his prize agates to Grant Silverton, and apparently it caused some hard feelings down the road."

Strauss nodded. "Yeah, I heard about it. Grant said he'd paid him easily two or three times what the specimen was worth—at least that was his estimation. Anyway, I guess Fontaine changed his mind. Wanted the agate back."

"And?"

"As far as I know, Grant told him no. That a deal was a deal."

In Renard's mind it was yet one more example of Silverton getting what he wanted, even though his tactics seemed to result in collateral damage in the form of enemies made or, at least, feelings hurt.

As if reading his mind, Paul Strauss said, "You know, if there was a tragic flaw in Grant, it was that he thought money could buy anything. That everything had a price. It would have been part of the culture he worked in—investment banking, mergers and acquisitions—but he also grew up privileged. I know that from the things he said about his parents and his early years. Sad in a way, since the best things in life can't be bought. I don't think he ever understood that."

Renard nodded. "You may be right about that. Tell me, did you ever see this agate he bought from Maurie Fontaine?"

"Sure. Grant kept it right there on his mantel in the living room. It was a beauty, that's for sure."

"Did he ever mention moving it?"

"No, far as I know it was always there on his mantel."

"Well, that should be all, Mr. Strauss. I'll get out of your hair."

"No problem. I hope you and the sheriff's department find the person who did this."

"That's the plan, Mr. Strauss." He pocketed his notebook and headed out the door and back down to his squad.

Chapter 15

Before pulling away from Paul Strauss's house, Renard called Deputy Gunderson.

He answered on the third ring. "Gunderson here."

"Hank, I'd like you to go back to Grant Silverton's residence and interview the folks who live within sight of his house. See if any of the neighbors saw anyone coming or going from Silverton's house over the past few months. Especially anyone they might have seen more than once."

"Man or woman?" Hank asked.

"A woman in particular. But that said, I'd be curious about anyone, man or woman, who was seen coming or going on a regular basis. If you get any hits, see if the neighbor recognized the person, or if not, if they can give you a description."

"Roger that, Claude. I'll get on it right after I finish lunch."

They ended the call.

The last thing on Renard's mind was lunch, but his stomach had been sending up flags—telling him he had already skipped one meal. So he decided to head down to the Harbor Café. But his reason for going there was as much about talking to Willow Tall Grass as it was about lunch. Willow, in her role as waitress at the café, was in a position to hear things, since the village grapevine had its roots firmly planted in the Harbor Café. He pulled out and drove around the end of the block and headed south toward the waterfront.

Down the block on the left, he saw Maggie Norlund, whom he'd met outside the café yesterday, coming down the walk in front of a two-story house. As he approached, she made her way around to the driver's side of an SUV parked at the curb. When she saw him, she waved and turned as if expecting him to stop. He came to a stop and powered down his window.

"Hello, Maggie. Nice to see you again. So this must be your new digs." Willow Tall Grass had told him yesterday that Maggie had just recently moved to Grand Marais after taking a job at Lutsen Mountains.

"Home sweet home." She turned and gestured toward the house. "I rent the first floor. Plenty of space for me."

She walked over to the driver's side of the squad where he sat. Close enough that he could smell the scent of citrus.

"I'm just heading to work, but I'm still looking forward to that tour of the area," she said.

Renard ignored the tour comment. "So you start work in the afternoon."

"At 3:00, normally, but I'm headed in a couple hours early today because someone went home sick."

"Puts you home pretty late."

"After midnight, but I don't mind. I'm a bit of a night owl, so I actually like the hours. Gives me a chance to sleep in." She gave him a sly look. "Sleeping in can be nice, Deputy."

Renard turned his head and stared out the windshield. Having just spent the night with his old love, Maggie's charms were lost on him. She seemed to sense that her allure was not having the desired effect. She stepped back and studied him as if trying to understand why. As if something didn't compute.

"So do you work at the lodge or up at Lutsen Village?" Renard said, trying to redirect things. He realized it was sounding a bit like an interview, which hadn't been his intent.

"I work in the office at the lodge," Maggie said. "Such a lovely atmosphere."

"It's quite a place, all right. Lot of history there." He thought his response sounded canned.

She nodded and brushed aside a strand of silky dark hair that had blown across her face. "Yes there is."

"Well, I should roll, but I'm glad you're settling into our community."

"Of course, I won't keep you." She seemed to have gathered her pride around her like a small fortress. "I'll see you around, Deputy."

He started to say goodbye, but she had already turned toward her car. He powered up the window and drove on down the hill, wondering just who Maggie Norlund really was.

He parked his car along the curb next to the small park that fronted on the frozen harbor. Out on the breakwater, the lighthouse stood its lonely watch over the frigid waters of Lake Superior. Renard crossed 1st Avenue and ducked into the café. The sign said *Seat*

Yourself, so he sat in his favorite booth next to the windows.

He spotted Willow Tall Grass just coming out of the kitchen. Her hands were full, but she smiled and nodded—code for *I'll be right there.*

In a few moments she arrived with a carafe of hot coffee and a menu.

"How's it going, Claude?"

"About like you'd expect, Willow. Lots of questions. Few answers."

"It's only been one day, though."

"The first days are critical, Willow."

She poured hot coffee. "What can I get you?"

"How about the Country Benedict?" He hadn't prevailed yesterday, so he thought he'd try again.

"How about the BLT instead?" Willow counseled. "The tomatoes look wonderful today."

"You know what, Willow, I know it's not the healthiest, but I'd really like the Country Benedict."

She studied him for a moment as if divining what lay behind his request. "Okay, Claude. One Country Benedict coming up."

He sipped his coffee and stared out the window. The immensity of what lay beyond the harbor always brought calm to his spirit.

Before he knew it, Willow was sliding a steaming plate of everything that made for a wonderful breakfast, or lunch, all of it smothered in sausage gravy. Claude understood the concept of too many calories but, truth was, he just didn't have to worry about it. He had a habit of skipping meals, whether that was bad or good. What was more, his days off were frequently spent snowshoeing or cross-country skiing—both big calorie burners.

Willow reached for the carafe and refilled his coffee.

"I'd like to talk to you, Willow. Can you sit down for a few minutes?"

Willow glanced around the café, taking stock of who might need what. The place was pretty empty.

"I'll ask Tammy to keep an eye on things for a few minutes."

She walked toward the kitchen, her long black ponytail in motion.

Tammy was one of the owners. A sometimes sous chef, waitress, cashier, or hostess, she wore all the hats and filled in where needed.

In a few moments, she appeared in the dining room, and Willow came over and slid into the booth opposite him. There was no one in the booth behind them, so he didn't have to worry about anyone over-hearing what they said.

Willow studied him for a few moments as he ate his food.

"I've heard about what happened yesterday at the folk school, Claude. The death of Grant Silverton. It's a terrible thing. The townspeople come in here in pairs or groups, and it's pretty much been the only topic of discussion. People are saying he was murdered. Is that true?"

"Yes, Willow. It is true. It would have been nice if that fact hadn't gone 'round like wildfire, but you may as well tell a genie to stay in the bottle once you pull out the cork."

Willow smiled at the analogy. "Doing what I do, I can't help but hear it all, and let me tell you, some of the theories folks are coming up with are pretty wild."

Renard smiled. "I'm sure they are. But because you encounter just about everyone in town, I consider you a valuable resource."

Willow got a little taller at the sound of that.

"I'm happy to help in any way I can, Claude."

He set his fork down. Willow had brought a cup of coffee with her, and he topped it off from the carafe on the table.

"I assume you knew Grant Silverton, or at least knew who he was."

Willow nodded. "He's lived here in town for about two years, hasn't he?"

"Yes, a little over two years."

"He seemed like a nice man. Very kind and polite, and he always left me generous tips. He would come in alone sometimes, but often, in the mornings, he was with Paul Strauss. They would come in for breakfast, and they seemed like really good friends."

"Paul is relatively new to the town as well," Renard said. "He moved here about three years ago. Big fisherman. That's what brought him up here to live."

Willow nodded. "Yup. He talks a lot about fishing. Sometimes Grant—Mr. Silverton would just sit and listen to his stories about his angling adventures. He used to joke that he needed to get a hobby so he could do some of the talking. But then I think they both got into woodworking, because I used to hear them talking a lot about that."

"Did you ever see Grant Silverton come in here with anyone else?"

Willow stared out the window, thinking. "You know, I want to say I saw him come in with Sandy Grainfeld a couple of times. The woodworking teacher from the folk school. It's been a while though. That was probably a year ago."

Renard had been forking in sausage and hash browns as she talked, but now he stopped and studied her. "You've got a good memory, Willow."

"It's from being a mom. You have to remember everything for everybody."

He smiled. He knew Willow had a lot on her plate, figuratively speaking. She had two kids approaching their teens, and her mom lived with them too, up in Grand Portage.

"Did Grant Silverton ever come in to eat with a woman?"

"You mean like a girlfriend?"

Renard nodded.

"Not that I ever saw."

"Ever see him around town with anyone?"

"You mean a woman?" Willow paused and looked at him. "No, I've never seen him with a woman to my recollection. In fact, the only woman I've ever heard talk about him is Kristin Fontaine."

Renard's ears perked up at that. Kristin was the wife of Maurie Fontaine—the guy who'd sold Silverton the storied agate.

"Can you tell me more about that?" he asked.

"Well, there's not much to tell. I just know that she cleaned his house."

"Really?"

"She has a small cleaning business, Claude. Works for a number of the townspeople."

"I did not know that. That's helpful information, Willow. Can you remember what you might have heard Kristin say about him?"

Willow stared out the window again, thinking. After a few moments she turned back to Renard. "I do remember one day—I think it was on the weekend— she came in with her sister, Kate. I remember because she seemed upset. I heard her talking about Maurie being really angry with Grant Silverton. It was some-thing about rocks. He teaches earth science up at the middle school. My kids have had him as a teacher. He's really into Minnesota geology and rock hunting."

Claude nodded. This was not new information, but he let Willow talk, hoping something more might come to light.

"Kristin seemed really worried that Maurie would make her stop working for Grant Silverton. She told her sister that day that Grant was her best customer and that he would occasionally leave extra money as a tip for her." Willow gazed out the window again. "There was something else that day, too. Maybe I'm remem-bering it now because of what has happened to Mr. Sil-verton, but Kristin told her sister that she was really worried Maurie would do something stupid."

"Huh." Now it was Renard's turn to stare out the window.

"That's all I heard. I tend to pick up bits and pieces of things when I'm circulating around the dining room, waiting on the customers, but I mostly never know the whole story behind what I hear."

"No worries, Willow. This has been very helpful. You've given me some information I can follow up on.

Right now, I'm just trying to get the best picture I can of who Grant Silverton was, and what you've told me helps flesh out that picture."

Willow nodded. "I need to get back to work." She started to stand up and then stopped and sat back down. "This is weird, but there's something else I just remembered."

"What is it?"

"This happened about six months ago, I'd say. Grant Silverton had stopped in for lunch by himself that day. I had come over to take his order, and he seemed happy. I remember I dropped the menu as he handed it to me, and he bent down to pick it up. When he handed it to me, he looked like he'd seen a ghost. It was so strange that I asked him if he was okay. He said he'd just remembered something he had to do and that he'd have to cancel his order. I told him not to worry about it, but he was already on his feet, headed out the door."

"That's pretty strange. Did he seem frightened?"

"I'd say alarmed."

"Did you notice who else was in the diner? What might have spooked him?"

"It was July, Claude. The place was full of tourists. Every table was packed. It could have been anything— anyone."

Renard nodded. "Still, I'm glad you told me about it."

Willow nodded. She stood up and placed his ticket on the table and headed back toward the kitchen.

Renard finished his meal and laid money on the table for the bill. He headed out the door and back to his squad. He hoped he could catch Kristin Fontaine at home and interview her before Maurie got home for the day. He drove back out to the highway and headed up the hill toward the Fontaines' house, west of town.

Chapter 16

Highway 61 rose steeply as it left downtown Grand Marais. Maurie and Kristin Fontaine's property lay a short ways beyond the town line. As Renard headed west, he was thinking about what Willow Tall Grass had told him. He wondered why Kristin Fontaine had not informed him yesterday that she'd worked for Grant Silverton. It seemed odd she wouldn't have mentioned it.

He was also thinking about what Paul Strauss had said. Could Kristin Fontaine be the woman he had heard in the background the night he called Silverton's house? Strauss had said he'd heard a phone ring and then a woman say hello. Was it Kristin Fontaine? If so, had she been there cleaning, or was she there for some other reason?

He saw the turn coming up. He took a right and followed the long driveway up to the house. The pickup truck was not there, which told Renard that Maurie was still at the school, but there was a white minivan there with Kristin's business name—*Make It a Clean Sweep*—on the side. He climbed out, went to the door, and rang the bell, and a few moments later Kristin opened the door. She seemed startled to see him.

"Maurie isn't here, Claude. He won't be home for probably another hour."

"That's okay, Kristin. I actually wanted to talk to you. Could I come in for a few minutes?"

"Of course. Where are my manners. Please, come inside."

Kristin had a can of furniture wax and a dust rag in her hand, and the vacuum sat in the middle of their family room.

"Can I get you some coffee, Claude? Would you like to sit down?" She gestured toward the sofa and chairs over by the fireplace.

"No thanks, Kristin. I just had lunch, so my coffee tank is topped off."

She smiled at that.

"We can just talk here, if that's okay?"

"Of course." She set the dust rag and can of Pledge on a small table that sat next to the door. "How can I help?"

Renard took out his notebook and pen.

"How well did you know Grant Silverton, Kristin?"

"Not well at all, really."

He waited for her to mention that Silverton had been her customer. That she had cleaned his house.

"He had quite an interest in rock collecting," she said. "That's how he got to know Maurie. Maurie actually helped him set up some rock cutting and polishing equipment."

"But wasn't Grant Silverton one of your customers? Didn't he hire you to clean his house?"

"Well, yes. That's right." The way she said it, it sounded like that fact didn't matter at all.

"It just seems odd that you wouldn't have mentioned working for him yesterday when I was here."

Her eyes slid sideways. "I guess it just didn't come up. Your focus yesterday seemed to be on accusing Maurie of stealing back the agate he'd sold to Grant Silverton."

"Did he?"

"Did he what?"

"Did he go to Silverton's house and take back the agate he'd sold him?"

"Of course not. That's ridiculous."

"Are you sure, Kristin? Maurie was in the crowd down at the folk school yesterday morning. He knew Grant Silverton had died."

The color came up in her face. "If Maurie said he didn't do it, then he didn't do it. You can take that to the bank. Or back to the sheriff's office, or wherever."

She gave Renard a hard stare. "What are you implying, Claude? What are you really saying? Where that agate went seems pretty unimportant, considering a man has been killed. Here's what I think. I think you believe Maurie killed Grant Silverton just to get that agate back. And that is ridiculous."

"It may seem that way, Kristin, but believe me, people have died over less." He studied her. "As an investigator, all I can do is follow where the evidence leads. Maurie is not the sole focus of this investigation. But sadly, because of the unpleasantness about that agate, he does have a motive. He was overheard saying he would get that rock back no matter what he had to do."

Kristin had stepped back and crossed her arms on her chest. She was actually glaring at him.

"Maurie is the most honest man I've ever known. Most men lie. Sooner or later, they all lie. But not Maurie. That man is honest as the day is long. That would be a June day, by the way. And I love him for it."

Renard studied her. Up until that moment, he had wondered if she might possibly be involved with Silverton. After all, she was a very attractive woman, and Paul Strauss had had the feeling that maybe Silverton was involved with someone—someone he didn't talk about. But Renard put that thought to the back of his mind. This woman appeared to love her husband. But as to the part about lying, he knew first hand that Maurie *did* lie. He had lied to him about several things yesterday, at the beginning of the interview.

"Was your working for Grant Silverton a bone of contention between you and Maurie? Is that why you didn't mention it yesterday?"

Kristin looked down at the floor, and Renard could see he'd struck a nerve.

"I'll admit he wasn't happy about my working there. He asked me to drop him as a customer. But this isn't a huge community, and Grant Silverton was a good customer. Frankly, I wasn't going to alienate one of my best customers, and I told Maurie so."

Renard looked up from his notes and studied Kristin. She was a force to be reckoned with. He could picture her telling Maurie that and Maurie just having to accept it. Maybe the reason Maurie never lied to her was that he was afraid to.

"Did anyone ever come to visit Mr. Silverton at his house when you were there working?"

She thought for a moment. "Paul Strauss came by on occasion. They were friends. Seemed like good friends. Have you talked to him?"

"Yes, I've had two interviews with Mr. Strauss. You're right, they were good friends. Was there anyone else you ever saw at his house, or maybe heard him talking to on the phone?"

"Occasionally, I'd hear him on the phone, but I never knew who he was talking to. If he was in the same room as me and the phone rang, he'd always walk to another area of the house to talk. He kept to himself a lot."

"So, he wasn't in the habit of visiting with you when you'd be there?"

"Not at all. Like I said, he kept to himself. He'd usually be working on his computer when I was there cleaning."

Renard nodded.

"I assume, since you cleaned his house, you knew where Grant Silverton kept the agate that Maurie had sold him."

"Of course. He kept it right on the mantel in his living room."

"And when was the last time you saw it there?"

"I cleaned his house Monday—the day before he died. The agate was there on the mantel. I picked it up when I dusted the mantel."

"Kristin, I'm going to ask you this question one time, because I have to." He looked her straight in the eye. "Did you take that agate from Grant Silverton's house?"

Her blue eyes turned to ice, but she never looked away. "I—did—not."

Each word fell heavy as stone, and, in Renard's estimation, each carried the weight of truth.

The only two people with motive to take that rock were Maurie and Kristin Fontaine. If he were to believe them—if they spoke the truth—it only deepened the mystery of where the agate had gone. And why. There was one thing of which he was certain, though. The disappearance of that agate was somehow connected to Silverton's death. He did not believe that the timing of its disappearance was coincidental.

So, did the killer take it to cast suspicion on Maurie? If so, it had to be someone who knew he desperately wanted the agate back. Someone who possibly had heard his threatening words that night up at the Harbor Light Bar & Grill—*I'm going to get it back no matter what I have to do.*

Renard closed his notebook and put it in his pocket.

"That's all for now, Kristin. Should anything come to mind that relates to Grant Silverton—anything you might remember or think is important, please call me." He took a card out of his pocket and handed it to her, thanked her for her time, and left.

He climbed into his squad, backed around, and headed down the driveway, where he turned left onto Highway 61 and drove back toward town.

Chapter 17

Renard came down the hill into Grand Marais. As he passed Northern Arts Folk School on his right, he noticed that Sandy Grainfeld's truck was parked outside the woodworking building. He was glad to see it there since he was hoping to talk to Becca Grainfeld alone.

The Grainfelds lived on Devil Track Lake, north of Grand Marais. Renard drove through town and turned left onto the Gunflint Trail. Devil Track Lake lay west of the Gunflint and fifteen to twenty minutes northwest of Grand Marais. On an icy day that time could double, but today the roads were in pretty good shape.

The Gunflint climbed with ear-popping steepness as it snaked north of Grand Marais through frozen walls of snow, pushed up by the plows as winter deepened. The view of the town and its signature tombolo that separated East Bay from Grand Marais Harbor was spectacular from the Pincushion Mountain overlook a few miles up the road.

Ten minutes along, Renard turned left onto Devil Track Road and followed it west, through dense forest for another six miles to where he turned onto a snow-covered drive that would take him down to the Grainfeld property. Being law enforcement, he knew the roads up here like the back of his hand.

The Grainfelds' acreage lay along a narrow private road that tunneled through spruce and balsam forest. The property had been in the family for three generations now. Sandy's grandfather Nels had purchased the tract of land up here in the early 1940s and built his homestead on it. Nels had been a colorful character in the town's history. Before there were roads out to Devil Track Lake, he had traveled by dog sled during the long, cold winters when he'd needed to get supplies in Grand Marais. The tradition of mushing had been passed down to his great-grandson Ethan—Sandy and Becca's son—who still kept dogs on the family homestead.

The tires crunched on compacted snow as Renard pulled up behind the house. There were two vehicles there—Becca's Jeep and an older model Ford pickup that Renard had seen Ethan around town in. Renard parked behind them.

Sandy's father had inherited the homestead and, in the 1990s, rebuilt the house. But about ten years ago, Sandy's parents had decided to move to warmer climes, and word was Sandy and Becca had drawn up an agreement to buy the house from them.

The large, half-log timbered house was stained dark red-brown and stood in sharp contrast to the deep snow and evergreen forest. As he climbed out of the cruiser, Renard heard the barking of dogs and the sound of an ax at work. He saw Ethan Grainfeld splitting wood about twenty yards from the house. He was wearing heavy boots, a red flannel shirt, brown overalls, and a Sherpa hat with ear flaps. He had shed his parka, due to the heaviness of the work.

Renard started toward him and the dogs went wild.

"No bark," Ethan shouted over the din.

Renard stopped three feet from him.

"Sheriff One Step." Ethan nodded a greeting.

Ethan Grainfeld had been a young boy the last time Renard had been sheriff hereabouts, but some things just stick.

Ethan had a neatly trimmed beard and mustache, and although he wore a hat, Renard knew he buzzed his hair. While taller, he looked like his father, or at least a well-put-together version of him. Sandy Grain-feld tended to lean toward scruffy.

"Running in the Beargrease this year?" Renard asked.

Ethan nodded toward the dogs. "We're training every day now."

The John Beargrease Sled Dog Marathon is run from Duluth to Grand Portage, Minnesota every January. It honors the memory of John Beargrease, a mail carrier who delivered the mail along the north shore of Lake Superior by dogsled and rowboat from Two Harbors, Minnesota to Grand Portage in the late 1800s, up until his death in 1910. At 400 miles, it is the longest sled dog race in the lower forty-eight states and draws racers from all over the world.

"My friend Martin Running Wolf will be racing."

"Sure, I know him. Good guy. All the mushers just call him Wolf." Ethan leaned on his ax. "Suppose you're here about the murder of Grant Silverton."

"That's right," Renard said. "He was a student in your dad's class."

"Dad told us about it. It happened at the woodworking building. Freaked him out bad."

"How do you know that?"

"Dad was the one who found him. Mom and I went down there to the school yesterday morning when someone called to tell us something was wrong. When Dad came up the hill to meet us, he looked like he was eighty years old. His face was gray. We got home—he couldn't sit down, wouldn't talk to us."

Renard waited to see if he would say more, but he didn't.

"The night before—Tuesday—the night Grant Silverton died, were you here when your dad got home?"

"Yeah. I was just getting ready to leave—to meet some buddies up at the Harbor Light."

"What time was that—I mean, when your dad got home?"

"I don't know. Probably about 8:30. You can ask Mom. She'd know."

"How did he seem?"

"Tired. He seemed tired. But he's always tired. Hey, why are you asking all this stuff?"

"It's my job to ask, Ethan. That's why we call it an investigation."

Renard moved on. "Did you know Grant Silverton at all?"

Ethan turned and picked up his ax. "Nah, not really." He reached for a log. "I talked to him a few times, but hey, he was older—not like I would have hung out with him." He started his swing. A second later the log split in two.

Renard smiled to himself. God forbid you would hang out with an elder. So different from his heritage where young people were taught to seek out the elders —to learn from them. 'Ask an elder' was like a mantra to the Anishinaabeg.

"Is your mom home?"

Ethan waved his head. "In the house."

Renard nodded. "Good luck in the Beargrease."

He turned and headed toward the house. As he did so, he pulled out his cell phone to see if he had reception. At that moment there were two bars showing outside the house. He stepped up to the door and rang the bell.

With lake homes the main door of the house is actually the back door, because the front of the house, where the living or great room is, looks out on the lake and often has sliding doors out onto a deck.

In a few moments, Becca Grainfeld opened the door. She had large gray eyes and fine facial bones. Her dark blond hair was plaited into a French braid along the top and down the back of her head. Wisps of hair had escaped in an attractively unruly fashion. He knew that she and Sandy were in their 50s, but, whereas Sandy looked a bit weathered, the years had been kind to Becca.

"Hello, Claude. I've been expecting your visit. Howie told me you would be coming."

Sandy was the moniker the town had given her husband, and it related to his woodworking. But to Becca, who had known him since their school days, he would have been Howard. Renard had never heard her call him anything but Howie in all the years he'd known them.

She held the door open, and he stepped into a large tiled entryway to the left of the kitchen. The wall on his left was filled with coats hanging on pegs, with lots of boots underneath, some neatly lined up, others piled higgledy-piggledy. A shelf above the coats held bins for hats and mittens.

He removed his boots and followed Becca into the large bright kitchen that had a vaulted ceiling and pale yellow walls. Two skylights flooded light into the work area.

She turned to face him. "We're very sorry about what happened to Grant Silverton."

Her words seemed to cast a shadow of sadness in the light-filled room.

"It's a terrible thing for the community and for all who knew him," Renard said.

Becca looked down at the floor. "Howie told me he was murdered."

Renard thought he detected a slight shiver when she said that last word.

"It's horrible to think about. I'm glad I didn't see him . . . like that." She looked up. "Howie is so upset about it."

"I've been told that he and Grant Silverton were friends."

Becca's eyes slid to the side.

"I guess you could say that. Grant . . . or should I call him Mr. Silverton?"

"What are you comfortable calling him?"

"Grant, I guess. The thing is, he hadn't lived here long."

"More than two years," Renard said.

He understood what she was saying, though. In a small community like this, where people had grown up together—known each other forever—two years hardly seemed like enough knowing time to call it a friendship. It would have been different for Paul Strauss and Grant Silverton. They were both big city boys. Both had imported themselves here. Their forming a close friendship would have been natural, even though the townsfolk might have considered two years an unnaturally brief span of time.

Renard took out his small notebook. He hoped it signaled that they were just getting started.

"Let's start at the beginning. How long *had* Howard known Grant Silverton?"

Becca thought for a minute. "Over a year. Might be a year and a half, I guess. These are questions you should really ask Howie."

"That's all right, Becca. Your best guess will do."

"Well, I'd say a year and a half then."

"And did they spend time together?"

"Grant was his student at the folk school. He'd taken two or three woodworking classes from Howie."

So far, that tracked with what Howard had told him. "Did they spend time outside of class?"

"I think Howie helped Grant set up a woodworking shop at his house."

"You think or you know?"

Becca looked surprised. "I know . . . I mean, he did."

"How long ago was that?"

"A while ago. I'd say over a year. I think that happened soon after Grant Silverton took the first class from Howie."

"So, as far as you know, things were friendly between them. Even during this current class?"

Again, Becca's eyes slid sideways as if she was making a decision. She looked back at him. "Howie was a little miffed at Grant for wanting special favors in the class."

"You mean the wood? Because he wanted walnut, not pine for his coffin?"

"Yes."

"Was there anything else?"

Becca hesitated. "Howie didn't like that Grant was falling behind and asking to stay after class and work."

"Did you know Grant had stayed after class the night before last?"

"Yes. Howie mentioned it when he got home."

"Was he upset about it?" Renard asked.

Now Becca actually turned her head and stared out the window for a moment. Renard knew why.

She turned her eyes back to him. "He said Grant was being a pain in the ass."

"Anything else?"

"No. I asked if he wanted to talk about it. He said no, that he just wanted to eat his dinner. So I left it alone."

"And what time did Howard get home?"

"At 8:20."

The answer had come too quickly, as if rehearsed.

"Not around 8:20?" Renard asked. "Exactly 8:20? Could it have been 8:30?"

Becca appeared flustered but quickly collected herself.

"It was 8:20. I was prepping dinner for Howie, and I looked at the clock when he came in." She pointed to a decorative clock on the kitchen wall, as if to say *discussion ended*.

Theoretically, if Sandy Grainfeld was the killer, Renard figured he would have stabbed Grant Silverton before he left the woodworking building at the folk school—not gone back later. But since the last three students left shortly after eight o'clock, it wouldn't have left time for him to commit the murder and still arrive home by 8:20. Change his arrival time to 8:30, though, just a ten-minute difference, and he would have had time to commit the crime.

Renard looked up from his notes. "What time do you and Howard go to bed at night?"

Becca looked at him for a moment like it might be a trick question.

"Between ten and ten thirty. Why?"

"At 10:30 p.m. the night of the murder, Dave Isaacs was out for his run before going to work up at the hospital. As he came past the folk school, he saw someone running from the woodworking building. He immediately called Howard to report that there'd been a break-in at the school. Did you hear that call come in, Becca?"

He watched her study his eyes as if she might read the answer there.

"No, I didn't. Did Dave Isaacs say which number he called—Howie's cell or our landline?"

"He said he called Howard's cell phone. I'm wondering why he didn't answer that call?"

"We have bad reception up here. The call probably didn't come through."

Renard took out his phone and looked at it. "I have two bars showing."

"That's fine, but reception can be poor up here. It's very hit and miss. If there's wind or a front approaching, reception evaporates. Or maybe Howie had turned his phone off. Did Dave recognize the person he saw?"

"I can't comment on that."

Her face clouded. "Why not?"

"Because that's the nature of a homicide investigation."

Even if protocol had allowed for it, he never would have mentioned that Dave Isaacs had recognized the Dinkovich boys. In an investigation, there are certain facts that are kept under wraps.

Renard decided he'd learned as much as he was going to about the phone call. He moved on to the next part of the interview.

"How well did *you* know Grant Silverton, Becca?"

"Only through Howie. That seems like an odd question."

"Why? He must have been at the house here occasionally."

"I don't think he was ever here. He and Howie met at his house when they got together."

"And what about Ethan? Did he know Grant Silverton at all?"

"You'd have to ask Ethan that."

"I'm asking you, Becca."

"He knew who he was, but I don't think he *knew* him." She put air quotes around the word "knew." "He's right outside, though. You can ask him yourself."

Renard nodded. "I'll do that." Of course he'd already asked Ethan, but that was the nature of investigation—asking different people the same question. Seeing what jibed and what didn't.

"I saw the dogs outside. Looks like Ethan keeps them here."

"Ethan still lives here," Becca said, unapologetically. "Hasn't found the right girl yet. Howie and I are fine having him here, until he finds the right spot for himself. After all, he can't live in town with the dogs. He'll need a place with land. We have ten acres here, so why not? Right now, he's training for the Beargrease."

"He mentioned that. It's coming up fast."

"Two weeks," Becca said.

"Where does Ethan work?"

"He works for Nordic Logging Company," Becca said.

"Ah. I have an acquaintance who works there. Boyle Bouchard."

Becca nodded. "I think Ethan mentioned him. Said he was an odd guy. Thinks he's a Buddhist monk or something."

"Well, Becca, Boyle is on his path just like all of us."

"Ethan doesn't plan to make a career of the logging company."

"No?"

"He's actually taking an online course."

"In what?"

"He's learning about investing."

"What got him into that?"

"One of his buddies at the lumber company does this online investing. What do they call it?" She thought for a moment. "Day trading. That's what it is. Anyway, he got Ethan excited about the prospect of doing it." Her face darkened a bit. "It's a bone of contention with Howie, though."

"How so?" Renard asked.

"Howie claims it's not a real job. Tells Ethan he needs to work at getting a real job. Earn an honest living. Of course, Ethan bristles at that and tells Howie he's doing that, but that you don't have to break your back to earn an honest living."

She shook her head. "It's sad, really. They used to be so close. Always going fishing and ice fishing in the winter. Now they just seem to butt heads. It's changed Howie. Now, when he finally stops working at the high school and the folk school, he's like a couch potato."

Renard heard a bit of disgust in her voice.

"Does Ethan ever do any woodworking? Help his dad at the folk school maybe?"

Becca shook her head. "Never. I used to tell Howie if he wanted Ethan to love woodworking, he had to start teaching him about it when he was a young boy. But he'd never take the time. And sure enough, by the time Ethan became a sulky teenager, it was too late. Howie tried to get him involved then, but Ethan would have nothing to do with it."

"That's really too bad," Renard said, "because Howard is very talented."

"Thank you, Claude. I'll tell him you said that. It will mean a lot to him."

"Well, Becca, I think that's all for now. We'll be in touch if we need anything else."

"I can't imagine what that would be."

Renard heard a note of hostility in her voice. He studied her for a moment before speaking. His silence seemed to unnerve her.

"Howard was the last person to see Grant Silverton alive, as well as being the person who found him dead. That makes him a significant person in this case."

"Are you saying he's a suspect?"

"I'm saying what I just said, Becca." He pocketed his notebook and thanked her for her time. She walked to the door with him.

Renard stood outside the back door for a few moments. Like a number of the other interviews over the past two days, there seemed to have been growing hostility in Becca as the interview proceeded. As a law enforcement officer, he was in the unenviable position of knowing many of the townsfolk—having grown up with many of them—but still having to police them when necessary. So he approached these situations with the utmost respect. However, he would not be cajoled or coerced because of those relationships. When he had become a cop, he'd had to draw a line in the sand. There was a loneliness about that line. Nonetheless, the line had to be upheld.

No matter how close his connection to any one of them might be, his commitment to the truth came first. *Truth* was the last of the Seven Grandfathers Teachings —the Seven Sacred Laws. It was last, he believed, because it was the most important of them all, and if you followed the path of the other six, it would lead you to truth. Over time, Renard had come to believe that the great spiritual traditions are all roads that lead to the same destination—truth or God. What his people called Gichi Manitou—the Great Mystery.

Renard walked to his cruiser. He had been going to ask Ethan something, but both he and his pickup truck were gone. It would have to wait until later. He climbed in, backed the SUV around, and headed out the long, snow-compacted gravel drive to Devil Track Road.

Chapter 18

Renard stopped at the junction with Devil Track Road and called Deputy Gunderson.

"How did the interviews with the neighbors go, Hank?"

"Except for one house, directly east of the Silverton property, we managed to talk to everyone who could have had a view of the property."

"What did you learn?"

"Not much. Several neighbors had seen the cleaning service come and go regularly. They reported that the name on the business van was 'Make It a Clean Sweep.' Two people told me that Kristin Fontaine is the business owner."

"Yes, I know about Kristin's business. How often is regularly?"

"Sounded like she cleaned once a week. House looked like it too, didn't you think?"

"It did," Renard said. "A lot cleaner than my place. Anything else?"

"Guy across the street reported seeing a Toyota Highlander come and go. Said an older guy was always driving it."

"That's the make of SUV Paul Strauss drives. No surprise he'd be a regular visitor at Silverton's house, since they were good friends. Anything else?"

"That was about it," Hank said. "My take on it— there may have been other people who visited, but folks tend to remember things they see more than once. That seemed to be the case here."

"Did any of the neighbors you spoke to seem to know Grant Silverton?"

"Didn't seem like it. They all said that beyond 'Hi, how are you?' Silverton kept to himself."

"Where are you now, Hank?"

"Len and I are back at headquarters."

"I just finished interviewing Becca Grainfeld up at Devil Track Lake, so I'm heading back down now. I think I'll swing by the Silverton property and see if I can catch that neighbor you missed, since folks are getting home from work and school this time of day."

"Anything you want me to do? I'm just here working on reports."

"There is something I thought of. Could you call Northern Arts Folk School and request a schedule of classes and who taught them for last year and the beginning of this year? We're just a few weeks into the new year, but see what they have. Okay?"

"On it," Hank said.

"Also, would you tell Merlin Waters to wait until I get back to headquarters so the three of us can go over a few things?"

"I'll tell him."

"And Hank. If Merlin's not busy, could you send him to get some food for the three of us? Maybe Subway."

"Sure. What time?"

"I'll plan to be back there by six, so let's shoot for that timeframe."

"On it, Boss. See you then."

They ended the call, and Renard pulled out onto Devil Track Road and headed back toward Grand Marais. Darkness was closing in behind him as he drove east. No spectacular sunset, just a morphing from gray to black as the day died behind him in the west.

At this point he had little mind space for anything but the case. He thought about the interview he'd just had with Becca Grainfeld. He'd picked up a vibe—an uncomfortable one—that told him she was hiding something. Did it relate to her husband and his connection to the victim? Was she covering for him in some way? When he'd asked what time Sandy got home Tuesday—the night the murder occurred—she'd been too quick to answer. Like she might have rehearsed what she would say when asked.

Sandy Grainfeld certainly had means and opportunity. He was irritated with Silverton for wanting favors in the class. Could it have escalated to an argument after the other students left that night? Renard thought about the weapon—a wood chisel. A weapon of convenience. That told him the crime was not premeditated. But stabbing is an act of passion, the result of extreme anger. Grainfeld's motive just didn't seem to mesh with such an act.

The Gunflint Trail dropped in steep curves toward Grand Marais. When Renard reached the intersection with 5th Avenue, he turned right and drove down toward Silverton's property, which lay on the west side of town.

He pulled up in front of the property immediately east of Silverton's house, climbed out, and headed up to the door. It was a modest-looking two-story house, far less grand than Silverton's imposing log home next door.

After a few moments a woman opened the door. Renard placed her at early thirties. He recognized her immediately. She worked as a waitress at My Sister's Place, where he sometimes ate. Her name, he recalled, was Sue, and right now, she looked stressed. He heard children rampaging around in the background—the probable cause.

"Sheriff One Step. Hello."

She looked surprised, but then the look changed to, *Oh, of course.*

"You must be here with questions about Mr. Silverton, I mean, since he lived right next door and all. It's so terrible what happened to him. There's been nothing but talk of it at the restaurant since yesterday."

"If you have a few minutes, I'd like to ask you some questions, Ms. . . . ."

"Oh, it's Jamison. Sue Jamison. Do you remember me from My Sister's Place?"

"Yes, I do. Could I step inside?" Renard asked. "Might keep the house warmer."

"Of course, please." She held the door open and he stepped in.

Just then a young red-caped boy came charging through the living room pursued by his sister, wielding a wooden sword.

"The battle rages on," Sue said with a wry smile. "Not sure why I'm still alive." She looked back at Renard. "How can I be of help?"

"We're talking to the neighbors that surround Grant Silverton's house to see, first, how well any of you knew him, and second, to get a sense of who may have visited him at his house. My deputies were around earlier but didn't find you at home, so I thought I'd try this evening."

"Yes, I had to work today. I usually work evenings, after my husband gets home, but someone was out sick today, so I went in to cover the lunch hour."

Renard nodded and took out his notebook. "How well did you know Grant Silverton?"

"Not very well. He was always very polite, though, whenever we'd be outside and he would arrive home, or if he was out in his yard. He would always talk to the children if they were there and ask Mike and I how we were doing. Mike is my husband. Mike Jamison. Just mentioned it because sometimes married couples have different names. But we're both Jamison."

Renard nodded and let her talk.

"Anyway, Mr. Silverton—that's how we made the children address him—was very kind. A gentleman, I guess you'd say. At Christmas he'd always bring over a fancy box of food he ordered from a company called Harry & David. It was something we never would have bought for ourselves. Fruit, chocolate, fancy nuts and cheeses. I used to bring baked goods over to his house at Christmas, too. He always made a fuss about that. Said he loved home-baked goods. Once or twice he invited us into his house. It's quite a grand place."

"Did he ever talk to you about his life at all?"

"Oh, no. Nothing like that. He was kind and polite, but there was a line, you could tell. He kept to himself. Very private, if you ask me."

"Living next door, you must have seen people come and go," Renard said. Just then the forces of good and evil rampaged back through the living room pursued by a barking dog—one that looked like a border collie mix.

Sue Jamison proceeded to tell him that she had seen the cleaning service there once a week. The same information that deputies Blake and Gunderson had gathered.

"He had a friend who seemed to visit often," Sue said. "We even met him one time when we were out in the yard and he arrived. If I recall, his name was Paul."

"Paul Strauss?" Renard asked.

"Yes, I think that was it. Seemed like he and Mr. Silverton were good friends."

"I believe they were. Is there anything else you can remember, Ms. Jamison? Anyone you may have seen visiting the house, especially yesterday morning."

"Well, I saw the police cars over there yesterday morning."

"But before they arrived? Did you by chance see anyone approach the house from the backyard, like they might have come from the woods at the back of the Silverton property?"

Sue Jamison shook her head. "No. . . ." Then all of a sudden her expression changed. "There was something odd, though, now that you mention the backyard and the woods beyond. I did see something a couple of times. Not yesterday, though. I didn't see anything like that yesterday."

"Tell me what you *did* see," Renard encouraged. "And when."

"I saw someone approach the house the way you just mentioned—from the backyard. Not yesterday, but a couple of other times in the past few months."

"Tell me about that," Renard said.

"Well, the baby's room is on the back corner of the house, upstairs. We have an infant, six months old. Anyway, that room looks out toward the back of Mr. Silverton's property."

"Go on."

"So on two or maybe three occasions, when I was putting the baby to bed, I saw someone approach the house from the backyard. Usually it's pitch dark out there, but one night there was a moon, and I happened to look up after I laid the baby down, and I saw someone walking toward the back of the house next door. I moved to the window and saw the person just walking in the back door, like they lived there, but it wasn't Mr. Silverton."

"Did you see what the person looked like?"

"No, you know, it's winter. Everyone dresses the same—boots, parkas, stocking hats."

"Was this person a man or a woman?"

"Oh, I'd say a woman, even though I didn't see her face. But that was my impression, so she must have moved like a woman."

"You said you saw someone approach that way two or three times. Do you think it was the same person each time?"

"I couldn't say for sure, except that I think it was a woman. It was dark, though. If there hadn't been snow on the ground, I likely wouldn't have noticed anyone at all."

So, whoever it was, they could have been visiting for months and not been noticed until the snow fell, Renard thought.

"Any impression of how tall this person might have been or anything distinctive you might have noticed?"

"I couldn't judge as to height. I only ever saw the person from upstairs. That's the only room in the house with a view of the back of Mr. Silverton's property."

"Do you recall what time this occurred?"

"Well, right around 7:30, I'd say. I always lay the baby down then so I can start getting the other children ready for bed."

"Do you recall if it was a weekday or the weekend when you saw this person?"

"I can't remember. Probably because all my days are about the same."

Renard heard a tinge of desperation in her voice.

"There is something I just remembered, though." She looked up at Renard. "The person wore a stocking hat with a pom pom. You know, those fur pom poms that are popular right now. Maybe that's how I knew it was a woman. Not too many men wearing those."

"Did you notice color of clothing?" Renard asked.

"It was too dark to see colors accurately. It just looked like dark clothing. But now that I think about it, I think the hat was white or light colored, anyway, and that's how I saw the pom pom on top."

"Can you think of anything else that might be helpful?"

"I don't think so," Sue Jamison said. At that moment the baby started to howl from another room.

Renard took out his card and gave it to her. "If you happen to remember anything that might relate to the case—no matter how small—please call me."

"I will." She was edging backwards now toward the baby's cries.

"I'll let myself out," Renard said. But Sue had already turned and headed toward the back of the house.

Outside, darkness had fully descended along with bone-penetrating cold. The wind was light but dead out of the north. Renard walked around to the back of Grant Silverton's house and looked up at the window on the corner of the Jamisons' house. From there, Sue Jamison would have had a clear view of Silverton's back door. But it *was* dark. Visibility was only possible because of the snow reflecting the ambient light. Head down, against the wind, Renard made his way back to his squad and climbed in. He turned over the engine, pulled out, and drove east toward the Law Enforcement Center.

He was thinking about what Sue Jamison had told him, but also what Paul Strauss had mentioned about hearing a woman's voice on the phone in the background when he had called Silverton one night. Was Silverton in a relationship with this woman visitor? If so, why all the cloak and dagger? Was she married? Was Silverton having an affair with a married woman? If so, that narrowed who she might be down to about half the town.

Under normal circumstances it wouldn't have mattered who this woman was, but these were not normal circumstances. Grant Silverton had been murdered. It was imperative that they learn who he was in contact with, and why, those last weeks before his death.

Chapter 19

Renard parked alongside the Law Enforcement Center. He headed up to the door, punched in a code, and let himself in. Partway down the hall he stuck his head into Merlin Waters' office and lab.

"You here, Merlin?"

Merlin stuck his head out of the back room. "I'm here. Hank told me to hang around until you got back."

"Give me a couple of minutes and then we'll all meet back in the conference room. Bring anything you've got so far, and we'll put our heads together."

"Will do."

Renard went into his office to collect the murder book, which had the reports on the case, pictures of the crime scene, etc. He also checked his emails to see if there were any updates from the BCA. There were none.

Within a couple of minutes Deputy Hank Gunderson stuck his head in the door. He was carrying sandwiches and drinks from Subway, which was a stone's throw from the Law Enforcement Center.

"Thought you'd send Merlin," Renard said.

Hank smiled. "Remember what happened the last time we sent Merlin?"

Renard paused for a minute and then laughed. "Yeah, I remember. We all got the wrong kind of sandwiches."

Hank nodded.

"You can take everything down to the conference room. I'll be down there in a minute and we'll get started."

"I'll tell Merlin."

"Already did," Renard said.

Hank headed down the hall, and Renard followed a couple of minutes later. Merlin was already there with his notes. He had brought along his jar of gummy bears. Dessert maybe?

"Let's eat," Renard said. "It's been a long day out there."

Hank had bought foot-long subs for everyone along with bags of chips, coffee for Renard, and drinks for himself and Merlin. They dug in, and mostly there was silence. The no-nonsense mood in the conference room fit the seriousness of the case. When they had finished eating, they cleared away the wrappers and got down to business.

"The autopsy results came back today," Hank said.

Merlin Waters brought them up on his laptop and pushed it over to Renard. Renard scrolled through the autopsy report and the photos of the victim.

"No surprises here, really. Cause of death is sharp force trauma or stabbing. The weapon, as we know, was a wood chisel. Mechanism of death is blood loss-induced cardiac arrest. Estimated time of death is between eight and eleven p.m. on Tuesday. But we know from the Dinkoviches' account that Silverton was dead by 10:30 p.m."

"So, the killer did not bring a weapon with him," Hank said.

"That we don't know. But assuming he or she did not, it would mean that the crime was not premeditated."

"Do you have a theory?" Merlin asked.

Renard turned to him. "One of two things happened. Either someone snuck up on him and stabbed him with one of the wood chisels that was lying there—a possibility, since the door to the building was unlocked. If he was making noise while working, someone could have approached without his knowing."

"And the other possibility?"

"Someone came into the building—someone Silverton knew. An argument ensued, and Silverton made the mistake of turning his back on the person—maybe to signal he was done talking to them. The perpetrator grabbed one of the wood chisels and stabbed him. Silverton fell forward, and the perpetrator pushed him into the coffin."

In his gut, Renard believed this second scenario was how things had unfolded.

"Sounds like an act driven by rage," Hank said.

"I would guess most murders are, but stabbing, in particular, is an act of extreme anger or passion. Then the killer took the time to push Silverton's body into the coffin. That certainly makes a statement."

"Suspects?" Hank asked.

Renard slid the murder book across the table. "My reports are in there, and I'll be writing more tonight. Right now, the focus in on Maurie Fontaine, Jules and El Pierre, and Sandy Grainfeld. They all had motives of one sort or another, and three of them knew Silverton was alone at the woodworking building that night.

"The Dinkovich boys are also in the picture. Dave Isaacs saw them running from the woodworking building down at the folk school the night of the murder at about ten thirty. I've interviewed them, and they also came in and gave statements. And while I don't believe Darrell and/or Duffy Dinkovich is responsible for the murder, they are definitely part of the picture and so, cannot be eliminated from the investigation. I intend to stay in communication with them on the off chance they may remember something. But for now, other than polluting the crime scene, I don't think the Dinkovich boys are connected to Grant Silverton's murder.

"How are you doing with the phone records, Merlin?" Renard asked.

"I have the digital data from Grant Silverton's cell phone and landline. I've also accessed his laptop and worked through his email threads. There's nothing in his emails to raise any flags. He doesn't have much of an email presence."

"Does that seem odd?" Hank asked.

"Not really. He was retired. Email is more of a business tool."

"Texts?" Renard asked.

"Again, not much. Quite a few between him and someone named Paul."

"Paul Strauss," Renard said. "Silverton's friend."

"Okay," Waters replied.

"Anything between him and a woman?" Renard asked. "Something that might indicate he was in a relationship?"

"Nothing recent. How far back do you want me to go?"

"At least six months, for starters," Renard said. "I just interviewed Silverton's next-door neighbor, and she saw a woman coming and going by way of the back yard on occasion."

"Seems odd," Hank said.

"Yes, it does. One would have to park below the hill at the back of the property to approach from that direction. Why do that unless you don't want to be seen? So, we need to find out who this woman is, if possible.

"I also want to get a subpoena for phone records and digital data for Jules and El Pierre, Maurie and Kristin Fontaine, and Sandy Grainfeld. Both landline and cell data."

"Should I contact the county attorney tonight?" Hank asked.

Renard looked at his watch. "It's not too late. So, yes."

"Anything from the BCA?" Hank asked.

"Nothing yet. I checked as soon as I came in tonight."

"So, what's next?" Hank asked.

"First off, see if you can round up that subpoena tonight, so Merlin can get to work on that data."

Gunderson nodded. "I'll call the attorney as soon as we're done."

"Tomorrow, I'd like you and Len Blake to recanvass the neighborhood around the folk school to see if anyone saw anything Tuesday night. We interviewed the neighbors yesterday morning, but it doesn't hurt to cover that territory once more. I'd also like you to interview any of the staff who were on the campus at the folk school Tuesday night. See if anyone noticed anything that seemed out of place that night. Maybe a car or truck that shouldn't have been where it was. Or anyone walking in the vicinity of the woodworking building between 8:15 and 10:30 p.m.—the window of time during which Grant Silverton was murdered."

"We'll take care of it," Gunderson said.

"Did you get the schedule from the folk school for times and dates of last year's and this year's classes and who taught them?"

"I'm picking that up tonight."

"Make a copy of that for Merlin, as well."

"Will do."

"I'm going to call Switzerland tomorrow and talk to the dean at the University of Geneva where Grant Silverton worked before moving here. I want to know more about his time there."

"That sounds like a scary call." Merlin Waters looked panicked at the mere thought of it.

Renard smiled to himself. Merlin was a brilliant guy, but introverted to the point of being socially awkward. He was pretty sure the thought of having to call strangers in Switzerland would have given Merlin a sleepless night.

"It helps to pretend you're just talking to someone in the next county," Renard said.

"Hard to do once you hear their Swiss accents." Merlin opened the jar of gummy bears and took a few for comfort. He offered the jar to Hank and Renard, but they declined.

"Well, I think that's it for now, unless either of you have anything to add."

Merlin Waters and Hank Gunderson shook their heads.

"You have our assignments for tomorrow, so I'll see you in the morning. We'll continue to work the case."

Hank and Merlin gathered their notes and laptops and left the conference room, and Renard headed back to his office to write up his reports. He settled in at his desk, took out his notebook, and brought up a blank report form to record what he'd learned from his second interview with Paul Strauss.

The day had actually started with his call to Chicago to the Harold Wallace Firm where Grant Silverton had worked. But he had already written up his report on that. He hoped Silverton's friend from Chicago, Owen McGraw, would remember the name of the woman Silverton had been involved with. The woman who had spooked him so badly that he'd decided to move to Switzerland and take a teaching position at the University of Geneva.

Renard pressed on, filling out reports in the order the interviews had occurred and referring to his notes where needed. What he had learned from Willow Tall Grass at the café about Kristin Fontaine's cleaning business and his subsequent interview with Kristin at the Fontaine property. Next the interviews with Ethan and Becca Grainfeld up at their home on Devil Track Lake. Finally, he filled out a report on his interview with Sue Jamison, Grant Silverton's next-door neighbor, in which he detailed her account of seeing a person come and go, on occasion, by way of the back of the property. Ms. Jamison had been unable to give a description except that, from the style of hat the person wore, she thought the visitor was a woman.

It was nine thirty when he finished his last report and shut down his computer. He stood and stretched his arms overhead, put on his coat, and headed for the door. Exhaustion that had shadowed him since evening was now winning the day. He'd had little sleep last night due to the wonders of Adrianna Tomebay. Renard had endurance, and in his mid-forties he could still weather losing a night's sleep. But these had not been a normal two days at the Cook County Sheriff's Department, and the needle on his tank was closing in on empty.

He headed out the door and was stopped in his tracks. The night had cleared, and the Northern Lights —*Waawaate*—crackled across the sky with near audible brilliance. This far north, it was not uncommon to see the aurora, but the wonder of it never grew old. Anishinaabe legend taught that when one leaves the earth, he will dance through the doorway to the next world in spirit form. He will find the spirits of his ancestors, and they will rejoice and dance in the sky.

But Renard was also aware of the legend of the Meskwaki people—an Algonquin-speaking tribe that had lived in the forests of what is now Northeastern Wisconsin. They believed the lights were the restless spirits of their dead enemies, and an omen of war. Tonight, with a killer at large here in Grand Marais, Renard was loath to ignore such symbolism. He watched the show with wonder for a few minutes, then climbed into his squad and headed for home.

Chapter 20

At the bottom of the hill where the Gunflint intersected Highway 61, Renard turned right and drove toward the center of town. He made a left at the light and, three blocks down, pulled into his driveway. He climbed out, headed up the steps to his house, and let himself in.

The heaviness of exhaustion weighed on him. And not just physical exhaustion but a kind of psychological fatigue, born of worry. Or, if he were honest, fear. Fear that he—they—would be unable to solve the case. That it would go cold. The thought was intolerable to Claude. In his mind, failure was not an option. If he failed to find the killer, how could the town return to normal? How could people here feel safe? No, that was not an option. He was a guardian of the people. Had been since his time in the military.

He made a conscious decision to set aside his dark thoughts about failure. He knew he was tired and that fatigue always makes things look worse than they are. He hung up his parka and headed upstairs to his room at the back of the house. East Bay, outside his window, lay still and dark. No wind tonight to rile the great watery giant that was Superior. He undressed and stowed his leg between the bed and the nightstand. A pair of crutches leaned against the wall in case he had to get up in the night, but he almost never did. He switched off the lamp and rolled under the covers. The room was black, and he was gone before any thought, good or bad, could interfere.

*   *   *

He wasn't sure what woke him, but he came fully awake. His eyes, now adjusted to the dark, could make out shadows around the room. He had the oddest feeling of being watched. He reached for a small flashlight he kept by the bed and panned it around the room. His clock read 12:42. He sat up, reached for his leg, and snapped it on. He moved to the window and looked out. The moon was just rising. It cast its ghostly light across the dark waters of the bay and illuminated the snow-covered ground.

Renard moved silently out into the hall, stopped and listened, and then moved across the hall into the bedroom on the front of the house. He could not shake the odd feeling of being watched. He moved over to the side of the window and surreptitiously looked out. The street below was dark, but he could make out a car parked across from his house. Odd, because there were no houses there. The car windows were dark, but his gut told him there was someone inside. The shape of the car seemed vaguely familiar.

He left the window and moved back across the hall into his room. He opened the closet and reached up on the shelf where he kept two pairs of binoculars—one regular set and the other, night-vision. Even in the dark he knew one from the other by feel. Back across the hall, he moved over to the front window and furtively trained the binoculars on the car below. The figure inside was a woman, and, through the night-visions, he recognized her immediately. It was Maggie Norlund.

He stepped back from the window. *Why was she out there? And why at this time of night?* Then he remembered that she worked the second shift at Lutsen Lodge. She would have finished work at around midnight. But that didn't answer what she was doing here or how she knew where he lived. It was creepy.

He had definitely gotten the feeling, the couple of times he'd encountered her, that she was interested in him. And were it not for the urgency and demands of the current case, along with the return to his life of Adrianna Tomebay, well, who was to say? Maybe he would have pursued the situation with Ms. Norlund. But now, with this occurrence, he had to wonder if there was something else in play here. Some other dynamic at work.

He thought about getting dressed and going down to her car and confronting her. But then the cop kicked in, edging the man aside, and he wondered if maybe she needed help or was in some kind of distress. He had just turned to go and get dressed when he heard the car start up. He returned to the window in time to see her making a U-turn and heading up the street in the opposite direction.

He stood for a minute in his boxers and tee-shirt, thinking about the odd occurrence. It might not have been as creepy under normal circumstances. But circumstances weren't normal. He was in the middle of a murder investigation with a killer at large. The wood floor was cold, and he needed his sleep. He would deal with this situation tomorrow. He headed back across the hall and sat on the edge of the bed to remove his prosthetic leg. He rolled over and pulled the covers up. It took a while to send his thoughts packing, but eventually he drifted off to sleep.

*　　*　　*

Wind whispers through the thick pine forest, sounding like a thousand ghosts have been let loose there. The darkness is complete. Still, Renard can just make out shapes against the whiteness of the snow. Up ahead, an amorphous shadow lurches through the forest. With each labored step, the figure sinks knee-deep in snow, staggering from left to right, as if injured. Renard struggles to move faster, but try as he will, he cannot close the distance between him and the shadowy figure. Now the shadow stops and turns. His face is illuminated as if by the moon, but there is no moon. It is Grant Silverton. Blood drips from the corner of his mouth, and in the ghostly light, Renard sees something protrude from his back. The murder weapon. Silverton reaches into his pocket and flings out a handful of money, then turns and lurches on. Now Renard sees a hooded shadow off to the east, approaching fast, on an intercepting course with Silverton. Renard knows the shadow is Death. He strains to run faster but now he is frozen in place—can only watch. Up ahead, Silverton lurches on through the snow, flinging handfuls of cash behind him, but the hooded shadow is nearly upon him.

Renard sat up with a jolt. His heart pounded and sweat covered his body. Phantom pain shot down his nonexistent leg. He swung his other leg out from under the covers and sat on the edge of the bed, the dream still close around him. Silverton, somehow alive, running through the deep snow. The hooded Shadow of Death, or so Renard had interpreted it, moving to intercept him. Silverton flinging handfuls of money behind him as he ran.

He thought about what Paul Strauss had said to him in the second interview yesterday. *You know, if there was a tragic flaw in Grant, it was that he thought money could buy anything. That everything had a price.*

Renard knew one thing, though. Death comes for all. He himself had seen its face. You may be able to dodge it or, with enough money and medical support, postpone it, but it's coming for you nonetheless.

Chapter 21

After the unsettling dream, Renard had no desire to go back to sleep. His clock said 5:45. Daybreak was still two hours away. He snapped on his prosthetic leg and headed into the shower. He hadn't been taking care of himself the past few days. This morning, since he had time, he planned to make himself a proper breakfast.

Ten minutes later he stepped out of the shower and took a deep breath of warm, steamy moisture that filled the bathroom. While the dream had receded a bit, its occurrence only drove his resolve to find the solution to this complicated case. He toweled off, wiped the mirror clear, and shaved. Back in his bedroom he dressed in a fresh uniform and went downstairs to the kitchen.

He walked over to the window that faced the bay and looked out. A nearly full moon was still up, casting its ghostly illumination across the face of things. Overnight the thermometer had slid down to a bone-chilling minus twenty degrees, and an icy silence spread across the vast surface of Gichi-gami.

Claude turned on a small lamp on the table next to the window. From the back of the counter, he took the large abalone shell that he used for smudging and set it on the corner of the table. From a leather pouch, he sprinkled into it the four sacred medicines—sage, sweetgrass, cedar, and tobacco.

Native American tobacco is not really tobacco. It is made from the inner bark of the red dogwood, called "red willow" by the Indians. It is dried or toasted over a fire and then powdered.

As smoke rose, Claude used his hands to sweep it over his head and around his body. The smoke from the sacred medicines would cleanse any darkness that lingered around him from the dream. When he had finished the ritual, he started some coffee and got out a small saucepan.

He poured in water and oatmeal, and set it on the stove to cook. He took down a small skillet from its hook over the stove, chunked in some butter, and cracked in two eggs. He cut a thick slab of wheat bread from a bakery loaf and popped it in the toaster, then scrambled the eggs around, while keeping an eye on the oatmeal and turning the toast over a couple of times. He smiled to himself. Maybe, if he ever stopped being a cop, he could invent a toaster that actually did the job. You'd think if they could build the stealth bomber, they could make a toaster that worked.

He always thought about his Swedish mother while cooking breakfast. When he was twelve, she had taught him how to cook a "proper breakfast," extolling the importance of a hot breakfast in the cold climes of Minnesota.

Within ten minutes everything was ready. He poured the oatmeal into a bowl and topped it with maple syrup, slid the eggs onto a plate, and buttered his toast. He poured out a mug of coffee and sat at the table by the window to enjoy his meal.

When he had finished, he washed the few dishes and pans, left them in the drainer to dry, and headed out to the entryway to don his boots and parka. He carried a knife in a sheath, strapped in his left boot next to his prosthetic leg. A backup weapon. He ran his hand down inside the boot to make sure it was there.

It was 6:45 when he pulled out of the driveway and headed for the sheriff's office. Darkness still held total sway as he drove through town, but lights in houses were beginning to come on, signaling that, for some, the day was beginning.

Renard parked outside the Law Enforcement Center, buzzed himself into the building, and headed straight for his office. As usual, he was the first one on board, except, of course, for the folks back in the detention center and the 911 operator.

His first order of the day was to call Switzerland—the University of Geneva—where Grant Silverton had taught for a couple of years. He found the website for the university and soon zeroed in on the Geneva School of Economics and Management, where he assumed Grant Silverton, having a background in finance, would have taught. He wrote down a phone number he found there, as well as the name of the vice dean for Research and Faculty Affairs at the school. Nils Steiner. Then he brought up a Google page to see what the time difference was between Minnesota and Switzerland. Seven hours. He did the math. It would be around two p.m. there. He picked up the phone and dialed the number in front of him.

After a brief wait, the number rang through, and after three rings a woman answered. Renard had also Googled how to say in German, "Do you speak English?" It was, *Sprechen Sie Englisch?* But he didn't need to use it as the woman spoke English, albeit with a Swiss German accent.

"Geneva School of Economics and Management. Ursula Meier speaking."

The words "school" and "speaking" sounded like *shchool* and *shpeaking*. And the inflection of her vowels told Renard he wasn't in Kansas anymore. He smiled. Merlin Waters would be running for cover.

Renard identified himself, telling Ms. Meier where he was calling from.

"I'm hoping to speak to Nils Steiner, the vice dean. Might he be available to take my call?"

"Let me ring his office," Ms. Meier said.

After a couple of rings, a man answered. "Dr. Nils Steiner."

Renard greeted him and gave him his credentials and told him he was calling from the U.S., from the state of Minnesota.

"It's very nice to talk to you, Chief Deputy. How may I help you?"

Dr. Steiner also spoke with a heavy German accent, but the connection was good and Renard had no trouble understanding him.

"I'm calling to inquire about someone who worked at the university. I learned from the university's website that you are the dean of Faculty Affairs."

"That is correct. About whom are you inquiring?"

"His name is Grant Silverton. I've been told he taught at the University of Geneva. This would have been two to three years ago."

"You are correct. He did teach here at the School of Economics and Management. You have come to the right place, Chief Deputy. What can I tell you? As I recall, Mr. Silverton was from Chicago, so it is surprising to get a call about him from Minnesota."

"Grant Silverton moved to Grand Marais, Minnesota, two and a half years ago, to retire here."

"That would have been fairly soon after he left Switzerland, then," Dr. Steiner said.

"I believe it was. The reason for my inquiries, and I am sorry to report this, is that Grant Silverton has been murdered."

Renard thought he heard Steiner draw in a sharp breath.

"I am leading the investigation into his death, so anything that I can learn about his life, especially in recent years, may be helpful."

"First of all, I am very sorry to hear of Grant's death. It is quite shocking and sad. So, if I can be of any help, I will be."

"Can you tell me about his time there as a professor?"

"Of course. As I recall, Mr. Silverton had a very fine academic pedigree. I'm pulling up the records now."

There was a pause, and Renard assumed Nils Steiner was studying the file.

"He taught classes in finance and investment, including investment banking," Steiner said. "He was only here for two years, but he was a popular teacher. The position was a non-tenured one. They typically run for four to five years. So he certainly could have stayed longer."

"Do you know why he left after only two years?"

There was silence at the other end. It stretched on, and finally Renard said, "Dr. Steiner? Are you still there?"

"I am here," he responded. "How do I say this?" Another pause. "There was some unpleasantness that arose involving Mr. Silverton."

"Can you tell me about that, Dr. Steiner?"

"I am not a purveyor of gossip, Chief Deputy Renard, but I understand this is different. You are dealing with a murder. Of course, it must be investigated."

"I appreciate your understanding of that, Doctor. Here's the thing, and maybe this will help. In order to understand what has happened, and why, we must reassemble the pieces of the victim's life. Of Grant Silverton's life. It's a bit like putting a puzzle back together that someone has dropped on the floor. In a sense, we must bring the victim back to life, piece by piece, so we can understand what led to his death."

"That was very eloquently stated, Chief Deputy."

Renard continued. "In the case of Grant Silverton, he had not lived very long in this community. Many of our residents have lived here all their lives, and this is not a large town, so, had it been one of them, our job might be a bit easier. In the case of Grant Silverton, though, I feel it is quite possible that something from his past—before he moved here—may be important."

Renard hoped he'd said enough to compel Nils Steiner to reveal more about what he had called the "unpleasantness involving Mr. Silverton."

There was a slight sigh at the other end of the line.

"Grant Silverton had an affair with one of the other professors' wives," Steiner said. "The fact of it got out, as such things do. It seems information of a salacious nature is born with an extra set of legs. It caused a lot of animosity among some of the faculty here in our branch of the university. People took sides.

"Of course, Grant Silverton was an outsider of sorts, which somehow made the whole situation worse. Sadly, the affair led to the couple's divorce. In spite of the situation, though, we could not base Mr. Silverton's continuing employment on anything but his work ethic and history, and those were beyond reproach. In other words, he could have stayed and continued teaching had he so chosen. But he did not. He put in his resignation, effective at the end of the spring term that year.

"I don't know if this is of any help, Chief Deputy, but if the information can in any way aid your investigation, then I am happy to pass it on."

"I appreciate your frankness, Dr. Steiner. The information helps us to continue to flesh out a sense of who Grant Silverton was, and what may have led to his murder."

"Then it has been time well spent, Chief Deputy."

"Can you tell me the name of that professor and his wife?" Renard asked.

"Yes, of course. It was Dr. Geoffrey Keller and his wife Elise. The good news is that they reconciled about six months ago. They have remarried."

"That's good to hear," Renard said. Also takes them off the list of any potential suspects, he thought.

"Is there anything else you would like to tell me, Dr. Steiner?"

"There really is nothing else. Nothing I know of, that is."

"Then I won't take up any more of your time. If you do happen to think of anything, though, please call me here at the Cook County Sheriff's Office in Grand Marais, Minnesota." Renard gave him the phone number, and they ended the call.

As he hung up the phone, Renard smiled to himself. Dr. Steiner's title—vice dean of Faculty Affairs—suddenly took on a new and mildly humorous aspect. The thought was funny enough to lift a bit of stress off his shoulders.

Renard had been scribbling notes as Dr. Steiner talked. Now he sat back and thought about their conversation, and as he did so, a number of details from previous interviews suddenly came into sharper focus. Was there a pattern to Silverton's behavior?

He thought about his second interview with Paul Strauss, Silverton's friend. Was Strauss right in his suggestion that Grant Silverton was afraid of commitment? If that were the case, it made sense that Silverton might become involved with a married woman. Then there was the mysterious female visitor that Sue Jamison, Silverton's next-door neighbor, had mentioned, who had been seen approaching from the back of the Silverton property after dark. Was *she* a married woman? If so, that would certainly create a motive for her husband, whoever he might be. *Was* there a pattern of behavior here? One that might have led to Silverton's murder?

He thought about Kristin Fontaine and her cleaning business. She was regularly in touch with Silverton. Might something have developed there? Kristin was an attractive woman. Might there be more going on with Maurie Fontaine than just a grudge about selling his agate to Silverton? Might he have had a much bigger motive to kill Silverton?

Renard was mulling over all of this when his phone rang. He picked it up.

"Chief Deputy Renard."

"Chief Deputy. This is Owen McGraw from Chicago. Do you remember who I am?"

"I certainly do, Mr. McGraw. You were Grant Silverton's friend at the investment firm where he worked. What can I do for you?"

"I believe I've remembered the name of the woman we discussed in our interview. The one who was stalking Grant Silverton."

"Go ahead," Renard said.

"I'm sure her first name was Maggie. I'm not sure about the last name, though. Something like Norgard or maybe Norbert."

Renard felt his heart rate tick up. "Was the name Norlund, by chance?"

"Why, yes. I believe that *was* the name. Maggie Norlund. But how did you . . ."

Renard felt the blood drain from his head. The case had just taken a dark and unexpected turn.

"This is very important information, Mr. McGraw. Thank you for calling with it. Is there anything you'd like to add?"

"No, that's it. I'm glad it's of help."

They ended the call.

Renard sat back in disbelief. So, Maggie Norlund was the woman whom Silverton had depicted as a stalker. She'd followed him to Chicago. Most likely been the reason for him moving to Switzerland. And she had tracked him here. This was a serious turn of events.

He grabbed his coat off the chair. Before he brought her in for questioning, he needed to drive to Lutsen, where she worked. Interview her manager there. See if she had been at work the night of the murder.

On the way out of his office, he nearly collided with Deputy Gunderson.

"Hank, I'm following up on a lead." He didn't mention Maggie Norlund because her name wouldn't have meant anything to Hank.

"After you and Len recanvass the neighborhood around the folk school and interview the staff there, I'd like you to help Merlin with the phone logs. Look for patterns—who was in contact with Silverton and when."

"Will do." Hank started to say something else, but Renard was already past him, heading for the door.

Chapter 22

Renard rolled through town and up the hill at the far end. Within minutes he was out of Grand Marais, heading west on 61 toward Lutsen Mountains. Confounded by the fact that Maggie Norlund was the mystery woman from Grand Silverton's past, he tried to carefully recall the few encounters he'd had with her. The first had been at the Harbor Café the morning after the murder. She had been there eating breakfast, and he had seen her talk to Willow Tall Grass. If she were the killer, what better place to learn what was unfolding, to pick up the scuttlebutt, so to speak?

Then she had stopped him outside the café as he was heading for his squad. The encounter had been flirtatious on her part. She had given him a note with her phone number on it. That would certainly be a bold move if she were the killer. But what better way to divert attention from oneself as a potential suspect than to flirt with the chief investigator? Or was it? In his mind, such an act only called attention to the fact that she was new in town, which of course begged the question, why had she moved here? Was it just to take a job, or did she have another motivation? Was she innocent or extremely clever and manipulative?

He had encountered Ms. Norlund again yesterday when he happened to drive down the street where she lived, just as she was leaving for Lutsen. She had mentioned that she was going to work early to fill in for someone who had called in sick. Renard had learned that she worked the second shift at Lutsen Lodge—the shift that runs from three o'clock to midnight. Question was, had she been working the night Grant Silverton was murdered?

Then there was the odd occurrence in the middle of the night last night, when he awoke with the feeling of being watched. He had gone to the upstairs window that overlooked the street and seen Maggie Norlund parked across from his house. Certainly behavior that might classify as stalking, depending on why she was there. He had every intention of getting the answer to that question.

Other questions rolled through his mind. Had Silverton known that Maggie Norlund had moved here? Grand Marais was a small town, so Renard couldn't imagine that Silverton wouldn't have encountered her or at least seen her. Had she contacted him? The unexpected discovery that she was here certainly would have been upsetting for him.

He thought about what Paul Strauss had told him —that Silverton had said something about moving away. Was it the arrival of Maggie Norlund that had motivated those thoughts? Was he once again planning to run away from her? Why not just confront her or take out a restraining order? These were questions for Grant Silverton, but *he* could not answer them. That was now Renard's job.

The drive from Grand Marais to Lutsen Lodge was only twenty-five minutes. Before he knew it, Renard was approaching the turn. He took a left onto the road that wound down a long steep hill. The historic red timber lodge sat in a sandy cove, yards from Lake Superior. Just beyond the lodge a picturesque covered bridge, rare as an albatross in Minnesota, spanned the small gorge where the Poplar River emptied into the lake. The setting was one of great beauty.

Lutsen Lodge, the oldest resort in Minnesota, went back to the late 1800s, fifty-plus years before the road from Duluth ran up the North Shore. Guests arrived only by boat in those early years. Renard knew that this was the third incarnation of the lodge, the first having burned down in the 1940s and the second a few years later.

He parked to the side of the lodge and headed up the steps and into the main lobby. A fire burned in the massive stone fireplace. The interior walls, floors, and ceiling were of rough-hewn pine timber construction— timber that would have been cut in the region and crafted by local carpenters and craftsmen.

Renard went to the desk and asked if the manager was available. The young woman there seemed alarmed by his presence.

"Is there a problem?" she asked.

"No reason for alarm," Renard said. "I just need to speak with the manager, Megan," he said, reading her name tag. He handed her one of his cards.

"Of course. I'll get her."

The young woman disappeared into the office behind the desk and was back out in a minute.

"She's back in the pool area with a contractor. If you'd like to take a seat, I'll go find her right away."

She disappeared around the corner of the desk, and Renard went and sat in front of the fireplace on one of the leather sofas. He was thinking about Grant Silverton making his escape to the north woods, only to be followed once again by the notorious Maggie Norlund, or at least that was the reputation that had preceded her. He reminded himself not to jump to any conclusions. Coming from Chicago, Grand Marais, Minnesota, must have seemed so far off the beaten path that Silverton thought he'd be safe here.

"Chief Deputy Renard? I'm Ingrid Hagen. I'm the day manager here at the lodge."

Renard stood and shook her extended hand. She was a tall woman of fifty or so, with blond hair pulled back in a bun and serious glasses.

"What can I help you with, Chief Deputy?"

"Is there somewhere we could talk privately? I have some questions."

"Of course. Follow me."

She led him across the lobby and through a door around the corner from the main desk. The room was about the size of his own office, but Ms. Hagen's desk was far more orderly than his. But then again, she wasn't in the middle of a murder investigation.

"Please, take a seat. How can I help?"

Renard sat across the desk from her and took out his small notebook.

"My visit is connected to an investigation currently underway in Grand Marais."

"Is this connected to the man who was murdered?"

"Yes, it is."

"We've heard about it, of course. It's shocking. What was the man's name?"

"Grant Silverton."

"Yes, that's right. But how does it connect to us here?"

"You have a Maggie Norlund who works here. Is that correct?"

"Why, yes. She's relatively new to the resort, but has so far been a good employee."

"Can you tell me how long she has worked here?"

"Of course." Ingrid turned to her computer. "Let me get into the employee records." After a few moments she said, "Maggie started working here in late October, nearly three months ago. I'm the one who interviewed her for the job. She moved here from Chicago. There's a note here, though, that she was born and raised in Minnesota."

Ms. Hagen looked over at him, concerned. "Surely, she can't be connected to what happened to Mr. Silverton."

"There's no reason for alarm, Ms. Hagen. We're interviewing many people who had a connection to Grant Silverton." He didn't want to jeopardize Maggie Norlund's reputation until he knew a whole lot more about her connection to the victim.

He steered the conversation in a different direction. "Can you tell me what Ms. Norlund does here, and how she found out about the position she applied for?"

"Well, Maggie actually has a number of duties. She works the second shift from three p.m. to midnight. Her background is in payroll and accounting, but right now she covers the desk out front during those hours. Lately, we've been moving her into some accounting duties in preparation for a position that will be opening in that department in the near future."

"Can you tell me if Maggie Norlund was working Tuesday night?"

Ingrid tapped the keys. "No. It shows here that she had Tuesday and Wednesday off."

Renard made a note. That put Maggie Norlund firmly in the suspect pool, since Grant Silverton had been murdered on Tuesday night.

"Employee schedules are staggered so that most of our employees are working Wednesday through Sunday," Ingrid offered. "Those are our busiest days in the winter."

"Can you tell me how many people are normally working at or near the front desk during second shift?" Renard didn't really need to know this, but asked anyway as a way to divert focus from Maggie Norlund.

Ingrid turned from her screen. "We always have a manager in the office and one to two people at the desk, depending on the day. And of course, the staff in the dining room would be working until dinner service is finished. The dining room closes at nine o'clock, but at this time of year, dinner service usually wraps up by around eight o'clock."

Ingrid Hagen stopped speaking and studied Renard for a moment. "What night did you say Mr. Silverton was murdered?" she asked.

"The crime occurred on Tuesday night." He could see the wheels going round.

"At what time?" she asked.

"I'm not at liberty to give details on the case."

"No. Of course not. I understand. But you said Maggie Norlund knew the victim."

"Yes. That's correct."

"But she couldn't have known him very well, since she just moved here."

Renard was not about to comment on the particulars and instead asked another question.

"You said you interviewed Maggie Norlund for the job. Do you recall when that took place?"

"I can look that up." She returned to her screen. "Yes, here it is. I interviewed her on July 12th of last year. She actually met with staff over two days. She had very good credentials, and we thought she was a fit for working here. I think she spent a couple days in Grand Marais as well, looking at where she might live."

Renard thought about what Willow Tall Grass had told him. About what had unfolded at the café last summer on a day when she was waiting on Grant Silverton. How he had suddenly acted frightened or panicked and had gotten up and abruptly left the café. Had he seen Maggie that day? If so, he could imagine how shaken Silverton might have been. But, more importantly, had Maggie seen him? Or did she already know he was here? All questions he intended to ask her when they brought her in for questioning.

He looked at Ms. Hagen. "Has Maggie seemed like herself this week? Have you noticed anything out of the ordinary?"

Ingrid thought for a moment, then shook her head. "No, nothing I can think of. She didn't work on Tuesday or Wednesday. Yesterday nothing seemed out of the ordinary. She came in early, at my request, to fill in for someone who was sick. Other than that, she seemed like her usual friendly self."

Renard nodded. "Could you give me the phone number you have for Ms. Norlund?"

"Of course." She read it off to him, and he jotted it in his notebook. Maggie had actually slipped her number into his hand the other day in front of the café, but he wasn't sure what he had done with it.

"Well, I think that's all for now, Ms. Hagen. Thank you for your time." He handed her one of his cards. "If you happen to think of anything that you feel I should know about, please call me."

Ingrid Hagen looked like she wanted to ask more questions. He knew that she, like everyone in the community at large, was curious about the investigation. But she restrained herself from asking anything else.

She stood. "I'll walk out with you, Chief Deputy."

Back outside in his squad, Renard looked up Maggie Norlund's address in the DMV records. Next he radioed Hank, gave him Maggie Norlund's phone number, and asked him to get a subpoena for her digital cell data. He needed to find out if there was a record of her calling or texting Grant Silverton.

"Once that's done, I need you to go to Ms. Norlund's residence and bring her in for questioning."

"Will do." There was a pause. "Who is this woman, Boss?"

"Some information has just come to light that she knew the victim. I'll fill you in when I get back to headquarters."

He signed off, turned over the engine, and headed back up the hill to the highway.

Chapter 23

Renard arrived back at the Law Enforcement Center within thirty minutes. He went directly to his office and found Merlin Waters waiting there for him.

"Merlin. What can I do for you?"

"Hank asked me to fill you in. We are waiting for the subpoena for the Norlund phone data. As soon as it arrives, I'll get on analyzing the digital data—calls and texts coming in and going out from her phone. See if I find any pattern of activity that connects to Grant Silverton's numbers."

"Good. I'm eager to know what that shows. It will tell us some important things about this suspect."

"Hank has gone to bring Maggie Norlund in for questioning. He left about five minutes ago."

"Good. I want to do some checking in the NCIC database before they get back here."

Merlin nodded. "I've been cross-referencing data from the various phone records we subpoenaed. There are some points of interest."

Renard nodded. "Let's meet later on and go over that information. I want to get through this interview with Ms. Norlund first."

Merlin nodded and headed back down the hall to his lair.

Renard went to his computer and logged in to NCIC —the National Crime Information Center—a national database where criminal justice agencies can search for a variety of information, including criminal histories. He typed in Maggie Norlund's full name—Margaret Kay Norlund—that he had obtained from the DMV record. Nothing showed up under her name. No arrests, no criminal history, no domestic violence protection orders.

Renard logged out and retrieved a yellow legal pad from his desk. He started writing a list of questions for the interview with Maggie Norlund. He tried to group them in a logical sequence, starting with her past connection to the victim, Grant Silverton, and then moving forward in time to her decision to move to Grand Marais.

Partway through this prep, Deputy Hank Gunderson knocked on the open door. Renard looked up.

"Hank. You're back. Did you locate Maggie Norlund?"

"I did. She's in the interrogation room, and she's not happy."

"I don't think I've ever seen anyone smiling ear to ear in one of those rooms."

"She wanted to know why she was being brought in. I told her you would fill her in on that."

"Good. I'll head in there in a few minutes. I'm just outlining what I want to cover. You're free to get back to your work with Merlin."

Hank nodded and headed down the hall, and Renard continued writing his notes and questions for a few more minutes. Hopefully, the wait would give Maggie Norlund time to consider the gravitas of her situation.

When he was finished, he took his legal pad and pen with him and went to get two bottles of water. He had activated the recording equipment before entering the room where Maggie waited. He walked in without knocking and sat at the table across from her.

She wore dark blue jeans and a red turtleneck sweater that looked both cozy and expensive, and set off her straight dark hair. Her face was a study in anxiety, but Renard sensed anger simmering just below the surface.

He was right. As soon as he sat down, she fired the first question at him.

"Why am I here?"

There seemed to be an accusation inside that question. Renard sat back and looked her dead in the eye. "Why do you think you are here?"

Whatever answer she had expected, that wasn't it. She looked to the side for a moment and finally down at the table.

"I suppose it must have something to do with the death of Grant Silverton."

That answer signaled that she wasn't going to play games and pretend that she didn't know Silverton. That was a positive sign, Renard thought.

"You're right. That is exactly what this is about."

"Am I under arrest?"

"No, you are here to be questioned," Renard said.

"Do I need an attorney?" Maggie asked.

"That's up to you. Do you think you need an attorney?"

"I don't know why I would. I've done nothing wrong."

Renard studied her silently for a moment. "Very well then. We will proceed. First of all, would you state your full name and address for the record."

"Margaret Kay Norlund." She followed up with her address.

"This interview is being recorded, Ms. Norlund. You can have access to any part of it if you wish."

She nodded. "It's all right to call me Maggie. I mean, we kind of know each other, even if only in passing."

Renard was happy to call her whatever she wanted if it meant he'd get answers to his questions.

"Very well, Maggie. Let's get started. Can you tell me about your relationship with Grand Silverton?"

"That's easy," Maggie said. "There was no relationship."

"But you obviously knew he lived here in Grand Marais. Isn't that right?"

"Yes. I became aware of it recently."

"How recently?" Renard asked.

"About a month ago. I was driving through town and I saw him coming out of the café with another guy."

"So, you're saying that you did not know Grant Silverton lived in Grand Marais when you chose to move here."

"That's what I'm saying."

"I have to remind you, Maggie, that it's a crime to lie to law enforcement."

"I'm not lying. I'm telling the truth. I didn't know that Grant had moved here."

Renard studied her for a few moments. He was inclined not to believe her. It was just too much of a coincidence, and cops don't like coincidences. Especially when they connect to a murder investigation.

"Okay. Then tell me what did bring you here if it wasn't the presence of Grant Silverton."

"Two things. I love to ski and I love the winter. I know lots of Minnesotans whine about it, but I was born here, in Minnesota, I mean. I've always loved the winter, and I've skied since I was ten years old." She looked him in the eye. "I hated living in Chicago. The people are brash. The weather can be nasty, and the pace of life is too frenetic for me. I grew up in St. Paul—that's enough city for me."

"But why Lutsen? Why Grand Marais? Why not go out west to the mountains, if you love to ski? I know from information I've gathered that you used to go there —possibly lived there. And I know that's where you met Grant Silverton originally."

Maggie Norlund looked at him like he'd stripped off a piece of her clothing. Her eyes darkened.

"How do you know all of this? Who have you been talking to?"

"This is a murder investigation, Ms. Norlund. We talk to many people and, most importantly, people who knew the victim. Those people—his friends and acquaintances—know things. Just like your friends would know things about your past. This is your chance to set the record straight. To tell your story."

He paused and studied her in steely silence. "Did you kill Grant Silverton?"

Maggie shot up out of her chair.

"No! No, no, no, no, no. How can you think that? I cared about Grant. Even though I knew, from the time I moved to Chicago, that it wasn't going to work with him, I still cared about him."

"So you moved to Chicago without his knowing, just like you moved here without his knowing."

"No. That's wrong. He knew I might move to Chicago. I told him I was interviewing for a job there."

"And didn't that interview, that job, have everything to do with the fact that he lived there? Be honest, Maggie. Weren't you stalking him? Isn't that why he moved to Switzerland?"

"Yes—I mean, no." She sighed, looking defeated. "Yes, I moved to Chicago because he was there. I was in love in him. But no, I wasn't stalking him, as you say."

Potato, potahto, Renard thought. Everything is open to interpretation, especially human behavior and motivation. He remembered what Paul Strauss had said about Silverton not seeming to understand commitment and marriage. He also thought about what Owen McGraw, Silverton's friend from Chicago, had said about Silverton seeming terrified of Maggie. So terrified that he moved overseas, cutting all ties, to get away from her.

Maggie was talking again. "And then one day he just disappeared—up and gone. I never knew where he went. I asked his friends and co-workers, but no one would tell me anything." She sat back in her seat. "Switzerland." She appeared dumbfounded by that bit of news.

"Tell me something, Maggie. What were you doing parked in front of my house in the middle of the night?"

He wouldn't have thought Maggie was the kind of person who would be capable of blushing. He was wrong. But as he studied her, he decided the color on her face might be caused by anger. The same kind of frantic, irrational anger that could cause one to plunge a sharp tool into another's back.

He leaned in. "You have to admit it looks a lot like stalking—you being out there in the middle of the night."

Something dark moved behind her eyes when he said that. Something that chilled him to the bone. Then in a flash the menacing look was gone.

Maggie leaned back in her chair and took a breath. "Look, you say it was the middle of the night, and maybe it was for you. I'm sure your days start a lot earlier than mine. But I had just gotten off of work. So, for me it didn't feel like the middle of the night."

"It was a quarter to one." He softened his tone a bit. "Can you tell me why you were there?"

She sighed again. "I just thought . . . I just thought you might still be up. You know, we've talked a couple of times. You must have seen that I was interested. I just thought, maybe . . . Oh, I don't know. Haven't you ever done anything impulsive in your life?"

That question hit Renard unexpectedly hard. *Impulsive? Yes. What else could you call what had happened between him and Adrianna Tomebay two nights ago?*

He looked at Maggie, hoping she hadn't detected the chink in his armor. "Let's return to a question you never answered. Why move here and not to the mountains out west, if you want to work in the ski world?"

"I wanted to stay in the Midwest. And Lutsen, well, it's really king among Midwest ski resorts. In my opinion, anyway. And it's only three and a half to four hours from the Twin Cities, where my parents live. They're getting older. I don't want to be more than a few hours away by car. So I inquired last summer to see if they might have a position that would suit me. My experience is in accounting and payroll. They asked me to send my resume, and that led to an interview in July, and the rest, as they say, is history."

"And wasn't it when you came for that interview last summer that you saw Grant Silverton in the Harbor Café? And didn't you know he saw you as well, because he suddenly bolted out of the café?"

"No. I told you before I didn't know he lived here until just recently." She leaned forward like she meant business. "He may have bolted out of the café, and it may have been because he saw me, but I did not see him that day. Period."

"I'm not sure I believe you, Maggie."

"Fine. I believe me, and that's all that matters."

"Is it?" He let the question hang there, knowing it would not receive an answer. The weight of it pressed down on them like a storm-filled sky.

After a few moments, he moved on.

"Were you working Tuesday night?"

Renard already knew the answer to this but wanted to see what she would say.

Maggie's eyes narrowed. "My guess is you already know that I wasn't."

"Fair enough," Renard said. "You're right. I've already talked to your manager at Lutsen."

He saw the anger rise up in her, and he saw her try to tamp it down.

"You'd better not have jeopardized my reputation there."

It sounded like a flat-out warning.

"There's a job opening in their accounting department that I'm in line for," she continued.

"You have nothing to worry about if you are innocent," Renard said. That, in his mind, was a big "if," though. "I told Ingrid Hagen that we were questioning lots of people who had known Grant Silverton, as well as looking into their whereabouts the night of the crime."

Suddenly, Maggie Norlund looked miserable.

"I wish I had never met that man," she said. Her eyes glazed with tears. "I wish I could erase the past four or five years. Start fresh." She looked down at her hands.

Renard didn't know what to say. A part of him felt bad for her, but the greater part was determined to stay objective. He moved on to the next question.

"What were you doing Tuesday night between 8:15 and 10:30 p.m.?"

"I was at home. I had the night off. It was really cold that night, so I didn't want to go out anywhere. I baked cookies and watched T.V."

"By yourself?"

"Yes, by myself."

"So you've had no contact with Grant Silverton since you moved here in October? And before you answer, I want you to know that we will be checking your cell phone data."

"I told you before, no. I knew he was here, but I didn't contact him."

"Did you want to?"

Maggie stared at the wall behind him, and her gaze came unfocused.

"Yes. I wanted to."

Her tone told him she was ashamed of the fact. He could understand why. After all, Silverton had first encouraged her and then rejected her. Renard gave her points for being truthful.

"That's all for now, Maggie. This interview is confidential. Please keep it that way. I know you have to get ready for work this afternoon, so I'll have Deputy Gunderson drive you home."

After Maggie left, Renard returned to his office, where he sat thinking for a time about the interview and reviewing the notes he'd written as she had talked. At this point his gut wasn't telling him anything about her guilt or innocence. But there were a few things he didn't believe. For one, he did not believe that she had moved here oblivious to the fact that Grant Silverton lived in the community.

He also sensed a side to her that was needy and would not easily let go of something or someone once she had attached herself to that person. Still, he was inclined to believe what she had said about not contacting Grant Silverton since she'd moved here. The phone records that had been subpoenaed would shed light on that issue.

Maybe Maggie thought that if she placed herself in the community where Silverton would see her, he would not be able to resist getting in touch. He remembered what Paul Strauss had said about Silverton's obvious attraction to her, even years after they'd been an item.

There was no question that it had been a mutual attraction. The real question was, had it also been a fatal attraction?

Chapter 24

Renard had told Hank Gunderson to stop by his office once he got back from driving Maggie Norlund home. Within fifteen minutes Gunderson rapped on his door.

"Come in, Hank. Sit."

Hank slid his lanky body into one of the chairs in front of Renard's desk.

"Where are you at with interviewing the staff at the folk school and also the re-canvass of the neighborhood around there?"

"I talked to staff at the school this morning and phoned any of them who weren't there. Unfortunately, I came up empty. No one saw anything. It sounds like the campus down there is pretty much a ghost town by nine p.m. Now, Sandy Grainfeld, the woodworking teacher, could have killed Silverton before he left that night, and no one would have been the wiser. Anyone noticing him leaving the building wouldn't have thought anything about it, since he'd just finished a class."

Renard nodded, bracing himself for another dead end.

"There was something that came up, though."

"What was that?"

"Well, I asked each of the people I interviewed how well they knew Sandy Grainfeld, and one of them—name's Neil Nelson—who said he was Sandy's friend, told me that Sandy hadn't been his usual self lately."

"How long is lately?" Renard asked.

"Nelsen said a couple of months."

"Huh. Did he know why?"

"Said he had no idea. Said he'd asked Sandy if he was okay a couple weeks ago, and Sandy had said he was fine. Maybe just a little tired."

"And did Nelson believe that?"

"I don't think so. He said Sandy seemed down. Depressed like."

"So, we have to wonder what was causing that, and did it have anything to do with Grant Silverton?"

They sat for a few moments, not speaking. Mulling over what had just been said. Finally Renard said, "And the neighbors? Anything new?"

"I sent two deputies down there first thing to recanvass the neighborhood, hoping to catch anyone we missed on Wednesday—the day after the crime was committed. They're still at it, so we'll have to wait and see if anything turns up on that front."

"That's good work, Hank. Merlin has made progress on the phone data from the various suspects and wants to meet with us. We'll see if anything he has sheds light on the change Neil Nelson noticed in Sandy Grainfeld."

With that, they went to find Merlin Waters.

Ten minutes later they all gathered in the conference room. Merlin had come armed with his laptop, a stack of printed data, and his jar of gummy bears. He opened the jar and offered them to Hank and Renard, but they both held up a hand that said, "Thanks, but no."

"So, what have you come up with, Merlin? Has the phone data shown any patterns?"

"I believe it has," Merlin said. "With the subpoenas, I obtained landline and cell records for the suspects you requested. Maurie and Kristin Fontaine, Jules and El Pierre, and Sandy and Becca Grainfeld. I'm still waiting on the cell data for Maggie Norlund, but that subpoena just came through, so I should have those records later today."

"And what has all the data revealed?" Renard asked.

"First off, I looked back over six months of call data. For Jules and El Pierre, the data showed no calls at all between either Silverton's cell phone or landline and any of their phones. Moving on to Maurie and Kristin Fontaine, and going back six months, there are occasional calls from Kristin's cell phone to Silverton's phones —primarily his landline. A total of four or five calls over that time."

"So, not enough to be considered a pattern."

"I don't think so," Merlin said. "What's more, none of them was more than a minute or two."

"Silverton was one of her cleaning customers," Renard said. "So that could easily account for a few random calls over that time period. How about Maurie's cell data? Any lengthy calls there?"

"Just two. One, a couple months ago that was twenty minutes long. The call originated from Maurie Fontaine's cell. And then three weeks ago, another call to Silverton's cell number that lasted fifteen minutes."

"I'll bet those were repeated attempts by Fontaine to talk Silverton into letting him buy back his prize agate. I don't think he had any intention of letting the issue go."

Renard made a note on his pad, then looked back at Merlin. "What about the Grainfelds?"

"This is where things get interesting," Merlin said. He popped in a gummy bear and reached for a different stack of data.

Hank Gunderson sat forward in his chair, poised for some kind of a break in the case.

For Renard's part, his mind was still on the Maggie Norlund interview. Right now, to his way of thinking, *she* had moved into the prime suspect seat. She had motive and opportunity, and no alibi. She'd been home alone Tuesday night—the night of Silverton's murder.

"In the case of the Grainfelds, there's much more landline data than cell phone data," Merlin said.

"That may be because reception is spotty up on Devil Track Lake," Hank said. "They may have to rely more on their landline."

"Problem is, it's impossible to know which of them was placing or receiving the calls," Merlin said. "Anyway, a pattern quickly became apparent as I looked at the data. When I began to see a lot of calls between the Grainfelds' line and Silverton's, over the past six months, I went back a full year to see if there was a point where the activity began."

"And was there?" Renard asked.

"There were occasional calls between the numbers going back a year, but the number of calls increased about eight months ago. Some were very short. Less than a minute. While others were long—some thirty to forty-five minutes. What's interesting is the times they were placed. There's a pattern. Always on weekday nights between six p.m. and eight p.m."

"But isn't that the time when most people call each other?" Hank asked. "You know, after dinner in the evening?"

"Were the calls placed by the Grainfelds or Silverton?" Renard asked.

"Most of the time they were initiated by someone at the Grainfelds' end. But here's the thing. When I looked at the class schedule for the past six months from Northern Arts Folk school, where Sandy teaches, and compared it with the phone data, there was a correlation."

"What was it?" Renard leaned forward.

"Those calls from the Grainfeld residence were always placed during the time that Sandy Grainfeld was teaching at the folk school. So, we know he couldn't have placed them. It could only have been Becca Grainfeld."

"Or Ethan Grainfeld," Hank offered.

"Yes, possible," Renard said. "But my money's on Becca."

"What are you thinking?" Hank asked.

"Remember what I learned from Sue Jamison, Silverton's next-door neighbor? Over the past several months, she had seen a woman approaching and entering from the back of his property. It seems like an odd and covert way to approach his house. So, why all the cloak and dagger unless that woman is married? And right now, my money's on Becca Grainfeld. I think the phone records are revealing. And the short calls—seems the perfect amount of time to set up a liaison.

"What's more, there are other facts that have turned up in the case that indicate Silverton may have preferred relationships with married women." Renard went on to recount what he had learned from Nils Steiner, vice dean of Faculty Affairs, from the Geneva School of Economics and Management in Switzerland.

"If you're right about Becca Grainfeld, that would give Sandy Grainfeld a strong motive," Gunderson said. "Assuming he had found out about the affair, that is. It could also shine a light on why he had appeared depressed lately to Neil Nelson, his colleague down at the folk school."

"Well, this feels like forward progress," Merlin Waters said.

"Good work analyzing all the data, Merlin, and finding that connection to the folk school schedule. As soon as you get hands on Maggie Norlund's cell data, I want you to search for any calls or texts between her number and Silverton's."

Merlin nodded. "Will do."

"That's all for now. I'm going to head up to the Grainfelds' and interview Becca."

Merlin gathered all his data and headed back to his office.

"I want you to go down and check in with the deputies who are working the neighborhood near the folk school. See if they've turned up anything, and give them a hand finishing up down there."

"On it, Boss. I'll contact you if we come up with something new."

Renard went back to his office to collect his coat. He grabbed a protein bar out of his drawer and headed out the door to his squad.

Chapter 25

Renard turned left onto County 12, the Gunflint, and wound his way up the hill toward Devil Track Lake, where the Grainfelds lived. The temperature had climbed to a balmy ten above zero today, and the wind came strong out of the east. Usually an omen of a storm brewing. The higher he climbed on the road, the more the wind buffeted the squad.

Today had certainly held its surprises. First the appearance of Maggie Norlund as a suspect, and then what Merlin Waters had turned up in his search of the phone data. Renard was also thinking about the original suspects in the case. With the advent of this new information, some of them had slid down his list, but he cautioned himself not to eliminate any of them prematurely.

There was one thing he knew for certain. This was not a crime of cold premeditation. This was a crime of hot anger. He believed a violent argument had ensued at the woodworking building on Tuesday night, and one party—Grant Silverton—had made the mistake of turning his back on the other.

There were several suspects who fit into this profile. Maurie Fontaine, who had expressed the intention of getting his prize agate back, no matter what it took. Now Silverton was dead and the agate was missing. Maggie Norlund, a victim of unrequited love, who couldn't shake her obsession with Grant Silverton. And now, the focus had come to rest on Sandy Grainfeld, whose wife Becca, chances were, was having an affair with Silverton. They all had motive, and they all had opportunity.

The turn for Devil Track Road was coming up. Renard slowed to a crawl and turned left. There was something else rolling through his mind, too. He was thinking about what his friend Martin Running Wolf had said to him the other night when he was up in Grand Portage. Martin had taught classes at the folk school and so, knew Sandy Grainfeld.

When Claude had asked him about his dealings with Sandy, Martin said that he had known Sandy long enough to have a sense of him. He'd also said that Sandy had played an important role in the development of the folk school over the years and that he was very loyal to the mission of the school. "Maybe too loyal, if that's possible," had been Martin's words.

Claude had read between the lines and asked him if that meant Sandy's family might be getting the short end of the stick. Martin had replied that it was not his place to judge.

Now Renard had begun to wonder if maybe he was late to the game, and some folks in Grand Marais knew about Becca and Silverton. Maybe Martin had heard something through the rez grapevine. Fact was, the Grand Marais and Grand Portage communities were linked in so many ways. Kids from the rez went to middle school and high school here in town. They took jobs here—some married local girls. So, often, what was known here in town was known up on the rez.

Renard slowed and took a left onto the gravel road and followed the tunnel of spruce and balsam down toward the house. The closeness of the forest seemed to have the effect of focusing his mind, and he cleared away all that did not pertain to the approaching interview. He had known the Grainfelds for many years, and he did not relish what he had to do. Sometimes he longed for the anonymity of a big city police force—one where the likelihood of ever having to question your friends or neighbors was slim.

He parked next to Becca's Jeep in front of the garage. Ethan's and Sandy's pickup trucks were both gone, so he knew only Becca was at home. He'd picked up a vibe in their first interview—an uncomfortable vibe. To him it had meant one of two things. She was protecting someone, or she was somehow involved. The meeting with Merlin Waters had confirmed his suspicions. He climbed out of the cruiser, walked up to the door, and rang the bell.

He stood there longer than he would have expected, and was beginning to wonder if Becca was outside somewhere or just not responding, when the door opened.

"Claude. This is a surprise."

But the look on her face told him she knew who it was before she'd opened the door.

"Becca. How are you?"

"Just fine. What's this about, Claude? I think I answered everything I could yesterday, and Howie's not here."

"It's you I wanted to talk to, Becca. I have some more questions, if I could come in for a few minutes."

Becca hesitated, like she didn't want to let him in. As if not letting him might keep the status quo intact.

Finally she said, "Well, all right, but I have somewhere I have to be in an hour, so this can't take too long."

Renard doubted that Becca had planned to go anywhere. She was dressed in baggy sweats, and her braided hair was coming undone like she'd slept on it and hadn't recombed it.

Becca led him to the table at the end of her large kitchen. He could tell this room was loved. While it was spotless and functional, there were little touches of warmth and character everywhere that reflected the Becca Renard knew.

"Would you like coffee, Claude?"

"No, that's okay. But thanks." A part of him wanted to accept, just to forestall the inevitable.

They sat across from one another, and Renard took out his small notebook.

"I need to ask you some more questions about Grant Silverton."

"I assumed that's why you're here. Go on."

There was a note of hostility in her voice. Or maybe it was fear.

"When we talked yesterday, I asked you how well you knew Grant Silverton, and you said you only knew him through your husband."

"That's right. He was Howie's student."

"So, you met him through Howie, but I'm asking how well *you* knew him."

"Not at all, really. Why are you asking this?"

"Look, Becca, we've subpoenaed phone data for your landline and yours and Howard's cell phones."

"Why would you do that without informing us?" Becca stood and crossed her arms on her chest.

"We're conducting a murder investigation. We're not required to tell suspects the details of the investigation."

"So you're saying Howie is a suspect?"

"Yes, Becca, he is. He was the last one to see Grant Silverton alive. He was alone with him in the wood-working building. He had means and opportunity."

"That's completely ridiculous, Claude. Howie doesn't have a mean bone in his body."

Renard thought about what Martin Running Wolf had said about Grainfeld's quick temper and seeing his anger flare at the folk school when something had set him off. But he wasn't here to get into that.

"I'm actually here to discuss something your land-line data showed that appears to have nothing to do with your husband."

Becca continued to stand. "Go on," she said.

"The data shows that there were many calls over the past six months between your landline and Grant Silverton's cell phone, with most of them initiating here."

"I have no idea what you're talking about. If there were calls, then Howie must have made them."

"Here's the thing, Becca. Almost all of those calls took place while Sandy was teaching down at the folk school. We've checked the times against the class schedules for the past six months. There are some lengthy calls, but most are less than a minute or two, as if something was being arranged. Maybe a meeting of some kind?"

Becca turned her back on him and walked over to the window.

"Becca, those calls could only have been made by you or Ethan. Are you telling me that Ethan made those calls?"

"No!" She whirled around. "No, I didn't say that."

There was something unreadable in her eyes. Maybe pain, maybe fear, Renard wasn't sure.

"Becca, I'm going to ask this because I have to. All due respect, were you in a relationship with Grant Silverton?"

She had started to say something when they heard the back door open, heard the stomping of feet, and Howard's voice.

"Becca. You here? What's going on?"

Becca shot Renard a look just as her husband came into the kitchen.

"Hello, Howard. I'm just following up on a couple of questions from my previous interview. You know I was here yesterday, right?"

"Of course. Any way I can help?"

"No, I think I have everything I need." He nodded at Becca before turning and walking toward the door.

But just before getting there, Renard turned back to him.

"Howard, just following up on something. At 10:30 p.m. on Tuesday night, the night Grant Silverton was murdered, Dave Isaacs tried to call your cell phone to let you know he'd seen someone running out of the woodworking building. Can you tell me why you didn't answer your phone that night?"

He watched Howard carefully to see if the question appeared to rattle him in any way.

"Who did he see?" The words came out machine-gun fast.

"I'm not at liberty to discuss any part of the investigation, but I do need to know why you didn't answer your phone that night."

"Well, that's easy. First off, I'm always in bed by 10:30. Second, I turn my cell phone off and put it on the charger at night. But reception can also be spotty up here, so even if my phone had been turned on, there's a good chance the call wouldn't have come through."

Renard nodded. It was just about what Becca had told him yesterday.

"Well, that'll do it, then." He headed for the door. No one followed, so he let himself out.

Chapter 26

Renard headed back toward Devil Track Road, turned right, and drove toward the Gunflint Trail. By now, the breakfast he'd eaten at 6:30 a.m. was but a distant memory. His stomach had been objecting for several hours, and the protein bar he'd eaten on the way up here had done little to end the protest.

He decided he'd stop in at the café for some food. He also wanted to ask Willow Tall Grass a question. She was his very best source for who knew whom in the town. If he could find out who Becca was close to—a best friend, maybe—he might possibly learn more about her relationship with Silverton. Because it was pretty clear she was not about to admit to having been involved with him.

In a few miles, Renard turned onto the Gunflint and followed it back down to Highway 61. He turned right and drove through town to the Harbor Café. He parked the squad in front of the café and headed inside. The place was virtually empty, it being too late for lunch and too early for dinner. The sign said *Seat Yourself*, so Renard slid into his favorite booth by the windows.

Jenifer LeClair

Beyond the ice pack in the harbor, Lake Superior stretched, vast and frigid, to the horizon.

Just then, as if she had sensed his presence, Willow Tall Grass appeared from the kitchen carrying a carafe of coffee and a mug. She set the mug on the table and poured out the coffee. He smiled to himself. She knew him well.

"Afternoon, Willow."

She studied him for a moment, concerned. "You look tired, Blue Fox."

"It's the weight of the case, Willow."

"Any breaks?"

"A couple possibilities, but I can't talk about any of it. I'm starving, though."

"What can I get you?"

"I'll have the deluxe burger and fries."

"How about some fruit instead of those fries?"

Claude appreciated Willow's nutritional concerns. She had always been like a sister to him—the one he'd never had. Even so, today, he was starving and not in the mood to negotiate for his French fries.

"How about I have the fruit in my pie after the burger?"

Willow gave him the stink eye for a moment. Then she laughed. "Oh, all right. Nothing wrong with a little comfort in the middle of January, I guess."

"You read my mind, Willow."

She disappeared back into the kitchen, and Claude enjoyed the comfort of the warm mug of coffee in his hands. He was glad the café wasn't busy and hoped Willow could sit down with him for a few minutes. Hoped she might know something that would help him on the Becca Grainfeld front.

He was lost in his thoughts about the case when Willow appeared with his food and set it in front of him.

"Could you sit for few minutes, Willow?"

She looked around at the mostly empty café. "I don't see why not. I'll just keep an eye on that couple over there in case they need anything."

She went and got another coffee mug and slid into the booth across from him. Claude poured out a cup for her and then waded into his burger. For a few minutes, nothing was said. Willow sipped her coffee and waited patiently as he devoured his lunch. When he'd finished his burger, he looked across at her.

"You know a lot about the town and its people, Willow. I'm wondering if you might know who Becca Grainfeld is close friends with?"

"Well, that's easy. As far as I know, Becca Grainfeld is close friends with Kristin Fontaine—you know, Maurie Fontaine's wife. She and Becca come in here fairly often for coffee or breakfast or lunch, and you can just tell there's that bestie vibe between them. But why do you ask?"

"Well, I can't really discuss that, Willow, but I appreciate the information. And please keep the fact that I have asked about it between us, okay?"

"Of course."

Just then Willow saw the couple on the other side of the café looking for her. She got up and went over to them. Claude finished his fries and drank some more coffee and was just getting ready to leave when Willow came back from the kitchen and slid a piece of banana cream pie onto the table in front of him.

"Here's your fruit, Blue Fox." She gave him a wink, set the check down, and disappeared back into the kitchen.

The banana cream pie at the café here was his favorite decadent treat, and Willow knew that. He finished off the pie, his taste buds doing their happy dance, and noticed the pie was not on his ticket, but he left Willow a nice tip—plenty to cover the pie and take care of her as well.

Renard headed out to his squad, turned around, and drove west out of town, toward where the Fontaines lived. It was just after two thirty, so he was hoping that Maurie would still be up at the middle school. If possible, he wanted to talk to Kristin alone. He hoped he could get her to confirm that Becca Grainfeld was having an affair with Grant Silverton. If the two of them were in fact best friends, then he assumed Kristin would know the truth of the situation. But would she be willing to tell him what she knew? That was the question.

Within a few minutes he saw the turn coming up, slowed, and turned right into the Fontaines' driveway and followed it up toward the house. Maurie's pickup truck was nowhere to be seen, but Kristin's van with her business name on the side was parked in the driveway. He pulled in behind it, walked up to the lower door, and rang the bell.

Kristin must have been downstairs, because within moments she opened the door. When she saw it was Renard, she looked like she wanted to shut it again.

"Maurie isn't here, Claude. And I told you everything I can about that night—Tuesday night—when you were here yesterday. I think it's best if I refrain from saying anything else."

"I understand, Kristin, but I'm not here to question you about Maurie or the missing agate. But I am hoping you might shine some light on another matter relating to Grant Silverton."

She studied him for a moment, suspicion narrowing her eyes.

"Well, all right," she finally said. She stepped aside and let him enter.

"So what is it you want to know?"

"I've learned during this investigation that you are good friends with Becca Grainfeld. I'm hoping you might shed some light on a part of the investigation that may involve her."

Kristin's eyes narrowed again. "If you have questions about Becca, you should ask her."

"I have. And it would be to her benefit to answer them, but she has chosen not to."

"Well, I certainly can't speak for her," Kristin said.

Renard saw no point in beating around the bush. "Was Becca having an affair with Grant Silverton?"

Kristin opened her mouth, startled by his question.

"I should remind you, if I haven't before, that it's against the law to lie to law enforcement. I also know this is a sensitive subject, and I appreciate that. But what you know could help the investigation and may, indirectly, help your husband as well."

Kristin let out a sigh. "Come in and sit down, Deputy Renard."

The formality of her words left little room for debate, so he slipped off his boots and followed her across the room to where a sofa and chairs were arranged in front of the fireplace and sat down in one of the chairs. Kristin sat across from him.

She studied him for a minute before speaking. "Becca is a bit of an innocent," she said. "I warned her that no good could come from getting involved with Grant Silverton."

"But she didn't listen."

"No."

"How and when did it all begin?" Renard asked.

"It started maybe a year ago—the meeting of him, I mean. Grant Silverton had gotten involved with the woodworking classes at the folk school after he moved here. Along the way, Howie had helped him set up a woodworking shop at his house. But Becca had never actually met him until about a year ago, when he stopped by their house one evening. He'd been up to the Red Rock Grill on Devil Track Lake for dinner, and since he was close to the Grainfelds' place, he called Howie to see if he could stop by for a visit. That's when it all began." Kristin looked around the room like she wanted to escape.

Renard clearly remembered Becca saying that Grant Silverton had never been to her house. That had been an outright lie.

"Please go on," he said.

Kristin looked at him like she hated him for turning her into a traitor.

"Becca said there was an immediate spark there. Nothing was done or said to create it. It was just there. 'Like the air in the room,' was how she described it. She was attracted to him, and she said she was sure the vibe was mutual."

Kristin wrung her hands. "You have to understand that this was completely foreign territory for Becca.

Since high school, Howie has been the only guy. But I have to say, I lay some of the blame at his feet. I think he's taken Becca for granted for some time now."

Renard had already reached the same conclusion, but he said nothing.

"It all started innocently enough," Kristin said. "Grant would call in the evening sometimes when Howie was at the folk school. He'd ask for him, and when Becca would tell him Howie wasn't there, he'd talk to her. I think Becca was flattered by the attention. Me, I think Grant Silverton knew exactly what he was doing."

"What do you mean?" Renard asked.

"I think Silverton knew perfectly well that Howie wasn't home when he would call. I think he knew the schedule at the folk school, and I told Becca so. But it was already too late. The flirtation had begun. The affair snow-balled from there. During one of the phone calls, Becca told Grant she'd love to see his house sometime." Kristin rolled her eyes. "That was the beginning of the end."

"And how long ago was that?"

Kristin thought for a moment. "Maybe seven or eight months ago."

"Do you think the affair was still going on?"

"You mean up until now? Up until Silverton was murdered? Yes, it was."

Kristin grew thoughtful for a moment. "But something had changed," she said. "I think the excitement was on the wane. Not for Becca—she was all in, and I think she had no plans to end it. Grant was an attractive man —no question—and that fed Becca's ego. I think she'd been longing to be noticed for a long time. It seems

Howie had forgotten how to do that. Really very sad. I tried to reason with her over and over."

"So, you say something had changed. Do you think Silverton had lost interest in her?"

"I have no idea. Maybe he grew a conscience. I just know that Becca had seemed a bit down lately—not on the high she'd been riding for six or eight months."

Renard thought about what Paul Strauss had told him. That Silverton had said something about leaving Grand Marais. It wouldn't have been the first time he had fled after entanglement with a woman. He had left Chicago to get away from Maggie Norlund, and then left his teaching post in Switzerland after the affair with the professor's wife. It seemed to be a pattern with Silverton. A pattern that may have begun to play itself out again with Becca Grainfeld. And, if that were the case, it made her a suspect in his murder. What was more, the affair also gave Howard Grainfeld a very strong motive.

"Do you think Howard knew about the affair? Did Becca ever say?"

"She was convinced he knew nothing about it. Me, I'm not so sure. Howie isn't stupid, and Becca has said over the past few months that he seemed to have developed a dislike for Silverton. So, it has to make you wonder. Right?"

"Seems to me, if he knew about the affair, he would have done something."

Kristin raised her eyebrows. "And maybe he did."

Then she appeared to realize what she'd just said. "Forget I said that, Claude. I don't really mean it. Howie's not capable of murder."

Renard wished that were the case, but he knew differently. Sadly, both Sandy and Becca Grainfeld had moved to the top of the suspect list, along with Maggie Norlund. He also thought back on what Hank had said about Neil Nelson, one of the staff at the folk school, noticing a change in Sandy over the past couple of months. Had Sandy learned about his wife's affair? Was that what was responsible for his change of mood?

Renard closed his notebook, put it in his pocket, and stood up.

Kristin stood too and looked at him. "Please don't tell Becca you learned any of this from me."

"I will do my best not to, but I can't promise it won't come out."

Kristin lowered her head.

"No matter what happens, Kristin, remember, all you have done is speak the truth when asked to do so. There is nothing to be ashamed of in that."

"I wonder if you'd say that were the tables turned."

Renard walked toward the door. It was a good question. One he didn't have an answer to.

Chapter 27

Renard sat in his cruiser, deeply troubled, thinking about the situation. He had known Sandy and Becca Grainfeld most of his life. The thought of one of them being a murderer was hard for him to accept. But the motives were there. And the opportunity. They both knew that Silverton had been down at the folk school alone Tuesday night. Even though Sandy had supposedly arrived home around 8:20 p.m., either one of them could have made up an excuse to go back out that evening. As it stood, though, they were each other's alibi, claiming they'd been home all evening and had gone to bed around ten p.m.

For a moment, he almost hoped that Maggie Norlund was the killer. The farthest thing from being objective, he told himself. *Wherever the evidence leads, that is where you must follow.* But, fact was, there was a strong case to be made for Maggie Norlund being the perpetrator, considering her past with Silverton and the fact that she had no alibi for the night of the crime. She had been off work and home alone that evening. Still, something about the interview bothered him. She had answered some of the hard questions truthfully. That meant she had character. And character is something that often gets in the way of heinous acts.

But there was something else that had been playing around the edges of his mind. There was one person he'd interviewed who he knew had not been at home Tuesday night. The question was one of motive, though, and he thought he knew who might help him learn more. He turned the cruiser around in the driveway, headed back toward town, and followed Highway 61 north toward the village of Hovland, eighteen miles above Grand Marais.

Boyle Bouchard lived in a small log house in Hovland that he had inherited from his father and to which he had moved after being released from prison. Renard had first encountered him when investigating a case with Detective Brie Beaumont from Minneapolis the previous fall.

Boyle, having been a somewhat godless man, had gone on a search for meaning while in prison and had found Buddhism.

Renard would never forget the surprise of arriving at his modest abode for that interview and finding Bouchard dressed like a Buddhist monk, and his living room set up as a Buddhist shrine. Renard had been so at a loss for words that Detective Beaumont had had to conduct the interview.

Once he had found his path, Bouchard had embarked on a mission to acquire knowledge, reading most of the books in the prison library. After moving up North, he had taken up a job at Nordic Logging, where his father had worked. But his real work seemed to be helping the community in any way possible. In the process he had become fast friends with Father Jim George up at the Catholic church in Grand Marais.

Renard remembered talking to him in the café the morning after the murder. Boyle had asked if there was any way he could be of help, and Renard had told him that, although he meant well, he could not interfere in the investigation. Ironically, now it appeared that he might be able to help.

Twenty minutes along the road, Renard crossed the Flute Reed River and turned right on Chicago Bay Road that ran through the village of Hovland. He followed the curve of the road for a short way and pulled over to the side near Boyle Bouchard's residence. The log cabin was modest, but the setting, studded with tall pine and spruce, was lovely. A short distance behind the cabin, the Flute Reed River tumbled over its rocky bed on its way down to Lake Superior.

Renard climbed out of the car. He was thinking about his first interview with Becca Grainfeld on Wednesday, and he was thinking about what Grant Silverton had done for a living. During that interview Becca had told him that her son Ethan didn't plan to keep working at the logging company—that he was taking an online course in investing. That one of his buddies at work had gotten him into the idea of it. The information hadn't seemed significant until today, when he'd found out that Becca was having an ongoing affair with Grant Silverton. Grant Silverton's career had been in investment banking. It could be coincidental, but being a cop, Renard did not like coincidences. That's why he was here. Boyle Bouchard worked with Ethan Grainfeld.

He stepped up on the small porch and knocked on the door. He could smell the sweet tang of incense from within the house. A moment later Boyle Bouchard opened the door.

"Chief Deputy Renard. How nice to see you."

It showed how far Boyle had come that he would greet the law with such enthusiasm.

"Hello, Boyle. I'm glad to find you at home."

"Please, come in." Boyle Bouchard gestured graciously with his hand, and Renard stepped inside, stood on the small mat, and slipped off his boots.

Everything was just as he remembered it. The room was empty except for a statue of the seated Buddha in the corner, surrounded by fresh flowers and bowls of fruit. A small oriental rug sat on the floor in front of the shrine, and a tiered stone fountain added the restful sound of moving water. Incense curled up from a bowl in front of the Buddha, the smell of it not unlike the sacred medicines his people burned for cleansing and peace. Boyle was dressed in a saffron-colored wrap. Renard had seen pictures of Buddhist monks, and Boyle's garb looked a lot like those pictures.

"Please come into the kitchen, Chief Deputy. I've just made some tea."

Renard followed him into the small kitchen with an even smaller dining table in the corner. He set the pot of tea there along with two small handleless cups. It was almost as if Boyle Bouchard had expected his visit.

"Please sit down, Deputy, and tell me what I can help you with."

Renard sat and Boyle poured tea into the cups.

"I believe you work with Ethan Grainfeld at the logging company," Renard said.

"That's correct. We aren't always on the same crew, but I've worked with him one way or another since I started at Nordic Logging last year."

"It's hard work, I know."

"Yes, it is," Boyle said. "But I'm lucky to have the job. It's not always easy to find employment when one leaves prison."

"I understand that, Boyle, and I admire your willingness to take on such physical work at your age." He knew Bouchard was in his late fifties.

Boyle nodded humbly. "Well, if it was good enough for my father, then it's good enough for me. I believe one can find joy and knowledge in any situation."

It was a good opening. "Does Ethan Grainfeld seem content in his work at the logging company?" Renard asked.

"He seems restless," Boyle said. "Like one who's searching." He set his cup down. "Young people often believe there's a pot of gold somewhere nearby. If they can just find it, they will be happy. They don't realize the gold is within. But it must be mined, and that can be hard work."

Boyle studied him for a moment. "Might I ask if this has something to do with the Grant Silverton investigation?"

"I can't really talk about the case, Boyle, but we are following several paths of investigation, and since you worked with Ethan, your input could be valuable."

Renard took out his pen and notebook. "Ethan's mother, Becca Grainfeld, has told me that Ethan was taking an online course in investing. Did he ever talk about that?"

"I've heard him talk about it with another young man on the crew. Peter Tillman. But that was several months ago. Peter moved from the Grand Marais area about three months ago."

Renard wrote the name in his notebook.

"Did you ever hear Ethan mention a connection to Grant Silverton? Ever get the impression he might be connected to him in any way? Maybe something to do with his interest in investing?"

Boyle Bouchard suddenly looked very uncomfortable. It was clear he didn't want anything he might say to create problems for someone else.

Renard broke the silence. "Did you know that Grant Silverton had been an investment banker?"

"I did not know that, but I'm not surprised. He struck me as one who'd had a successful professional career."

A sudden gust of wind rattled the window next to them and lifted a whirlwind of snow from the drift outside the window. A thousand tiny crystals refracted the light in a dazzling display.

Boyle looked back at Renard. "Ethan lost all his money. Twenty-five thousand dollars in the bitcoin collapse. I know nothing about that world—only what he said. That he had invested in bitcoin and had lost everything. He blamed Grant Silverton."

"Like you, I know nothing about bitcoin except that it is considered very risky to invest in," Renard said. "I can't believe an investment banker—one who had taught finance at the University of Geneva—would ever encourage such a thing."

"I'm not sure he did," Boyle said. "I think that encouragement came from his friend, Peter Tillman. But when Tillman moved away, Ethan may have looked for someone else to blame."

Renard looked up from his note taking. "As a member of law enforcement, I was interested in the collapse of that bitcoin company—FTX—a few months ago. Charges against the CEO range from wire fraud and bank fraud to bribery. Apparently, up until the collapse, FTX was considered one of the safer exchanges for bitcoin, until the CEO was exposed as just another world-class fraudster destroying people's dreams."

Boyle Bouchard's expression changed. "You know, Deputy. I remember Ethan saying something about six months ago. Something about how Grant Silverton had told him that if he was determined to invest in bitcoin, to at least put his money with a large company like FTX."

"So, Silverton *was* opposed to Ethan getting involved in bitcoin," Renard said.

"I believe that was the case. But, seeing that Ethan was determined to invest in it, no matter what, Mr. Silverton may have tried to direct him to what he thought was a safe company."

"That's what it sounds like," Renard said.

"I am surprised that, having been in the investment world, Mr. Silverton wouldn't have looked into that company more deeply," Bouchard said.

"Well, Boyle, you have to remember that Mr. Silverton had been retired from that world for a few years. And anyway, from what I've read, even the professionals were blindsided by the sudden collapse of that company. I think the world of bitcoin may be so bewildering that almost no one understands it. But maybe none of the big guns were willing to admit to that."

"So, it's a world of pretense," Boyle said.

"Exactly. And that usually leads to no good."

Renard stared out the window next to him. The fact was, Ethan Grainfeld had been in communication with Silverton. Something that both he and his mother, Becca, had denied. Had she encouraged him to seek investing advice from Silverton after she became involved with him? Did she also encourage Grant Silverton to help Ethan? It all added up to a strong motive for one of them to kill Silverton when Ethan lost all his money.

Renard wrote some more notes and then looked up at Bouchard. "This has been very helpful, Boyle. Thank you for sharing this information with me."

Boyle lowered his head, seeming troubled. "It's very sad, is it not? This whole terrible situation here in our community. I will meditate on love and hope surrounding Ethan and his family."

"Thank you, Boyle."

They sat together for a time, finishing their tea and watching the day fade outside, and then Renard took his leave, thanking Bouchard again for his input.

Chapter 28

Renard sat in his squad in the rapidly fading light, thinking over the information Boyle Bouchard had shared with him about Ethan Grainfeld and recalling his interview with Ethan yesterday outside the Grainfeld home.

Ethan had said he'd gone to meet his friends at the Harbor Light Bar & Grill on Tuesday night—the night Silverton was killed. He said he'd left shortly after Sandy Grainfeld had arrived home at around 8:30. Would he have heard from his father that Silverton was alone at the folk school? Most likely he would have. After all, Sandy had been upset about Silverton asking to stay and work on his coffin, and he had complained about it to Becca when he got home. Ethan could have overheard him.

Maybe Ethan went on to meet his buddies and had some drinks, which could have greatly altered his judgment. He thought he had a grievance with Silverton about the bitcoin situation. Had he seen that Silverton was still there as he was heading home? Had he decided to go in and confront him?

Renard could easily imagine the rest. An angry argument had ensued, maybe with Ethan accusing Silverton of causing him to lose his money. Maybe Silverton had been dismissive—told Ethan he had nothing to do with him losing his money. Maybe then Silverton had made the fatal mistake of turning his back on Ethan Grainfeld, and Ethan, in a fit of rage over being ignored by Silverton, grabbed the wood chisel that was lying there and stabbed Grant Silverton.

Or maybe the same scene had unfolded when he was on his way to meet his buddies. But it was hard to imagine Ethan killing Silverton and then meeting up with the guys for drinks, like nothing had happened. No, he suspected it had been sometime later.

It was one theory of the crime. But he reminded himself that Sandy and Becca Grainfeld also each had motive and opportunity, and Ethan losing his money could have been the final straw for either of them, if they bought into his belief that Silverton was responsible for the loss of his money.

He needed to re-interview the Dinkovich boys, who had entered the woodworking building Tuesday night around 10:30 and stumbled onto Silverton's body in the coffin. He wanted to go over exactly what they'd seen one more time, just in case there was some detail they had left out. He brought up the report he'd written after interviewing them, as well as the statements they'd given at the Law Enforcement Center, and read through everything. When he'd finished, he turned the car around and headed back toward Grand Marais.

Darkness was complete as he made his way through town. The car clock read 5:33. He had felt the wind buffeting his squad on the drive back down. His headlights revealed snow just beginning to fall—hit or miss for now—but the northeast wind told him more serious weather was on the way.

He turned on 3rd Avenue and drove up the hill to the outskirts of town. As he pulled to the curb, he saw what looked like flashlight beams out behind the house. The boys were obviously up to something back there, since elderly Mrs. Dinkovich wouldn't be out in the freezing cold with a flashlight.

He climbed out and followed a shoveled path up to the backyard, coming around the house just in time to see Darrell and Duffy scrambling out from under an old wreck of a car, dragging a driveshaft behind them. The car sat up on cinder blocks, its four flat tires frozen in place. A couple of hazard lights hung from the rusty frame underneath. Runnels burrowed into the snow revealed how the boys had gotten at the underside of the wreck.

They climbed to their feet, only then realizing Renard was standing there. He hadn't intended to surprise them, but he could tell his unexpected arrival had given them a start.

"Sheriff One Step. How long you been standin' there?" Darrell queried. "We was just pullin' this here old driveshaft to put on the good car over yonder," he said, as if feeling obligated to explain.

Renard turned where he pointed. The "good" car, resting on its own set of cinder blocks, appeared only slightly less dilapidated than its cousin.

The boys were both wearing headlamps over their tattered stocking caps, and Renard held up a hand to shield his eyes from the glare. Seeing this, Duffy whipped off his headlamp and nudged Darrell to do the same.

"Sorry, Sheriff. Didn't mean to blind ya there." Darrell pointed the headlamp toward the ground, where it cast just enough light for them to see each other.

"Would you like to come inside, Sheriff One Step? Mighty cold out here." Duffy looked concerned.

Renard thought about elderly Mrs. Dinkovich. No reason to worry the poor woman when it was clear she must have her hands full in the worrying department already, what with shepherding Darrell and Duffy here.

"I'm fine, boys. Maybe it's best we talk out here."

They glanced sheepishly at each other, but it was Duffy who spoke.

"Is weez in trouble?"

"No, boys, you're not in trouble. I just want to go over what we talked about on Wednesday. What you saw Tuesday night, down at the folk school. I just want to be sure I have all the details."

They nodded seriously in unison.

"Weez did like you said," Darrell offered. "We come into the sheriff's office and give our statements."

"I know you did, and I appreciate that, Darrell. But let's just go over the details again."

"Sure. Weez ready," Duffy said.

Renard took his phone out of his parka and started the voice recorder.

"So, according to our interview on Wednesday and also your statements given later that day, you didn't see anyone near the woodworking building on Tuesday night. Is that right?"

The Dinkovich boys looked at each other as if making a decision.

"Truth is, weez did see something, Sheriff One Step," Darrell mumbled.

Renard leveled his best stern cop face at them. A light had come on inside the house near where they stood, and he could see the consternation on their faces. Like they wished they could crawl back under their wreck and never come out.

He managed to keep his voice level. "Go on."

"Weez was comin' down the hill, there by the building . . ."

"The woodworking building?" Renard clarified.

"That's right. Weez was comin' down that hill there. . ." Darrell motioned with his hand, and it looked like a ski jumper going down the jump, "and we seen somebody walking out from behind the building."

"Walking?" Renard asked. "Not running?"

"Nope, they was walkin'. Fast-like. But not runnin'."

"A man or a woman?"

"Couldn't tell." Darrell shrugged. "They was in a parka with the hood pulled up."

"Weez only just seen him for a second and then he moved off into the shadows," Duffy added.

"You say 'he,' but you claim you couldn't tell if it was a man or a woman."

Duffy stopped, like maybe that was too many words to process all at once. Darrell came to his rescue. "Weez was up the hill. It was hard to tell how tall they was."

"I see," Renard said. "So why didn't you tell me this the other day—Wednesday—when I questioned you? It doesn't look good, boys. Omitting something this important. Calls your whole story into question."

"Weez thought you'd think we was lyin'," Duffy blurted out.

"Weez thought you'd think we was makin' it up," Darrell chimed in. "Tryin' to put the blame on somebody's else when we was the guilty ones."

Flawless logic, Renard thought.

"Did you?"

"No! No, Sheriff One Step. We'd never. Weez tellin' the truth."

"And what was that you were telling the other day?"

"That were the truth too," Duffy blurted. "Weez just left some out."

"I see." Renard looked from one of them to the other. "So, you couldn't see this person's face because the hood was pulled up. Is that right?"

They both nodded.

"What color was the parka?" Renard asked.

They shrugged. "Dark-like," Duffy offered. "Black, maybe. There was fur around the hood."

Huh, parka with a fur hood, in Northern Minnesota, Renard thought. *Now we're getting somewhere.*

"Anything else you can remember, boys?"

Darrell knit his brows together for a few moments, considering. "Nope, nothin' else. That was it, Sheriff."

"But wait, Darrell," Duffy blurted frantically, as if the question train might leave the station before he could jump back on. "There was somethin' else. He had them fancy boots, remember? You know, the ones like the Eskimos wear up there in Alaskie. Remember, Darrell? Weez both seen 'em. There was a light on the corner of the building, and weez both seen 'em. Remember?"

After a tick or two, Darrell nodded. "Yep. That's right. We seen 'em, all right. Come near up to his knees, they did—them boots. Tops was white with fancy lacin' down the front—crisscross-like."

The two of them nodded, clearly proud of their powers of recall.

Renard studied them for a moment. These were very specific details—not the kind he could see the Dinkovich boys making up. Had they caught a glimpse of the murderer? Or had they seen an innocent passerby? But Renard was thinking about a pair of boots he'd seen during one of his interviews, and they perfectly fit the description Darrell and Duffy had given.

"Think hard now, boys. Is there anything else you can remember about this person you saw?"

Duffy screwed up his face as if thinking hard took all his concentration. After a few moments, he shook his head definitively.

"Nope. That's all weez saw."

"How about you, Darrell? Anything else? Any other details you can remember?"

"Nope. Weez told you everythin' this time, Sheriff."

Renard looked from one to the other of them. "I hope so, boys, because this is important."

They nodded solemnly, and Duffy raised his right hand. "We swears."

For whatever reason, Renard had a hard time keeping a straight face.

"All right, then. I'm going to ask you to go into the Law Enforcement Center tomorrow, again, and each give another written statement of what you saw Tuesday night."

They both nodded. "Weez on it," Duffy said.

"Now go on inside and make sure your mom has had a decent dinner."

They turned and scrambled toward the back door, nearly tripping over each other in their race to obey orders.

As he walked back to the squad, Renard had to smile to himself. *Why did neither one of them ever speak about himself in the singular?* he wondered. It was like they'd come out of the womb at separate times but still joined at the hip. But what they had recalled was a possible break in the case. A big one.

Renard climbed into his squad and looked up Judge Amundson's phone number. After hearing the details of the case, the judge agreed to expedite the search warrant, telling Renard to come by his house immediately and he would get it ready for him. The judge also told him that, since this was a key piece of evidence in a murder case, he planned to authorize an after-hours search, in case he did not find the Grainfelds at home and needed to go back there after eight p.m.

Renard hung up and radioed Hank Gunderson. He asked that he and Merlin Waters meet him at the Law Enforcement Center in one hour. Then he put the car in gear and headed for Judge Amundson's house.

Chapter 29

Renard pulled to a stop behind the Grainfeld house on Devil Track Lake. Sandy's pickup truck and Becca's Jeep were both there. They were at home, but there was no sign of Ethan's pickup, nor did Renard hear the dogs barking. He turned off the engine and sat for a moment, collecting himself. The cop in him was excited about a possible break in the case, but the man, who had known these people for much of his life, dreaded what he had to do.

He tucked the evidence bag inside his parka, picked up one copy of the search warrant, and climbed out of the squad. He walked up the steps to the back door and rang the bell. He waited the better part of a minute and was about to ring again when Sandy Grainfeld opened the door.

"Evening, Howard. Could I come in?"

"What is this about, Claude? Becca and I were about to eat dinner."

"It won't take long, Howard." *But neither does pulling a tooth,* he thought.

"Well, it better not. You've bothered us enough lately."

Renard could hear fear behind the austerity in his voice.

Grainfeld held the door open, and Renard stepped inside. He immediately handed the search warrant to him. Howard looked from the warrant in his hand to Renard and his face turned scarlet red. Whether from embarrassment or fury, Renard was not sure. At that moment Becca stepped into the hallway. She saw Howard's face, and the warrant in his hand.

"What's going on here, Claude?"

"This is a search warrant for your property, Becca. It covers the entire property, but right now I am here looking for one specific thing."

Becca opened her mouth, but no words came out.

Howard had found his voice, though. "How dare you come here, harassing us like this. If this is about Grant Silverton's murder, you're barking up the wrong tree, and you should focus on finding the killer."

"I am focused on that, Howard."

"What motive could either of us possibly have?" Grainfeld stepped uncomfortably close to Renard.

"Please step back, Howard. Do it now." Renard looked past him to Becca. Her expression was one of horror mixed with pleading.

"Answer my question," Grainfeld demanded. "What possible motive. . ."

Renard turned and studied the collection of boots in the hallway. They were lined up along the wall, and he immediately saw what he was looking for in the corner. He pulled a latex glove from his back pocket, put it on and took the large evidence bag from inside his parka. He opened it up, stepped over and picked up the boots.

"What are you doing?" Grainfeld demanded. "You can't take those."

"I can, Howard. The search warrant specifically names and describes these boots." He placed them carefully in the bag, folded the top over and sealed it. He wrote his shield number and the time, date, and location the evidence was being collected on the bag. Then he turned back to Howard and Becca.

"Whose boots are these?"

Howard was fury personified. "We're done talking to you, and we're done answering any of your questions. From now on you will speak to our attorney. Do you understand?"

Renard looked past him to Becca. Tears rolled down her face. He turned back to Howard. "I will do whatever is required to solve this case and to find justice for Grant Silverton." He turned and opened the door and walked down the steps to his squad without looking back.

Renard sat in his squad for a few moments, breathing. Then he turned over the engine and headed back through the darkness of the forest to the main road. He was thinking about the Seven Grandfathers Teachings. He always reflected on them at moments like this. The practice brought calm—helped him to focus on what was required of him at a particular point in time and why. The teaching he reflected on now was respect. Respect for his position and for the law. Respect for the victim as well as respect for all involved—both the suspects and, yes, even the perpetrator, whoever that might be. Because that person must be considered innocent until proven guilty.

Five miles east, he turned onto the Gunflint Trail and headed down toward Grand Marais. He was picturing the boots he'd placed in the evidence bag. He hadn't taken time to inspect them at the Grainfeld home. His focus had been on getting them secured in the evidence bag. He would look at them more carefully back at the Law Enforcement Center with Hank Gunderson there as a witness. One thing he knew, though. The boots were too big to belong to Becca. Which meant they were either Ethan's or Howard's. But honestly, Renard could never recall seeing Howard Grainfeld in anything but Pac boots in the winter. The boots he had taken into evidence were Steger Mukluks—expensive outdoor footwear often worn by those who engaged in serious outdoor activities. Activities like dog mushing.

Renard saw Merlin Waters' car there when he pulled into the Law Enforcement Center. He buzzed himself inside and went directly to the evidence room, where he entered the boots on the evidence log and placed them in a locker there. He was just finishing when Deputy Hank Gunderson came in.

"Ah, Hank. Glad you're here." He took the evidence bag back out of the locker and told Hank about what the Dinkovich boys had seen the night of the murder that had led him to go to the Grainfeld house and take the boots into evidence.

"Before I call the BCA, I want you to witness me opening the evidence bag and inspecting the boots for a possible connection to the crime scene."

They both gloved up, unsealed the evidence bag and took the boots out. Renard turned them over one at a time and studied the bottom of each. They had deep treads for traction in the snow, and he immediately saw what he was looking for. Compacted in the treads of both boots was what looked like sawdust. There was no way to know if it was or not, or if it could tie these boots to the crime scene, but it was enough for him to take the next step of getting them to the BCA ASAP.

They resealed the evidence bag, and Renard made an entry in the chain of custody log, signing the envelope over to Hank Gunderson for transport. He also retrieved the sample of sawdust and shavings he'd collected from beneath Grant Silverton's coffin at the crime scene. He signed that evidence over to Deputy Gunderson as well. Adrianna's team would have collected a similar sample, but he sent it along nonetheless.

"I'll call Adrianna Tomebay at the BCA and tell her you're en route with the evidence." He gave Hank Ria's cell phone number and instructed him to call her when he was twenty minutes from the BCA.

"Will do. I'll grab my coat and get on the road."

"Good man."

Renard headed down the hall to his office. He was thinking about Grant Silverton and the coffin he'd been building. The wood he had chosen was walnut, not pine like all the other students' in Sandy Grainfeld's class. So the sawdust, generated by the work on his coffin, would have its own unique composition.

If that *was* sawdust in the treads of Ethan's boots, and it matched the walnut sawdust near Silverton's coffin in the woodworking building, it would be damning evidence. And making it even more damning was what Becca Grainfeld had told him when he first questioned her. She had said that Ethan never went near the woodworking building down at the folk school—that he would have nothing to do with his father's woodworking. So, he could never have gotten that sawdust in his boot treads accidentally. Finally, Ethan had gone out to meet his buddies that night at the Harbor Light. That might explain why he'd been wearing his good boots.

He walked up the hall and stuck his head into Merlin's lair.

"I just have one phone call to make, Merlin, and I'll be back. I need to know what you found in the search of Maggie Norlund's phone records."

"I'll pull up that information."

Renard went to his office and closed the door. He sat down at his desk and put through a call to Adrianna Tomebay from the BCA. She answered on the second ring.

"Hello, Fox. This is a surprise."

"I need to ask a favor, Ria."

"No 'hello, it's good to hear your voice'?"

"Sorry, Ria. What am I thinking?"

"Don't know, Fox. My best guess—there's been a break in the case."

He told her about the boots he'd taken into evidence and that they matched those seen on someone the night of the murder near the building where the crime had been committed.

"What can I do?"

"There's something compacted in the treads of the boots. It could be sawdust. If it is, the question is, does it match the sawdust from Grant Silverton's work station at the woodworking building, where he was murdered? His was the only walnut coffin being worked on. All the others were pine."

"I see where you're going," Ria said. "That sawdust would have a different structure and could place the wearer of those boots at the crime scene. Question is, could he have been there innocently?"

"I don't think so. From what I know about this suspect, it's not likely."

"Well then, what's next?"

"Hank Gunderson is already on the road, heading your way with the boots. But taking them into evidence will have put the suspect on alert."

"So time is of the essence," Ria said.

"It is."

"Is the suspect a flight risk?"

"My guess is he could be," Renard said.

"I'll plan to be at the BCA to run the tests myself when Hank arrives. Can you tell him to call me when he's fifteen minutes out?"

"I told him to call you when he's twenty minutes out."

"Perfect. As soon as I know something one way or the other, I'll let you know."

"Thanks, Ria. I owe you."

"Hmmm, we'll have to find some way for you to make it up to me."

Renard felt heat in his belly. "I guess we'll have to see about that," he said softly.

After they hung up, he sat back in his chair. It had been a long, stressful day, but the sound of Ria's voice —that brief flirtation—was a balm for his anxious spirit.

He sat for a few moments, eyes closed, picturing Adrianna. Then he rose and went to talk to Merlin Waters.

"Sorry to keep you waiting, Merlin. I know it's getting late."

"No worries," Merlin chirped. "I've got the cell phone data you requested for Maggie Norlund. I've also searched for her number in Grant Silverton's phone data and records."

"And what does all of it show?"

"There are no calls at all placed from Maggie Norlund's phone to Grant Silverton's over the past three or four months, since she's lived here."

So, she was telling the truth, Renard thought. She had not contacted Silverton, even after she saw him in town, supposedly discovering for the first time that he lived here.

"But there's something else," Merlin said.

"What is it?"

"Grant Silverton's phone records show several calls placed to Maggie's number over the past month. Very brief calls. Maybe long enough to leave a voicemail."

"But no indication that she answered or returned the calls."

"None whatsoever," Merlin said.

"Huh. So it looks like Maggie Norlund *did* refrain from contact with Silverton."

"Looks that way," Merlin said. He reached into his gummy bear jar and popped one in his mouth.

"Thanks, Merlin. That's all we need for now. You can head home."

Merlin nodded, pushed his glasses up his nose, and closed up his gummy bears. "We'll see you tomorrow then," he said. On the way out the door, he stopped and turned around. "You gonna be here awhile? Can I grab some food for you?"

"I'm fine, Merlin. Had a late lunch. You go on home."

Merlin nodded and disappeared down the hall toward the door.

Renard headed back to his office to start his reports. He was thinking about Maggie Norlund, who just that morning had seemed like the most likely suspect. But developments since then suggested something quite different.

Renard started writing his reports on the information he'd received from Kristin Fontaine, Boyle Bouchard, and the Dinkovich brothers, as well as on his seizure of the boots from the Grainfeld house. An hour and twenty minutes later he sat back and rubbed his eyes. He called Hank Gunderson to see what his ETA was at the BCA in Bemidji. Hank was still two and a half hours. It was going to be a late night for everyone involved.

There was one loose end that still bothered him. It was the disappearance of the prize agate from Grant Silverton's house the morning after the murder. Initially he had been sure that Maurie Fontaine had gone there and taken it, since he had been determined to get it back from Silverton. But now he wasn't so sure. More likely the killer had known about the bad blood over that agate and had taken it to cast suspicion on Fontaine—make *him* look like the killer. And it had worked. The disappearance of the agate, coupled with the threats Maurie Fontaine had made about getting it back "no matter what it took," had placed him high on the suspect list.

But one thing was clear now. Whoever took the agate from Silverton's house was most likely the killer.

Finding that agate was important, and Renard had an idea where it might be. He grabbed his coat off the back of his chair and headed out to his squad. He pulled around to the utility building where one of the sheriff's department snowmobiles sat on a trailer. He secured the trailer to the back of his SUV, drove out to the highway, turned onto the Gunflint, and headed north.

Chapter 30

Renard knew the owners of Skyport Lodge and Raven Rock Grill. It was a good point of access to Devil Track Lake and not all that far from the Grainfeld property. It was just after ten p.m. when he drove into the parking lot at the Raven Rock and off-loaded the snowmobile. He pulled his snowmobile suit out of the back of his squad and climbed into it. Then he walked into the lodge and headed for the bar. He caught the eye of Jim Todd, the bartender—nodded for him to come over.

"What's up, Claude?" Jim asked.

"My squad's out back, Jim. I need to access the lake with my snowmobile."

"Sure. No problem. You don't have to ask."

"It's always good to ask," Renard said.

"Is this official business?"

"It is, but I can't talk about it."

"Sure. Of course not," Jim said.

"Just wanted to give you a heads-up so you didn't see the squad out back and wonder."

"Thanks, Claude." Jim turned and saw someone at the bar looking around. "I should get back to it."

Renard headed out the back door, mounted the snowmobile, and drove slowly around the lodge and down to the lake. As he left the shoreline, he throttled the machine up and headed southwest across the frozen expanse. A full moon shone cold and white over the snowbound lake. The January moon—the Wolf Moon.

His destination was about three miles up the lake. One of the deputies, Len Blake, kept an ice house out here in the winter, and he and Hank often came out to ice fish with Len. Renard had passed the Grainfelds' ice house any number of times over the years and knew it was located about halfway up the lake. He also knew it was in sight of the Grainfeld house on the shore, so he intended to approach it with caution. The search warrant had been written for the entire property, including the ice house, but Renard preferred not to call attention to his visit, and with that in mind, he killed his headlight and slowed the snowmobile for the last hundred yards of his approach.

Gray, horizontal bars of cloud drifted across the moon, obscuring part of its light, but Renard could easily make out the ice house as he approached. The storm front that was slated to bring heavy snow by early evening had stalled, but now he could see a solid black wall moving in from the east. The temperature was falling, the wind building. It wouldn't be long before the storm hit with full force. There was no light coming from inside the ice house, so he drove around the back and parked the snowmobile out of sight. There was a small open trailer back there with firewood for the stove inside.

He walked around the ice house. To the north, a half mile across the lake, he could make out the Grainfeld house. There were no lights on there either. He doubted that Becca and Howard would have gone to bed after the search warrant and his visit. So, where were they? Maybe out looking for Ethan so they could warn him about what had happened? Depending on where he'd gone with his dogs, he could be well out of cell phone range.

Renard turned and tried the door to the ice house. It was unlocked. He pulled out his flashlight, stepped inside, and closed the door. The ice house was maybe twelve by eight. He shined the light around the perimeter. There were two cots with sleeping bags and, beyond them, two camp chairs set up near two holes in the floor where fishing lines could be rigged. A small woodstove near the back wall provided heat.

In the front corner a countertop held a two-burner Coleman stove. There were a couple of cabinets under the counter for supplies and one above. On the other side of the door were some hooks for coats and clothing. A gas-powered auger for opening up holes in the ice was propped in the corner, and next to it sat a picnic cooler for food or maybe storing fish.

Renard began his search with the cabinets up front. Inside were items that wouldn't be affected by the cold. Hot and cold cereal, pancake mix, ramen noodles, and boxes of mac and cheese. There were bags of chips, boxes of crackers and a stash of candy bars. "Good thing bears hibernate in the winter," he said to himself.

He moved things around in the upper cabinet, but it was quickly apparent that nothing was hidden up there. The lower cabinets were filled with an assortment of tools and fishing paraphernalia. There was a first aid kit, a box of fire starters and some matches, a bag of charcoal, and a small hibachi grill, just big enough for a couple of burgers or steaks. Renard foraged around in the cabinet, looking through everything, but there was no large agate to be found. He tapped on the bottom of the cabinet and tried prying up the bottom shelf, but it was nailed in place.

He moved over to the cooler and looked inside. It was empty. There were a couple of coats hanging on the hooks, and he checked those as well. Nothing. He walked to the back of the ice house. There was a box along the back wall that held kindling for the stove. He knelt and opened it and went through the supply of small wood there, making sure nothing was hidden underneath. No luck. He checked around and underneath the chairs and even took the covers off the floor holes used for fishing and felt around underneath the perimeter of the area under the floor.

He moved over to the cots, thinking this might have been a fool's errand, and felt the sleeping bags for anything inside. Nothing. But when he tipped the cot frame up, he felt something heavy in the back corner. He turned the cot up on its side. A nylon storage bag was velcroed to the underside of the cot.

Renard unzipped his snowmobile suit and took out a latex glove and an evidence bag he'd brought with him. He gloved up, pulled the nylon bag from the Velcro mounting and unzipped the top of the bag. Inside was a beautiful raw agate with colored banding that ran the spectrum from orange and white to pale green and lavender. He'd lived by Lake Superior his whole life, but he'd never seen anything like this. There was no doubt in his mind that this was the prize agate that Maurie Fontaine had sold to Grant Silverton. The one that had disappeared from Silverton's house the morning after the murder. A truly damning piece of evidence, especially since Becca Grainfeld had told him that Ethan was the only one who used the ice house— that Howard hadn't been out here ice fishing in a couple of years.

Renard *was* surprised the agate hadn't been hidden better. Clearly, Ethan was not worried about anyone discovering it, which showed he had little understanding of the all-encompassing nature of a murder investigation. *Did he really think I wouldn't find out about his connection to Grant Silverton?* Renard wondered.

He zipped the nylon bag closed and placed it in the evidence envelope. He labeled the envelope with the time, date, his shield number, and location of evidence collection, turned the cot back over, picked up his flashlight, and headed out the door. His peripheral vision caught a dark shadow. Searing pain shot through his head. Then blackness as he collapsed to the ground.

* * *

The roar of the snowmobile and the rough bouncing of the trailer shook Renard back to consciousness. His head was a boulder of pain attached to his shoulders. He moved his eyes around and recognized the trailer as the one that had been behind the ice house, holding firewood. He guessed it was a piece of that same firewood he'd been clubbed with. They were careening across the ice and, by the position of the moon, he knew they were traveling east. He had the sinking feeling he knew where they were headed.

His ankles were bound together with a length of rope and his wrists were zip-tied, but by patting his body, he discovered his firearm, radio, and cell phone were all missing. Pain split his head like a sharp spike, and his ears were ringing. But as he listened harder, he was sure he heard another snowmobile, or maybe two, approaching. He was lying on his left side and, since he could see no headlights, he knew the snowmobilers were approaching from the north side of the lake.

He tried to roll to his other side, but the violent motion of the trailer prevented it. All of a sudden, he thought he heard shouting over the noise of the engines. He tried to tune in past the ringing in his ears. There *was* shouting, and now he couldn't believe his ears. It sounded like the Dinkovich boys. *But what in the world are they doing out here?* Then he thought about all those ice houses on the lake—open for business.

Suddenly the sled jerked to a stop. The rider pulled out a handgun and fired it, first into the air and then north toward whoever was in pursuit. Renard was pretty sure that was his handgun and that the one firing it was Ethan Grainfeld. His heart sank as he heard the snowmobiles retreating.

He lay very still, feigning unconsciousness, as the crunch of boots moved toward him. He opened his eyes just a slit for a split second, but it was enough to glimpse the Sherpa hat Ethan Grainfeld had been wearing the other day when he'd interviewed him. The footsteps paused, and he knew Ethan was studying him—could sense the brightness of the flashlight on his face. Then the boots crunched away, the engine on the sled revved, and off they went again, across the frozen lake.

Renard was hoping there was one thing Ethan had missed in stripping him of his most vital survival items. He pulled his knees up and worked his gloved fingers down inside his left boot—the one covering his prosthetic leg. He kept a sheathed knife in that boot. When his fingers touched the knife hilt, hope spread through his veins like lifeblood, and he silently thanked the ancestors for watching over him.

Using his teeth, he pulled off his gloves, worked his hands down into the boot, and unsnapped the small strap that held the knife in the sheath. He carefully drew it out and went to work first on the rope around his ankles. When they were free, he maneuvered the knife around and started on the zip tie around his wrists. It was an awkward angle, and the bouncing of the trailer made matters worse. He managed to nick himself twice with the knife, but when the zip tie broke free, he knew his chances of survival had increased exponentially. He slid the knife back into his boot. No point in bringing a knife to what he knew would be a gun fight.

He pulled his gloves back on and lay there breathing for a moment, trying to think of a plan. His head still ached, but the ringing in his ears had retreated somewhat. The moon had been overtaken by the storm front, darkening the landscape—a fact that Renard knew could work in his favor. Then the snow and the wind arrived simultaneously, raging out of the east—cutting visibility down to yards. They were driving straight into the storm, and Ethan Grainfeld was forced to slow the snowmobile.

Renard was pretty sure where Ethan was headed, and he knew a miscalculation could be deadly. At the east end of the lake, the Devil Track River flowed out and south to Lake Superior. Because of the outflow, the ice there would be unstable. He suspected Ethan's plan was to put him through the ice near where the river flowed out.

He undoubtedly plans to send the snowmobile into the river as well, making it look like an accident, Renard thought. *Making it look like I got too close to open water and went through the ice.*

He needed a plan but had little time to formulate one. Any chance of survival would have to involve the element of surprise. The trailer had shallow wood sides—maybe eighteen or twenty inches tall—but they were solid, with no gaps between the boards. His plan was simple, and he estimated it had a fifty percent chance of success.

The wind was literally howling out of the northeast now, loud enough, he hoped, to cover his movements. Ethan slowed the snowmobile to a crawl, and as he did, Renard rolled onto his hands and knees and bunched himself up, preparing to move when the moment came. He was banking on Ethan dismounting the sled to the left as motorcyclists and snowmobilers are wont to do.

The instant the sled came to a stop and before Ethan Grainfeld had killed the engine, Renard made his move—one swift low vault over the right side of the trailer. In a moment he heard footsteps crunching down the other side of the snowmobile. Renard crept to the end of the trailer, staying concealed below the side.

"What the hell!" Ethan shouted.

Renard heard him rush to the end of the trailer—saw him peering down the lake. Now was the moment. Renard sprang, hitting him full force from behind, knocking him flat. The gun Ethan had been holding flew out of his hand and slid away across the ice. Before Renard could get to his knees, Ethan rolled over, scrambled up, and drove a gloved fist toward his face, stunning him. Ethan shot to his feet, grabbed Renard by the collar, and started dragging him.

Renard heard snowmobiles approaching in the distance and, farther off, sirens wailed. He threw his arms behind him, catching Ethan's feet, tripping him. Ethan scuttled backwards as Renard rolled over and grabbed for him. The snowmobile headlight illuminated the danger. Just ahead, Renard could see open water where the Devil Track River flowed out.

"Don't stand up," he shouted, but it was too late. He heard the ice crack and scrambled forward just in time to catch Ethan's arm. He pulled him to the surface and grabbed the back of his collar. Ethan fought violently to escape, and Renard wondered if his plan was to give up the ghost or try to float away down the river as a means of escape. But either way, it wasn't happening on his watch.

Seconds ticked by that felt like minutes. He needed to stand up to have enough leverage to haul him out of the water, but that decision could be deadly. He decided to stay prone. One or two minutes ticked by. They felt like hours. Ethan had gone still, and Renard thought the cold must be getting to him.

Then suddenly he was flailing again.

"I just wanted Silverton to pay me the money I lost," he shouted. "But he said no."

"So you killed him."

Ethan did not respond.

Renard thought about the dream he'd had of Silverton running through the forest and the hooded figure—Death—stalking him, and Silverton throwing money out behind him. He found the symbolism even more interesting now that he knew what Ethan's motive had been.

Ethan twisted his shoulders, trying to free himself from Renard's grip.

"I knew Mom was having an affair with him. I followed her one night. Saw her park below the hill and walk up through the woods to his house. She kept seeing him even after I lost my money. Made me furious at both of them."

Renard held fast to Ethan's collar, but his hands were starting to cramp from the cold. Fortunately, Ethan stopped struggling.

The snowmobiles were close now, and he heard shouting over the roar. "Weez comin,' Sheriff One Step."

The Dinkovich boys were coming to the rescue; Renard had never heard a sweeter sound.

And then they were there, stopping well back from the edge, and starting toward him.

"Get on your stomachs, boys. Just one of you crawl up here."

"You go, Darrell," Duffy said. "You's the skinny one. I'll pull you back."

Darrell infantry-crawled slowly up to the edge and grabbed hold of Ethan's collar. Ethan wasn't moving, and Renard knew the icy water was affecting him.

"Get a good grip, Darrell," Renard instructed.

Darrell nodded. "I got him, Sheriff. Start pullin', Duffy," he shouted.

Duffy was plenty strong from wrestling heavy car parts in and out. Slowly Darrell started to move backwards. Renard had hold of the shoulder of Ethan's suit with his right hand, and he struggled backwards, staying flat. His hands were going numb—the Dinkovich boys had arrived just in time.

Duffy kept hauling Darrell back until Ethan was clear of the edge by several yards. Renard got to his feet and went to help Duffy pull them back to a safe distance.

The sirens were close now. Renard turned and saw two sheriff's squads approaching from the north. They arrived almost simultaneously, one driven by Deputy Len Blake and the other by Thomas High Cloud, a young deputy who'd grown up in Grand Portage.

Ethan Grainfeld was conscious, so they patted him down and wrapped him in a survival blanket. Renard put him under arrest and read him his rights, and they put him in Len Blake's squad.

Renard leaned into the car. "What did you do with my radio and cell phone?"

Ethan didn't make eye contact. "I threw 'em away across the lake."

"Which direction?"

Ethan shrugged noncommittally. "Don't know. South maybe."

Renard studied him for a moment, then closed the door. "Take him to the ER at the hospital so they can assess him for hypothermia," he told Len Blake. "Stay with him and keep me posted. Once he's cleared by the hospital, we'll book him into the jail."

After Blake left, he told Deputy High Cloud about his gun being taken. With the Dinkovich brothers in tow, they walked back to the spot where he'd jumped Grainfeld. Renard indicated the direction he thought the gun had gone when it flew out of Ethan's hand and slid across the ice.

"Weez can help in the search, Sheriff," Duffy offered. "Weez good at findin' things."

Renard had no doubt of that. But more help was better, so he agreed.

"Okay, boys. Let's fan out. Use your feet."

The snow was accumulating fast, but he was sure they could locate the gun. It was just a matter of time. They'd been at it a good ten minutes or so when Darrell called out, "Weez found it, Sheriff One Step."

Renard smiled. Even though Duffy was five yards from him, it was still "weez." He headed over, pickup up the gun, and confirmed that it was his firearm that Ethan had taken when he knocked him unconscious.

He turned to High Cloud. "We need to go back to the Grainfelds' ice house. There's a piece of key evidence I need to locate along with my radio and cell phone."

Renard was hoping that Ethan had flung the agate back into the ice house after he'd clubbed him.

The snow had reached blizzard proportions, and they stood with their backs to the punishing wind. "It's about three miles west of here," Renard shouted over the wind. "I'll drive the snowmobile and you follow in the squad."

"I can take the sled, Claude. You drive the car."

"That's okay, Thomas. I'm dressed for it; you're not."

High Cloud didn't argue and headed for the squad.

"Weez comin' too, Sheriff. You needs our help, and weez in."

Renard hesitated for just a moment. "Sure, boys. Why not."

Leaning against the wind, they made their way back to the vehicles. Renard went first, then High Cloud in the squad, with the Dinkovich boys bringing up the rear. Renard smiled to himself. *An unlikely security detail if ever there was one.*

They drove down the middle of the frozen lake, and in approximately three miles, Renard saw the ice house loom out of the storm. He slowed as he approached it and came to a stop. There was a pair of cross-country skis in the snow, and Renard knew it would have taken an athlete like Ethan no more than a few minutes to traverse the half mile distance between the Grainfeld house on the shore and the ice house. He must have arrived home while Renard was searching the ice house and seen the glow from the flashlight inside.

Within seconds, the others joined him. He told Darrell and Duffy to wait there, and he and High Cloud turned on their flashlights and entered the ice house. Inside felt like a sanctuary from the fierce wind. It howled around the eaves of the tiny structure and shook the windows. They shined their flashlights around the space, and Renard immediately spotted the envelope under one of the camp chairs near the back of the ice house. He guessed Ethan had flung it in the door after he clubbed him, and that was where it had landed.

They headed back outside, and Deputy High Cloud secured the envelope in his squad.

The four of them huddled on the west side of the ice house out of the worst of the wind. "We need to try to find my radio and cell phone," Renard told the other three.

"Let's try calling the radio," High Cloud said. He keyed his radio and started calling, repeating himself over and over while the others listened.

Duffy stepped around the back of the ice house. "I hears it. Keep sendin'"

He and Darrell raced off in the direction of the sound, with Renard and High Cloud bringing up the rear. Duffy was beaming as he handed Renard the radio. Renard thanked him.

"T'ain't nothing, Sheriff. Let's find that cell phone of yorn."

They followed the same plan and called the cell phone. They all listened intently but heard nothing.

"Let's fan out," High Cloud said. "I'll keep calling. We're bound to find it."

After ten minutes of searching south of the ice house, they came back together and turned their search north of the structure, thinking that maybe Ethan had hurled the devices in opposite directions. Within five minutes, Renard himself found the cell phone directly north of the ice house, and they all headed for their vehicles.

"Let's get out of this storm, boys, and rendezvous at the Raven Rock," Renard said. Deputy High Cloud led in the squad to break the wind. Renard followed behind, and the Dinkovich boys brought up the rear.

Chapter 31

They looked like four refugees from the Yukon Territory as they bundled into the Raven Rock fifteen minutes later. The clock above the bar read 11:45 p.m. Jim Todd took one look at them and got some hot coffee going. He didn't ask any questions because, after all, seeing the Dinkovich boys in the company of the law wasn't all that surprising. But this was different; he could tell. There was pie left in the kitchen from the dinner service, and he plated up four large slabs and brought it out.

"Certainly was lucky you boys happened along when you did," Thomas High Cloud said.

"Warn't luck," Darrell said.

"No?" Renard looked at Darrell. "Tell us what happened."

Darrell looked at Duffy. Darrell usually spoke only when necessary, Duffy being the loquacious one.

"Weez had stopped up to the bar here, and weez saw your squad car and trailer." Duffy looked at Darrell for confirmation, but Darrell just nodded. "So weez asked old Jim here, 'Where's Sheriff One Step?' and Jim says you's was out on the lake on your snowmobile.

298

That it was something to do with the case. So, weez decided we'd best check it out. See if you might need ours help. Right, Darrell?"

Darrell gave one nod of affirmation, and on Duffy went.

"So weez lit out from here, and we sees a snowmobile pullin' a trailer out toward the middle of the lake, and we figures that was you. So we heads that away to see if weez could be any help."

Darrell gave the official nod to continue.

"So, off we goes, a-followin'. And when we gets closer, weez started yellin' your name."

"I heard shouting," Renard said. "I thought it was you boys, and let me tell you, it was good to hear your voices."

Darrell and Duffy beamed a hero's smile, and Duffy pressed on.

"But then comes the gunshots. Weez knew you wouldn't be shootin' at us, Sheriff One Step, so we hightailed it back to the bar here and called for help."

Jim Todd set down four steaming mugs of coffee and stood back, listening.

"Called 911 we did," Darrell interjected. "Told 'em we needed the deputies—toot sweet."

"Then weez headed back out there," Duffy said. "We knew's you was in trouble. Weez warn't gonna abandon ya, Sheriff."

"You boys were just the help I needed," Renard said. "I don't know how much longer I could have held on to Ethan Grainfeld."

Suddenly a thought lit Darrell's face. "Did he stab Mr. Silverton, Sheriff One Step? Be he the killer?"

"Looks like that's a good possibility, Darrell. But I can't really talk about it yet."

"No, 'course not, Sheriff. Weez wasn't pryin' or anythin' like that."

"It's quite all right, boys," Renard reassured them. "Best not to speculate about the case, though, till things wrap up."

Darrell made a motion of zipping his lips and turning the key. "You's can depend on us to be discreet, Sheriff."

Renard smiled and nodded.

They finished their pie and coffee and stood to leave. "You boys need to stop down at the Law Enforcement Center and give statements," Renard said.

"Right now, Sheriff?" Duffy asked. "Weez good with that."

"Right now would be fine." He turned to High Cloud. "Thomas, will you see to their statements when you get back there?"

"Sure, Claude."

They thanked Jim Todd and headed outside to their vehicles. High Cloud and Renard loaded up the snowmobile. By the time they'd finished, the Dinkovich brothers had already left. They climbed into their squads and headed out.

Fifteen minutes later, they pulled into the parking lot at the Law Enforcement Center, and Deputy High Cloud accompanied the Dinkovich brothers inside. Renard sat in his squad with the heat pumping out. It was over a four-hour drive to the BCA in Bemidji, but with the severity of the storm, he guessed it would have taken Hank Gunderson even longer to get there with the boots from the Grainfeld house. Still, Hank had left the Law Enforcement Center around 7:00 p.m., and it was almost 12:30 a.m. He should have heard something. He took out his cell, but it was dead. Whether the cold had killed the battery or the impact of being thrown had killed the phone, he had no idea. He climbed out of the squad, walked to the door, and keyed himself into the LEC. As he headed down the hall to his office, he heard the phone ringing and rushed to answer it.

"Renard."

"Claude, I've been trying to call you for the past half hour."

"There've been some developments," Renard said. He did not elaborate.

"Adrianna Tomebay is here. I'll let her explain things."

"Deputy Renard. I have the results of the tests."

He knew her formality had everything to do with Hank Gunderson's presence.

She explained that the tests had been positive. That the sawdust in the treads of Ethan's boots matched exactly with the walnut sawdust found under and around Grant Silverton's coffin at the crime scene in the woodworking building.

"That's good news, Ria. The final nail in the coffin, one might say."

"Oh my, that's really bad."

"Made you laugh, though."

"Well, at this hour, we could all use a laugh. I'll get my report on the results to you before I go home."

"Not necessary, Ria. Tomorrow will be fine. You head home."

A moment later Hank came back on.

"Listen, Hank, you find a motel and hunker down for the night. We'll see you back here some time tomorrow."

"I won't fight you on that," Hank said. "I'm beat."

They ended the call, and Renard headed back down the hall to the room where High Cloud was overseeing the Dinkovich boys writing their statements.

"I'm heading up to the hospital to see what's happening with Ethan Grainfeld."

"You have them take a look at your head," High Cloud said.

"Hey, maybe now it's on straight," Renard joked.

"You okay driving up there?"

"It's two minutes away, Thomas."

"I guess. See you when you get back."

Renard found Len Blake in the emergency department of the hospital with Ethan Grainfeld. He spoke to the ER doctor, who told him they would be keeping Ethan overnight for observation and treating him for hypothermia, since his body temperature was almost three degrees below normal.

Renard assigned Len Blake to stay with Grainfeld overnight and bring him back to the sheriff's office for booking once he was released the following day. But then he must have done the math.

"Actually, that's a lot of hours," he said. "I'll get one of the other deputies to spell you in about four hours."

Len nodded. "Sounds good."

Renard then told the doctor about the blow he'd taken to his head. The doctor ushered him into an examination area and proceeded to check his pupils, reflexes, and coordination. He also tested Renard's memory and assessed his ability to recall information.

"Seems as if you're okay," he told Claude when he'd finished. "But if you have any headaches, dizziness, or nausea, you need to get back in here right away and we'll do a scan."

"I've got a thick head, Doc. I'll be okay."

"This is no joking matter, Deputy Renard."

"'Course not, Doc. I'll pay attention."

The doctor gave him a sheet on concussion protocols and then told him he was free to go.

Renard drove back to the Law Enforcement Center. High Cloud was still in the room with the Dinkovich brothers. Seems the boys were taking their time getting everything written down just right. Renard smiled to himself and headed back to his office to write his own report on what had transpired the past few hours. It was nearly two a.m. when he finished the report, pulled on his coat, and headed for the door.

He stood outside for a few moments, breathing in the cold, clean air. The worst of the storm had passed, and the snow drifted down, silent and pure. He climbed into his car and drove toward home. For the moment the world was aligned. For the moment there was peace. It was enough.

Author's Note

Since the Publication of *Death in the Blood Moon* in 2019, I've made changes to the spelling and form of two Ojibwe names. After continuing research, I have discovered that the correct spelling of the name for Lake Superior in Ojibwemowin or Anishinaabemowin is Gichigami. The word *gichi* means great or the greatest, and the word *gami* means sea or water. Hence, the Great Sea, as it is known to the Anishinaabe. We sometimes also see *gitchi* written with a "t" as in the name for the Grand Portage Band—Gitchi Onagaming, so I believe the two forms are somewhat interchangeable.

Also, in Claude Renard's Ojibwe name, Blue Fox, Ozhaawashko Waagosh, I have reversed the order of the words in this book, as I believe that is the correct form.

Please forgive any errors in the past or future as I continue my study of the language and heritage of the Anishinaabe.

Acknowledgements

Many thanks to my fantastic team who help me produce such a wonderful finished book each and every time. To my editor, Jennifer Adkins, who works tirelessly with me to correct and iron out all the errors and changes that are always part of the editing phase of the book. We have worked together for 15 years now, and my appreciation of your work only increases with each book. To my fine artist, Rebecca Treadway, for her creativity and amazing ability to create covers that bring my stories to life visually. To my alpha readers, Christopher Valen and Jeanette Brown, for your invaluable help and insights. And to my wonderful husband, Craig—my sounding board, my listener. No novelist can succeed without such a person by their side.

I would like to acknowledge the following sources and works that have been invaluable to me in the writing of this book: *The Manitous: The Spiritual World of the Ojibway* by Basil Johnston. *One Story, One Song* by Richard Wagamese. The video recordings "Ojibwe Word of the Day" by James Kaagegaabaw. You truly bring the Ojibwe language to life in a most beautiful way. Chief Deputy Will Sandstrom, Cook County Sheriff's Office, for his insights and information about the workings of the sheriff's office. Thank you all.